THE GAME PLAN

THE GAME PLAN

ALISHA SEHGAL

NEW DEGREE PRESS

COPYRIGHT © 2021 ALISHA SEHGAL

THE GAME PLAN

ISBN   978-1-63676-708-6   *Paperback*
         978-1-63730-059-6   *Kindle Ebook*
         978-1-63730-161-6   *Ebook*

FURTHER PRAISE
FOR THE GAME PLAN

———

Life is never coincidental. Everything happens for a reason; trust that it is always for a good one.

Whom you meet in life, what events will take place as you grow, how these events will impact your perspective, are all part of the game that life has for you.

In The Game Plan, Alisha has very beautifully weaved in some very powerful messages on mind, gift, and of course, love.

Your powers are you.

Along with the adventures of Sam Bleu are repeated messages of courage, self-acknowledgement, patience, and utmost trust in one's device.

In this realm of life, choose to be the angel in your way…even if it means that you have to play the devil's role when the need arises, for one to own their own power."

JOYCE TEO, THE KICKASS STRATEGY MENTOR FOR YOU TO LEAD YOUR E.P.I.C. LIFE, A SELF-MADE MILLIONAIRE, BEST-SELLING AUTHOR, INTERNATIONAL SPEAKER, AND FOUNDER OF MULTIPLE BUSINESSES INCLUDING HER MANAGEMENT CONSULTANCY FIRM, SAGE GLOBAL PARTNERS.

For Surabhi Didi, my original creative muse. You told me that you hoped I'd fulfill all my dreams, and without you, this first step in doing so wouldn't have been possible. Love you and miss you!

CONTENTS

If my life is going to mean anything,
I have to live it myself.

RICK RIORDAN, *THE LIGHTNING THIEF*

AUTHOR'S NOTE

The children ran to get the magical fruits that grew on the tree...

They watched as the ball fell down the hill and crashed into the tree...

These were just a few phrases about my drawings that I wrote in my Crayola marker notebook set my mother had given me.

Trees and geometric objects were the few things I knew how to make. My parents were immediately surprised by the short stories I created through the images and started talking about how I could develop it into a full story.

I was five years old.

Even at a young age, I realized that becoming an author was a possible future goal.

However, like most five-year-olds, I was very scattered and excited by most things.

I'd pretend to be a hip-hop dancer as I watched my sister take dance classes. I would play every sport that I could get equipment for. I would conduct science experiments or participate in coding challenges.

Because of all these interests, I explored many careers, including artist, data scientist, dancer, software engineer, and researcher, but in the back of my head, I was always creating storylines.

Some were inspired by the type of life I wanted to live. Other concepts were inspired by the books I read and the shows I watched.

I remember watching several Bollywood movies and falling in love with the idea of living with the whole extended family. I also remember watching *Winx Club* with my younger cousins and being inspired by the huge group of girls and guys that would fight off evil in different magical realms.

Both of these concepts intrigued me greatly and I took a lot of inspiration from them when creating the main storyline of *The Game Plan*.

Throughout the years, my story evolved, and my characters came to life.

They started out as extensions of Greek gods and Titans with superpowers that I thought were cool. I've loved Greek mythology ever since my older sister gave me her book of Greek myths.

For instance, my main character, Sam Bleu, started out as Athena. She got a great deal of her personality from the Greek goddess' battle strategy and mental powers. Sam became an icon of self-defense and grew up hiding her all-too-powerful ability of mind control.

Her overprotective brother and cousin, Derek and Sky, took some inspiration from Prometheus and Zeus, respectively. Even without my realizing it, there arose some parallels among the characters' interactions and the legends revolving around the mythological beings they take after.

For instance, Sam represents the fire Prometheus gives humans against Zeus' will. This parallels with Derek's desire to liberate Sam so she can protect herself, versus Sky's need to protect her himself.

This book inadvertently takes these myths and begins to discuss the ripple effects the characters' actions create:

- Can any one person's definition of good stand for everyone?
- Would it be better to give someone power and let them control it, hoping they are good?
- Is it better to keep control and do things the way one thinks is good?

I wanted the book to inspire philosophical thought while also being a fantastical escape.

With over a decade of developing these themes and ideas, my book has intertwined several unique personalities and complex storylines into a world of fantasy.

I remember a trip I once took to India, during which my sister and I had to sit around waiting for our parents.

I had so many stories floating in my head waiting to be written that my brain had no time to sit idle. There was the story of four siblings navigating their powers in a world that didn't accept anything out of the normal, or the story about a siren left alone on Earth.

I looked to my sister and said, "I don't think I'll ever be bored again."

Whether it was sitting in class, lying awake in bed at night, or on long drives, my brain was constantly creating and connecting more scenes for all the characters, even those that seemed minor in the grand scheme of my novel. I remember throughout high school that I wouldn't let myself think of my book if I had major tests coming up so that I could focus on school.

The storylines became an alternate world I lived in—a place that I escaped to.

I realized that I had to write these stories into a series of novels. I wanted to share the characters and their struggles with sexism, power, confidence, and growing up. I spent a good part of high school and my early college years trying to write the novel and get it published.

However, much like my five-year-old self, I was very distracted by school and the crazy college lifestyle associated with it.

Then I found the Creator's Institute.

I came across Professor Koester's Book Creator Program by pure chance, and it truly changed my life. I saw a link on a quarantine college Facebook page for people interested in becoming authors.

On a whim, I set up a 5 a.m. phone call with a Georgetown professor across the country. And for all of those that have ever met me, getting up at 5 a.m. was no easy feat, but I joined Professor Koester's program and set out to fully write the novel in four months.

I would finally get to share the story of Sam Bleu, my alter ego for so many years.

In fact, putting Sam to paper came rather easily, since much of her character building and actions were so deeply engraved in my mind. I had grown up acting out scenes with my friends.

I called it "The Game."

My friends and I would write scenes with characters we had separately created and put on our own shows by acting them out. When my friends weren't free, I'd do the same thing through the Sims and other roleplay games.

Writing Sam's life story down felt like I was writing down an alternate life I had already lived.

Sam represented everything I wanted to be and lived the life I wanted to create for myself. It felt all too familiar, and the personal elements of it made it rather nervewracking to share.

However, getting over this fear and being able to share what I learned growing up, along with the entertainment this novel, has brought me has been a great experience.

I hope that YA fantasy readers can both relate to the struggles my characters face and also forge their own life paths from learning about the character's trials and triumphs.

I found my path to finding confidence, learning about myself, and struggling as a data scientist through writing a novel.

And each path is intertwined into *The Game Plan*.

—Alisha Sehgal

PROLOGUE

SEVEN YEARS AGO

"Get out! Get out now!" Derek screamed. Sam ran down the hallways of her beachside home. She rubbed her eyes, squinting as the sun rose outside. "Hurry, Sam. We have to leave now. Leave everything." Derek waved his hands frantically at the front door.

Sam looked to her bedroom on the left. She desperately wanted to crawl back into bed and pretend this was a nightmare. She looked towards her parents' room on the right. Her eldest brother, Keith, stood at the doorway laughing at her. His face had a menacing grin. She could see her mother fallen on the floor in a bright red dress. *The red dress from last night.*

"Who are you?" She yelled at Keith as she ran down the stairs and joined the rest of her siblings in their car. She watched as they drove away. In a period of three minutes, her mom was dead, her father was nowhere to be seen, but probably dead too, and her eldest brother was happily letting them leave without him. *What just happened?* A tear ran down her cheek.

PART 1

SAM BLEU

CHAPTER 1

NEW HOME, OLDER BROTHER

—

It was time to leave again. Sam knew it because once again her older brother Derek was whispering on the phone with their cousin, Sky. She leaned on her cabin room door trying not to make a noise on the creaky wooden floors.

"I think we need to move. Keith sent me a letter to call him," Derek muttered.

Keith? Why'd he send a letter?

"Are you going to?" Sam could clearly hear Sky's voice through Derek's mind. It was one of the few perks her powers gave her. Now if only she could access thoughts people weren't currently thinking, she wouldn't have to sneak around for answers. "I think you should cut off communication with him completely. Sooner or later, he'll find out about Sam, and I don't know how much longer we can keep her safe like this. And how'd his letters find you anyway?" Sky spoke with a stern voice.

"Talking to him is the only way I know what he's up to and how much he knows. I pretended to not know who has the gift, but I don't think he bought it."

Sam always wondered why her mind control powers were called "the gift." They seemed more like a curse if anything. She had been on the run now for seven years because of them. After her parents had died, she had moved around with her siblings trying to hide their powers. It wasn't easy trying to make it on a human-filled planet with an angel mother and the devil as their father. Especially since the eldest of all of her siblings, Keith, was mostly out of their lives. He only showed up a few times a year, but Derek had made it practically impossible for Sam to see him. Derek always said something about him being evil now or the reason their parents were gone, but Sam remembered the kind older brother she used to play with when they were all really young. She didn't understand how he went from being the one who trained all four of them with their elemental powers to ditching them when life got harder. Sam inched closer to the door she was hiding behind to see if she could see the letter Derek had mentioned. The wooden door creaked as she accidentally stubbed her toe on it. *Ow!*

"Sky, wait a second. I think someone's awake."

Shoot. She could see Derek walking towards her door tilting his head sideways to see if anyone was there. Sam ran to her bed and hid under the covers, pretending to sleep. She was tired of this forest cabin. It was impossible to sneak around since everything creaked or broke at the lightest touch. She missed her parents' beachside home, but even having her parents around seemed like another lifetime.

"Okay. We're fine. Sam's still asleep."

"Let me know how the meeting goes. I think it might be time to bring you guys home," Sky said and then hung up. *Home? Did home exist?* Her heart raced at the idea of a permanent place, but she forced herself to stay in bed and not get too excited. This wasn't the first time Sam had thought about settling down. She bit her lip and pulled the sheets over her face trying to make sense of the phone call.

"Sam! Wake up." Derek came running. "It's time." He peered through her room and began grabbing the jackets and books lying around. "Where's your phone? Don't forget it."

"What time is it?" Sam rubbed her eyes, pretending to wake up.

"5:30 a.m. We have to leave now."

"Where are we going this time? It's not another worn down cabin in the woods like this one, right?" She got up, picked up her duffel bag, and took a moment to look over the fading engraved name. *Sameera.* She stuffed her blanket in with the rest of the things she packed last night then tried to close it. She tried sitting on it, but Derek pulled it away and zipped it up.

"It's Malibu this time. Just a few hours." He walked out of the door. "Hurry up. We should've been in the car already."

Sam waited until he was out of the room, then grabbed her pillow in one hand and the bag in the other. She walked out of the house and a hint of laughter escaped from her as she saw her three siblings by their gray van. *Typical.* Her siblings all had the same routine before they moved from one place to another. Derek lathered on sunscreen anywhere his signature gray tee and jeans didn't cover him. His pale skin couldn't handle the long drives under the Southern California sun. Mia found the perfect spot in the car for all of the books she had to read or reread. Ethan looked through his bag, making sure he didn't forget anything. Even Sam had some things she had to get done before the move.

Malibu. She thought with her eyes closed. *Seth! Malibu this time. Can you meet me there?* She hoped her thoughts would reach her friend.

Malibu! That's exciting. I swam there last year. Find the blue lighthouse by the famous caves. You'll know what to look for when you get there, I promise. Seth's thoughts ran through Sam's mind.

Perfect. Sam responded to her friend's thoughts and smiled as she left the cabin, knowing she would never see it again.

"Sam, hop in. We saved you a seat in the back." Mia took Sam's bag and stuffed it in the trunk.

"Hey, you tell Seth yet?" Ethan whispered as he pulled Sam aside. He was the only one who knew about Sam's secret friend. She had met Seth a few years ago while she was practicing her powers by the ocean. They had instantly clicked over having little to no knowledge about their origins. She didn't know why she was given such important powers as the youngest. Seth didn't know what he was doing as a siren in Earth's oceans. Their misfortune marked their bond.

"One step ahead of ya." Sam pointed to her head and smirked. She got in the back seat and settled in for the journey.

An hour in, Derek parked the car at a run-down gas station. Sam looked out the window and saw no other cars nearby. It seemed to be one of the generic rest areas that popped up on the route between the Bay to LA. A tall and lean man wearing a gray hoodie walked towards their car. He rummaged through his jeans pockets and pulled out a key.

"You got the cash, kid?"

"Here." Derek held out a couple hundred dollars. "This should cover it."

"And your ID? Can't be selling to anyone under eighteen." The man clearly was doing illegal deals, but lucky for them, they needed someone willing to sell abandoned buildings to live in while they moved around California. "What kind of business are ya running anyway? I draw the line at child labor," the man said as he nodded towards the rest of them in the car.

"They aren't working for me. They're my siblings."

"Yeah, okay, sure. Just don't let anyone trace anything back to me." He pulled his hoodie farther down over his eyes and looked around "If you get caught, I know nothing," he muttered and ran away hiding his face.

Most people questioned whether they were truly related. Derek was significantly older than the rest of them, and none of them looked completely alike. Derek and Mia had light skin, while Sam and Ethan had a tawny brown skin tone. Their eyes were all different colors, which Sam found funny, since they matched their elemental powers. Derek's were stormy gray like the windy skies, Mia's were ocean blue, Ethan's were forest green with hints of earthy brown, and her own were grey with orange and red specs. In fact, the only thing they all had in common was their dark, almost black, hair color. She didn't blame the shady guy for not believing they were related. If she thought their parents were mortal, she wouldn't have believed it either.

"Where do you even find these people?" Mia laughed. "If we didn't need to be in hiding, I'm pretty sure these are the people we would be saving others from."

"Don't worry. Doing business deals with them is the best way to know where they're going next. You and I can go make sure they don't start any trouble for humans later." Derek smiled and continued driving.

"Can I come?" Sam asked with innocent hope.

"No, it's too dangerous right now. You and Ethan need to stay back together and train," Derek said with little to no emotion in his voice.

Typical. Mia and Derek go on fun quests, and I have to stay home. Why is danger only bad for me? Sam folded her arms against her chest and sat back in her seat. Mia turned, giving her a sympathetic smile but stayed silent as Derek continued to drive.

"We're here." Derek parked the car behind a defunct fire station. He pointed at the garage type door in front of them. "We should be set to stay here for a week. I know it's shorter than usual, but I think this will be one of the last few changes we make for a while." Sam sighed, still pouting over Derek's double standards. As a sign of rebellion against Derek, she stayed in the car as the rest left. Realistically, she was only punishing herself by staying in the hot, musty car. Mia and Ethan jumped out and started unloading the back. Ethan playfully nudged Sam's head with the bag closest to her seat.

"Come on. At least you aren't left out alone," Ethan said, walking away and helping Derek open the door to get in. Sam reluctantly got up and grabbed her phone. She was used to traveling, but moving from place to place with no say in her life never got easier. *Ethan's right though. At least I have him.*

"Okay. Perfect, let's settle in. This fire station has a few walls that we can use as room separators. Go find your own spaces." Derek dusted his hands off and looked through the now-open garage door. "Oh, and there are some areas for all of you to practice. Sam, there's a fire pit to the left. Ethan, there's an area around the corner with some dirt and shrubs."

Derek pointed to another exit on the opposite side of the station. "And Mia, this isn't the best accommodation, but there is a stream that runs behind the neighboring buildings. Be safe." He walked in and started settling, putting his things in his corner of the fire station. Everyone else followed and got themselves situated.

***

There was a fire blazing in the rather large pit. It lit up the room and smoke rose up to the tall ceiling, creating dancing shadows on the walls. Sam stood next to the pit. She played with the flames, controlling them through her fingertips. Suddenly the fire burst outward. She fell back, the color drained from her face. She looked down at her slightly scraped hands and sighed. *Maybe Derek's right about it being dangerous.* Derek came into the room and jumped back as the flames blew near him. *Oh no, he always walks in at the worst moments.* Sam clenched her shirt in her hands trying to dry off her palms. *Don't tell me I'm behind, please.*

"Sam, just focus. It gets easier."

She glanced back and frowned. Her whole body ached from waking up and traveling early in the morning. "Derek, how long did it take you to...you know, to master the wind?"

"A while. A little too long."

"Oh." Sam's face softened. She felt guilty, but knowing her overly capable brother, who made fighting demons look easy, had struggled, lifted her spirits.

"Well, anyway, you're doing well so far."

"Thanks. Have you seen Mia?" Sam asked in a hushed voice. *Phew. He isn't concerned about my progress.*

"Yeah, she's practicing too." Derek said looking towards the back alleyway door.

Sam tried to hide her smile. *Mastering our powers seems almost like a race. The faster I learn, the faster Derek will start taking me on quests.* Feeling encouraged, Sam went on playing with the fire. "Okay."

"Well, I'll leave you to it then." Derek left.

Sam decided to put a pause on practicing after taking a few more falls to the ground. She stepped out toward the garden Ethan was practicing in and quickly spotted him. He was searching for the wilting flowers that were slowly losing their petals as fall approached. At last, Sam saw him smile as he found a drooping sunflower.

Ethan raised his hand and tried to connect with the plant. He looked a bit ridiculous, but slowly they both saw the plant grow. It grew taller and wider. "Stop! No! Stop growing!" Ethan exclaimed. He palmed his forehead. The plant was now so big that its thin little body was unable to handle the weight and sadly began to droop low. "The proportions! And this is just...ugh..." He yelled out, his voice cracking.

"Don't stress too much. I almost blew up the building," she said trying to comfort him. Sam was all too familiar with the frustration of not being able to control herself. "I guess we'll learn soon."

"I hope. I'll probably kill the whole garden before I get anywhere."

"Why don't we try something?" Sam lifted her hand to the section of the garden that was limp and brown. A flame erupted and the largest dying sunflower fell down in ashes.

"Sam! What are you doing?" Ethan's eyes grew large. She continued to burn the dead half of the garden to the ground.

Sam could feel a knot in her stomach by the time she reached the last plant.

"If only I was as good at extinguishing the flame as I am at igniting it. This would have been a great plan." Sam looked towards Ethan.

"A great plan? Burning down the garden was your plan!" Ethan clenched his fists. Sweat dripped down the sides of his face. He looked at the flame. It wasn't too big, but it was growing.

"Quick. Give me that tablecloth." Sam pointed to the picnic table next to Ethan. He tossed the cloth to her and she threw it over the fire and stomped on it. "Don't worry. I wasn't going to start a fire without a contingency plan. I learned that the hard way." She smirked. "Here, now try to regrow this side of the garden. Wildfires are part of nature's cycle." Derek's homeschool plans really were becoming more useful for understanding her powers than she had anticipated.

He lifted his hand and focused on the now-bare ground. Seeds from the lively side of the garden started floating through the wind towards the ground. One seed enveloped itself in the dirt, and the rest soon followed. The surface of the dirt glowed as a stem reached out. Sam smiled. Her brother was getting better. The stem got taller, and leaves began growing. Finally a flower budded and the plant stood majestically.

"See? When you step out of your element, you get better at controlling yourself. Your mind tricks you into focusing more," Sam said but noticed Ethan wasn't listening. His forehead was covered in creases as he raised his hand towards her.

"Okay, now let's see you out of your element, Sam." Ethan grinned. Sam gulped.

"Um, I'm okay. I'll be fine learning on my own. I was just trying to help," she mumbled as she started moving backwards. Ethan raised his other hand and vines began growing rapidly towards Sam. "I'm sorry Ethan, chill!" Ethan dropped his hands and the vines returned to normal. He laughed.

"Thanks, Sam," he said, chuckling.

"For sure, brother." She sighed in relief and then ran back inside. *That was fun.* She smiled. She was coming to terms with this place even though she knew they had only a week to stay. *Maybe I'll go check on Mia too.* Sam walked out of the door that led to the block of business buildings. *Where is this stream?* She looked towards the buildings and all she saw was a dark alley. No water in sight. *Do I have the wrong door?* She started turning around to leave and out of nowhere she heard Derek's voice.

"Hey! Aren't you supposed to be training?" Sam didn't know what to say. She looked around and saw a pile of old newspapers next to a dumpster.

"Yeah. I was just looking for something that burns easy." She walked over and picked up the newspapers, trying to ignore how dirty and smelly they were. She wrinkled her nose and turned her face to breathe the slightly better air to the side of her. "All done!" She walked back towards the building.

"Uh huh. Okay." Sam knew Derek was always extra suspicious of her, but still she hoped he believed her. "I'll be back in an hour. Go back inside and try combining your powers. You know...fire and—" He looked around them before leaning in and making eye contact with her—"the gift," he whispered, his voice soft. Sam wondered why he was so cautious about his words. It didn't seem like there was anyone around. *Is he calling Keith today?*

"Yeah, okay, whatever." Sam walked back into the station and let the door close behind her. *He's up to something and he's never going to admit what it is to me.* She looked back at the door. *Should I...*None of her siblings were back yet. She walked towards the door again and slowly opened it enough to see outside. She could see Derek lingering around the trash cans, looking around. He glanced back at the door and Sam quickly moved away to avoid being seen.

Derek walked through the old dark alley. He seemed to be waiting for something as he cautiously walked towards one of the building's back entrances. He opened the glass door, took a deep breath, and entered. *What's he doing? Is he even allowed in there?* Sam slipped outside the fire station and let the metal door gently fall into place. She crept up to the door Derek had disappeared through. The building loomed tall above her. Its dark blue appearance and all glass exterior screamed, cold and intimidating, but her curiosity was stronger, so she followed her brother inside. She looked around, hoping to spot him without being caught. An aura of darkness and death surrounded her. She didn't even think that was possible, but something felt off about the building. Something dangerous was here.

Sam made her way down the long corridor. There was one flickering lightbulb dangling from the ceiling at the end that let her see piles of paperwork left on the floor. *Why is Derek interested in this building?* Sam felt a sense of responsibility to find out and make sure her brother wasn't in danger. She heard a thud and the sound of breaking glass coming from the right end of the hallway. *Who else is here?* She tip-toed up to the end of the corridor and peered to the side.

Derek was standing in the middle of an office-like room. He waved his hand and pushed the cubicles to the side wall.

Only a few printer papers lay on the ground. Derek placed a small compact mirror and began creating a misty fog in the center of the room. He raised his hand to create an air wave that lifted a piece of paper above the mist creating a rainbow effect. He then uttered a few words that Sam couldn't comprehend. A shadowy figure appeared behind him.

Oh no! What's that? She inched further behind the corner hoping the figure wouldn't notice her.

Derek jerked backward and raised his hand. A gust of wind raced and knocked the intruder unconscious. Another shadow appeared, but this one was faster. Still, Derek blew the figure away. More and more of the black shadowy creatures appeared. One by one Derek beat them. Then a larger figure materialized out of the rainbow. It was more human-like. Sam couldn't tell who it was, but next to it, Derek looked like a kid. Her usually tall brother with a stern face now looked small and timid.

"Ah, getting better, aren't we?" The figure's laugh sounded familiar.

"I've got the gift, haven't I?" Derek replied.

Sam held back a gasp. *Derek's telling people he has the gift? Why would he lie?*

"Oh, Derek. You've learned many things from our parents, but lying isn't one of them. I know you don't have the gift. You don't fight like it. Your eyes lack the confidence." Derek shifted nervously as the figure circled him through the misty fog. Sam had never seen anyone make Derek scared. He always carried himself like he had all the answers in front of her. "See? You're getting afraid of me, and I'm not even there with you. Anyway, I'll figure it out, whoever it is. Our parents had the time to train me, unlike you," the figure emphasized.

Our parents? Is that…no…it's Keith! Sam felt an urge to step in and give him a hug and catch up. She missed him, but she held herself back. The night her mother died rushed through her mind. She remembered walking into her parents' room to say goodnight. Keith was smiling as he and their father praised their mother's red gown. She had thought nothing of it, but the next day Derek rushed them out of the house. As Sam ran out, she caught a glimpse of her mother on the floor in the same red gown. Her whole life flashed before her eyes, but Keith just stood outside the door laughing, and their father was nowhere to be seen.

Derek had warned her about Keith changing and not caring about them anymore, but Sam wanted to know what had happened for herself. *Derek has some serious explaining to do if he has been calling Keith. And why didn't he ever let us message people like this? Seth would love to hear about this.*

"Why? It's not like you'll get the gift anyways. Mom didn't want you to have it. You'll never get it if I have anything to say about it," Derek declared.

"You talk like a young child. You know you could let me take care of the others, seeing as you're not fit to do so yourself."

Sam had always wondered why they didn't live with Keith, since he was the oldest. She cupped her ears with her hands to hear better. She couldn't tap into Keith's mind and read his thoughts through the strange messaging Derek had set up for some reason.

"I may be younger, but I'm not stupid. You would just torture them to death." Derek retreated a few steps.

Torture? Keith? Sam couldn't put those two words together. Her main memories of him were him teaching her how to ride a bike and helping her and Ethan sneak past their parents when the older kids did anything fun. *How and why would he torture us?*

"I'm still sad you don't trust me to meet you in person. At least message me from home and not in this dark, abandoned office building." Keith had a fake endearing tone that made Sam shiver.

"If you think I'd expose our location to you, then I'm not the child in this conversation. I'm leaving. I just wanted to tell you to stop sending me letters, and I won't be Iris messaging you again. Sky is just a call away, and you know you won't be able to take on all of us. Just mark my words. You're never getting the gift."

"Fine. You can do all the work of raising them, but mark my words," Keith sneered, "I will get the gift. Mom may have given it to someone else, but Dad wanted me to have it." With that, Keith's image rippled and vanished. Derek absorbed the mist in his hand as he groaned. He punched the cubicle next to him.

Can I Iris message people too? How much is Derek not teaching me? Derek turned around and headed for the hallway where Sam was hiding. *Shoot.* Sam quickly lit a flame in her hand to search for a place to go. She saw a door behind some papers on the ground. She scooted them to the side while blowing the fire away from her hand and ran in, accidentally closing the door too loudly. *I need to figure out how to get rid of the flame better.*

"Anyone there?" Derek went running into the hallway. Sam kept quiet until his footsteps seemed far away. She quickly got out of the room and retraced her steps out of the building. She had to make it back to the fire station before Derek did. *Where'd he go? He should have been right ahead of me.* Sam walked towards the station door when a hand grabbed her from the back. She jumped.

"Sam!" She turned and sighed in relief as Ethan ran towards her.

"Oh, thank the angels. I thought you were Derek. Or worse. I thought you were Keith."

"Keith? Sam, the whole reason we keep moving is so he can't find us. You're safe."

"Really? Or is that just what Derek told us?" Sam took Ethan's wrist and dragged him back inside the fire station. She knew she could trust him. After all, he was her twin. He only knew two minutes more of this world than she did. "I followed him into that building, and he just had a meeting with Keith. It was some weird Iris messaging, but it's only a matter of time before Keith finds us."

"What! Did you get to talk to Keith?" Ethan's smile turned into a frown. Sam knew he hadn't gotten any closure with their older brother either. "Is he really after your powers?"

"Yeah, and Derek tried telling him that he had the gift. Keith didn't buy it though." Sam looked around, worried that Derek or Mia would find them. "He said something about Dad wanting him to have the powers?" Sam struggled to keep her voice at a whisper. She desperately wanted to scream at Derek until he gave her answers.

"Do you think that Mom knew Keith was going to turn evil? Otherwise she would've given him the powers as the oldest, right?" Ethan looked at her wide-eyed.

"Yeah, maybe. But then Derek's the next oldest. Why me?"

"Maybe…" Ethan shrugged his shoulders just as Derek walked in with some letters in his hand. "Oh, hey! Been on any adventures recently?" Ethan rambled awkwardly. Sam nudged him.

Obvious much? She pushed her thoughts into his mind.

"Uh. No. I just went to get mail." He shuffled through the mail and his eyes widened as he saw a blue envelope. "Blue envelope's Sky, right?" Sam asked. *I wonder how he sent the mail to us before we even got here.*

"Yeah," Derek muttered and began opening it. "Guys, we'll eat dinner a little late tonight." He walked away while pulling out his phone and dialing a number. "Hello? Sky?" His voice trailed off.

"What's with the letter?" Ethan asked, confused. "He has a phone."

"No digital evidence, I guess. Derek's lying to us about a lot," Sam said. "Can we even trust him? I thought Keith was nice, but if he can turn evil so easily, how do we know Derek can't. Or maybe he made us hate Keith to hide his own motives."

"Okay, okay, wait." Ethan shook his head as he held it in his hands. "Let's figure out what's in that letter first."

CHAPTER 2

SPYING ON YOUR SIBLINGS GETS YOU A PENTHOUSE

It had been a few days since Derek had called Sky. *Is he not coming?* Sam sat on a bench in the garden. She felt warmth as she looked at the small lilies Ethan had grown. He always knew how to make a place feel more like a home. Sam knew that Sky and Derek had started getting suspicious of her and how much she knew, but she didn't care. She almost wanted to confront them and make them tell her everything. *But how well would that go over? Would they just get better at hiding things from me?* She had been venting to Ethan, who seemed to be the only other person who understood her pain. Mia was great to talk to, but she knew things that Derek wouldn't let her tell Sam or Ethan. *I wish Mia would just spill already. She should know how irritating Derek's secrets are.*

When their parents had died, Mia was the last to know. Sam had stumbled upon the information with Ethan when they found their mom dead and a new set of powers within her. Derek had forced them all to leave their home, but at first he refused to tell Mia why. Sam remembered going from place to place, moving every day, with Mia completely in the dark. Sam broke down on day three and told her that their mom died and dad was gone, but Derek didn't tell them anything about Keith for a few weeks. *I thought after all that Mia wouldn't hide things from me. What could Derek's plan be? Does Mia know what happened to Keith?*

"Sam, come here for a second." Sam jumped off the bench as she heard Mia call her. "Can we talk?"

Is she reading minds now too? She took a breath and answered her older sister. "Yeah, what's up?"

"Derek told me that you wanted to train together." Sam had forgotten that she asked Derek to try sparring with their siblings and combine their powers. *I can't believe Derek agreed. I bet he didn't ask Sky, because Sky would have never let me learn what Mia and Derek do on quests.*

"I want to see if we can battle with our powers." Sam smiled at her sister, excited to see what she was going to say, but Mia only frowned.

"Okay, so Derek made me promise that we wouldn't do anything dangerous when we trained. He heavily implied not using our powers against each other." Mia sighed.

"How am I ever supposed to use my powers for defense if every educational thing is too dangerous?" Sam snapped at her older sister. *I don't want to be afraid of my powers anymore.* "I'm not going to start battling for no reason, but I need to know how. I can't always have you or Derek protect me."

"Trust me, I agree, but I can't go against Derek or Sky. You know how they are." Mia shrugged. Sam knew all too well how they were. She barely had a relationship with Sky, and yet he seemed to dictate a lot of her life.

"Overprotective," she muttered.

"Overbearing," Mia added with a smirk growing on her face.

"In over their heads." Sam laughed. Mia joined, putting her hand around Sam's shoulders.

"Let's start training and see where things go, okay?" The two of them began leaving to go to the stream where Mia practiced. "Oh, and why don't you call Ethan, too?" Mia looked at Sam who nodded.

Ethan, come to the back. Mia and I are going to train at the stream, she projected.

On my way, Ethan thought back. Sam was relieved that Mia was sympathetic of her situation with Derek and Sky. At the very least, she knew that Mia had her back.

***

Ethan tapped Sam's shoulder as they returned from training and pointed towards Derek, who seemed to be packing a bag. *Is that my stuff he's packing? What's he doing with that?* Sam thought as Derek shoved their mom's old jacket into a bag. *He gave me that jacket to remember her. He better not be taking it back.* Once again Derek was up to something. Sam hated being the youngest. Well, actually, she hated being the one everyone took care of, sadly the youngest. To add to her pain, she had the gift. *Why couldn't it have been gifted to someone else?*

Sam saw Derek leave through the station's back alley door. She had begun to realize that the door he used always meant something. The garage door meant taking out the trash. The front door meant going to fight demons or problematic humans with Mia. The back door meant he was mad, but the back alleyway door meant he was doing something secretive, like calling Keith. Sam kept track of everyone's little habits, because if they were all watching her every move carefully, she might as well too.

Then, she saw a flash of platinum blond hair. Sam knew that this meant Sky was at the house. *Finally. He took long enough.* She quickly rushed outside and hid behind a plant so she could hear what they were talking about.

"When's the last time he called?" Sky muttered. He was wearing a tight black shirt and camo pants that were tucked into his combat boots. Although Derek was older and generally more muscular, Sky looked more threatening in his fancier clothes. *I guess having nice clothes comes with the whole home life thing.*

"A week ago." Derek shifted uncomfortably. "He wanted to see if we knew something, and I didn't know where to answer other than the office building next door," he stuttered.

"I don't know what we can do. Sooner or later, Keith will find out about Sam's powers." A slight rustle came from where Sam was hiding.

By now Ethan's powers made all the plants at the station grow into monstrous obstructions wherever they were placed. Another plant rustled when she shifted. Derek looked back. "Sky, did you hear something?"

"No. Does Sam know about our plan? She's too young to know about it. I don't want her to get more involved than she already is." Sky's voice was raised.

"Shhh. Keep your voice down. I don't want the others to worry," Derek whispered as he suspiciously eyed the plant Sam hid behind. "We need to figure out the plan first, and then I think we should train her." Sam tried to slip into the shadow behind the plant, but as she moved, she accidentally moved a leaf and some dirt fell out of the pot. She could see Derek eyeing the plant still. *Shoot, please don't notice that.*

"Derek, we can't. If she trains, she's going to want to fight the battles we fight. With her power it's too dangerous," Sky whispered.

"If she can learn to control her powers, then we can help her protect herself." Derek stood next to the plant and turned as he listened to Sky's next words.

Don't turn back!

"Her powers would help us so much against demons, too," Derek said. "We need someone like her on the quests."

"It's too risky, Derek. If she uses her gift, the demons will report it to Keith right away. I don't want her to know about any of this," Sky rebutted.

This is the last time I think I can deal with Sky saying he won't tell me what's happening. She pulled down a leaf to get a better look at Sky, but instead she made eye contact with her older brother. Derek quickly lifted the plant's leaves to reveal Sam covered in dirt and crouched in the corner. She glared at him brushing off the dirt. Flames flashed in her eyes, demanding answers.

"What plan? Why don't you guys ever let me in on things? I'm just as old as you were, Derek, when our mom died and you took responsibility. If you weren't too young then, I'm not too young now."

Sam had enough of the protective thing her family had going on. She wanted to be capable of taking care of herself. Derek looked at her and Sky. Sam's heart raced as she waited for their reply.

"You know what, fine. We'll take you to the new plan site. Get in the car." Derek went inside and grabbed his keys.

"What are you talking about Derek?" Sam asking, following him. She raised her eyebrows, but secretly she was excited for any new information.

"We can't let her in. The more she knows, the more danger she's in," Sky badgered.

"That's the most cliché thing you've ever said, and I'm fourteen," Sam said to her cousin.

"Sam, don't be rude." Derek opened the car's rear door. "Get in now. Both of you." He raised his voice. "Sky, take her to your home. I'll bring Mia and Ethan." *That's why he was packing my stuff? Sky wasn't in on it? Their plan involves a whole new location?*

"Fine, if you're sure." Sky started reversing the car. Sam wanted to be in on their plans. He looked back at her. "I don't know what Derek's up to, but I hope you know what you're getting yourself into."

"I get it. I'm young. I've heard this story before, but we were never meant to have normal childhoods."

Sky drove like an old man, following every speed limit exactly. She didn't think Malibu was this big, but it seemed to be taking ages to get to this "home" both Sky and Derek kept referring to. Looking outside, Sam could see forests on both sides of the car. A surprising number of trails flowed between the large cottonwood and sycamore trees. There was a marine layer above, so she knew they were quite close to the ocean.

Home! Home? Home. What even is home? Are Ethan and Mia close behind? It wouldn't feel much like a home without them. Sam's heart skipped beats at the thought of having a permanent home. She was tired of running. *I love adventure, but everyone needs a stable place to come back to, right? Maybe this could be it.*

"Sam, you still awake?" Sky asked.

"Yeah."

"Get ready, we're here." Sky had a cheek-to-cheek grin as he looked at her through the rearview mirror.

Large ivory gates welcomed them as Sky drove into the private residence. She squinted her eyes as she looked at the sun reflecting off of the glass buildings in front of her. *Is that a house?* It must have been a hotel at some point because it looked like it could house several families. As Sky drove further in, Sam could see a second hotel-sized house next door.

Both of the buildings had little wooden cabin-like structures in front of them. The cabins seemed big enough to be houses themselves. She wondered if they were for guests like her. As she thought about a life in the cabin, she got distracted by the sight of a hedge maze in the middle of the front courtyard and a large fountain that peeked through the top.

"Sky, what statues are on that fountain?" Sam asked.

"They're different Greek gods. Our neighbors have their Roman counterparts in their garden."

"Oh," Sam said, making a mental note to go look at them more closely later. She had no other words. She was mesmerized by the place. Sky pulled in the car to the drop-off loop in front of the garden. Sam watched in awe as she saw the trees deepen all around her and heard ocean waves. *Oh no! I have to find Seth today.* "Hey, Sky! Are we near that famous Malibu lighthouse?"

"Uh. I didn't know it was famous, but yeah, it should be somewhere around here." He stopped the car and gathered his belongings. She jumped out and turned, taking in the views.

How could people live here? Why haven't I seen this place before? She knew that Sky and Derek had secrets, but never did she imagine Sky living in a mansion was one. She had gotten used to the moving-around lifestyle. After all, it wasn't safe to stay in one place. *How weren't the people who lived here vulnerable to the dangers of the rest of the world?*

It was much harder avoiding demons and evil spirits when only a few people on Earth had magic. "Sky, how do you guys stay here? LA is just forty minutes away. Malibu is still a pretty popular city. This place can't be hard to find for demons."

"We all know how to protect the place. Usually, demons don't try to fight so many of us at once, and they sure as hell don't want to team up with each other to fight us. They can never get along. The best way to defeat a demon is to distract it with another one." All of this made sense to Sam. She had read a lot about her dad, the devil, hoping that he was still alive somehow and would someday come back for them. But all she had found was that nobody got along so demons weren't likely to take over. The divide and conquer strategy was working for the right side for once. However, even as a divided enemy, the angels couldn't fight enough battles to get rid of the demons for good. That would take more power than existed in the world.

"Oh."

"But that also means that, if there aren't a lot of us here, we're in danger. That's why the two families live so close to each other," Sky said and then turned to Sam. He noticed that she looked sad. "Everyone has been really excited to meet you, Sam."

"Are there really that many of us on Earth?" Sam felt butterflies form in her stomach.

"Quite a few. Don't worry if you don't get everyone's names down right away. I'll let you off here and go park the car. Travis is waiting for you at the door." He finally drove around all the hedges and parked in front of the mansion's doors.

"Travis?" She had no idea who these people were to her or why she was only meeting them now. "Hey, Sky, why haven't I met everyone before? It's my dad, isn't it?" Being the daughter of the devil meant everyone was scared of her before she even met them. She hoped that the rest of her cousins didn't know this about her.

"He definitely makes everything harder, but don't worry. We all are together now. And Travis is your older cousin. He'll show you around and introduce you to everyone. I'll be there soon." Sam jumped out of the car. All she had was her beat-up phone and a jacket. She walked up the steps to the doors. A tall boy with dirty-brown, wavy hair stood in front of her. He wore a tank with shorts that matched his blue eyes. He had sand covering his knees, and his hair looked wet. Sam could smell the ocean wafting off of him.

"Sam! Hi." He gave her a hug. "I'm Sky's brother." Travis paused. "His younger brother."

"I have a feeling he doesn't let you forget that you're younger," Sam said under her breath.

"Yeah, that he doesn't. You're pretty witty." He chuckled.

Sam looked up, surprised that he heard her, but she smiled and walked into the entryway. The ceilings hung high above her, and the house was filled with sunlight. "Wow. This place is gorgeous." She turned all around and just took the view in. Two marble staircases framed the entry to the main room. She walked through, landing in a huge open kitchen. There were a large number of people standing around the island smiling at her. She felt like she was on a reality show being introduced to strangers. In fact, they really *were* strangers despite being her family. Sam tried to smile and opened her mouth to say hello but fell silent. She just looked around. Everyone was at least a few years older than her, maybe late-teens. *Great, I'm the youngest again.*

A tall girl with brunette hair looked at her and her smile grew. "I'm Ashley! I was so excited to hear that we were getting more sisters. There are too many guys in this house. Here, I'll show you your room—well, your set of rooms. We're going to spoil you here," Ashley said, walking towards her.

"Um, okay, thank you," Sam replied and then turned to the others. "It was nice meeting you guys," she muttered, thinking she was being too formal. *How do you talk to family that you don't know yet?* She followed Ashley. Another girl began following too.

"And I'm Nikki," she said. Nikki was at least a few inches taller than Sam and extremely fit. They both were beautiful in their own very different ways. Ashley had warm ivory skin with dark, chocolate-brown eyes. Nikki on the other hand had darker, espresso-brown skin and extremely light gray eyes that complimented her matte brown lipstick.

Ashley walked with confidence in each step as they neared the elevator, and Sam could tell that Nikki looked up to her. The only girl Sam had ever been close to was Mia, so she was excited to get to know more.

"Okay, so I know an elevator is a bit ridiculous for a house, but trust me, you're not going to complain after a long day of training," Nikki quipped as the three of them walked into the lift. It was big enough to take fifteen people at a time, and Sam wondered how many rooms there were in the building.

"I guess it makes sense when the building is twenty floors high," Sam said with shock in her voice as she stared at the numbered buttons.

"Oh, wait till you see how this elevator works before you're shocked." Ashley pressed the right arrow button until the screen displayed the number four. Then she pressed level twenty. "Lucky for you, you get the penthouse."

"What? Um. Nobody else wants it?" Sam's eyes grew wide. She was used to taking the smaller or lesser of everything because she was the youngest.

"Everyone wanted it, but Sky got us all to give it up. Something about you deserving it and keeping lines of defense for the building." She smiled and looked at Nikki. "Anyway, we both were happy. Now the girls can hang out in the penthouse. Before you got here the older siblings used to use it as a party space, which really meant a place to do everything people under eighteen can't do."

"Ah, okay, I got it." Sam smiled as she realized what they were referring to. She knew where Derek hid the weapons and potions he didn't want the rest of them to see, so she was well aware of what Sky and Derek did at their training. Despite the fun banter, she couldn't help but wonder. *Do they know about the gift? Is that what she meant by lines of defense? Is everyone here going to treat me like I have to be protected?* She hoped not. The elevator reached the twentieth floor, but it kept moving. "Are we moving horizontally?" Sam asked.

"Yup. This elevator can drop you off at any part of the house. It's half really good engineering and half magic." Nikki winked as she said the latter half of the sentence. "A lot of this house runs on magic."

"Can't demons sense us more if we use all this magic?" Sam was confused, but also extremely curious about what other parts of the house were magical.

"Nope. That's a myth perpetuated by fantasy novels. Demons and other creatures can sense magical beings, but not the magic they use. No matter what we do, they'll be able to find us. So the use of magic is pretty free around here. Just remember to be careful when you leave the property these two buildings are on."

"Oh," Sam said. The elevator opened to a gorgeous two doors opening and revealing a room with a vaulted ceiling and gray-brown oak wooden floors. Floor to ceiling windows surrounded her.

"This is the primary bedroom of the penthouse." Ashley stepped out and walked inside. She gestured to the left. "This is the main bath of this floor. The view from the tub is amazing."

Maybe a view of a lighthouse? Sam followed her into what she expected would be a regular bathroom. To her surprise, it was the size of a bedroom. Inside, there was a large bathtub made of porcelain in the middle and a wall made of glass facing the ocean. There was a stainless steel rain shower head placed above it. She could see the forest and beach outside. Sam pressed her hand on the window and peered outside, but her heart sank as she saw no lighthouse anywhere. *How much time do I have 'til Seth is expecting me?*

"Come, let's see the closet!" Nikki pulled Sam's arm. She opened the double doors and was amazed to see a blank room.

"Oh. Sorry. I forgot to tell you that the closet is actually not done yet. Sky was leaving the project for Sam, actually. He didn't want to design everything until she got here." Ashley announced while Nikki pouted, looking at the bare room.

I guess interior design is where Sky thinks my opinion finally matters. Sam tried to suppress her bitter feelings and push this thought aside because, despite his annoying habit of hiding things, he was giving her this amazing place to live in. She didn't want to be ungrateful considering every other house she lived in barely had walls.

"Sounds fun. I'd love to design my own space," Sam said as she looked into the closet closely. *Huh. My own space sounds nice.* Her eyes quickly spotted a clock on the floor. Its hour hand was at four. "Um, is that clock accurate?" *Shoot. This tour is taking longer than I expected. I need to leave now.*

"Oh, yes," Ashley said as she checked her phone. "Sky probably left it there by accident."

"Oh, no worries." *Quick. Sam, how are you going to leave a mansion of people trying to welcome you? Maybe they'll take you back outside and you can slip away for a while?* "So, the house next to us…Do you guys know them?" *No, that's dumb. A dozen people will definitely notice you being gone.*

"Actually, we do. We're all pretty close to them. Sky and Maddi have basically taken the role of parents around here."

"Oh, so there really are more of us on Earth?" Sam was suddenly intrigued, but her excitement lasted only a few seconds. Her hands were getting sweaty and she could feel every minute passing get heavier and feel shorter.

"Yeah. So far, we only know of our two houses, but there has to be more out there you know?" Nikki said.

"Should we go back down to meet the others?" Ashley asked.

I have an hour to figure out how far away I am from the caves and get to the lighthouse to meet Seth. Hurry! She had to find out how to get to their secret spot. She remembered that there was a beach behind the house, which meant that she was closer to where she needed to be than before. She still couldn't believe that there was a mansion filled with her family so close to where she had been staying this past week.

"Wait, before we go, we were both really curious to ask about your name. Sky won't allow us to mention our names from the magical dimension here, but we had to ask." Nikki clapped her hands in excitement.

"Oh, yeah." Sam froze. She realized she had been tapping her feet in anticipation to leave. "Mine's Sameera." *Is Sky really that worried about mortals finding out our names?*

"Achara for me and Nikora for Nikki. We sometimes use them for our magic when the boys aren't paying attention, and now you can join us." Ashley smiled and then gestured for them to follow her down.

Using magic behind Derek and Sky's back sounds like the move. Sam walked to the room's door. *I might just have to stick with Ashley and Nikki.*

"Sameera's pretty. Just don't tell Sky we asked," Nikki instructed, raising one finger to her mouth and winking. The two of them walked towards the elevator and they all made their way back down to the first floor. Sam glanced at her watch again.

Forty-five minutes, Sam! She looked worried.

"Are you okay?" Nikki asked.

"Yeah. I...um, would it be okay if I just explored the place for a while? There's so much to cover, and the hedge maze looked pretty fun," Sam said, hoping their feelings wouldn't be hurt. She was really grateful for her cousins showing her around and giving her a space to live, but she hadn't antici-pated that eavesdropping on Derek would lead to a day-long journey to meet a family she didn't know. She had to meet her friend at any cost.

"Okay, we get this may be overwhelming for you, so if you want to have some time for yourself, we can distract the others," Ashley said.

"Yeah, don't worry. The sisters always help each other get away with stuff. You're soon going to learn that all of our brothers are way too overprotective. They have some weird older sibling complex." Nikki shrugged. "It's sweet, but we don't always need it."

"Tell me about it. Derek and Sky are a nightmare." Sam laughed and then hugged the two girls. The elevator opened and the girls motioned for Sam to sneak out through the mud room's side entrance. "Thank you. I'll be back around 6 p.m."

CHAPTER 3

SIRENS BLARING

How did I end up even closer to the beach than before? And where's the lighthouse Seth mentioned? She looked left and right and couldn't see anything. No lighthouse. All she saw was the side of a mountain cliff cutting off her view of the rest of the ocean. She decided she would try to see what was past the cliffside and walked next to the water. The sound of waves crashing filled her left ear. Soon she was behind the other mansion. *Who lives there? Is there anyone my age? I wonder what angels their family are related to.* She couldn't believe just how many people Sky knew from the magical realms.

Sam stared at the number of windows the house had. These houses seemed more like resorts. *So demons don't come here because we have a lot of people, but how do we draw human attention away from us? This place is huge and gorgeous, but this beach is so empty. Not a single human is here.* She kept questioning until her gaze landed on a window on the second floor. There was a young boy staring out at her. He had deep, piercing blue eyes and messy ruffled black-brown hair. She quickly looked away and began walking towards the cliffs. *Maybe he didn't notice me? No, he definitely saw me.*

The cliffs got closer, and the sun was slowly sinking in the sky. She climbed above some rocks. *Ow!* Sam brushed away the small pebbles that were rubbing against her knees. As she made her way across the shallow water to the other side of the cliff, the smell of the saltwater and fish got stronger. She looked above and luckily, found that the lighthouse was in front of her. She made her way toward it.

Slippery rocks made it hard for Sam to walk through the cove. Thankfully her hair stopped blowing around as she got deeper into the cave and left the sea breeze behind. "Seth?" she yelled, and her voice echoed. "I'm sorry I'm late. I got lost." She looked around the cave pool and saw nobody. Then something caught her eye. It was shimmering in the sunlight and Aegean blue. "Nice try. Your tail isn't that discreet, you know," she said, laughing as she dipped her feet in the ocean water next to Seth. He pulled his head out of the water and looked at her.

"I guess I could have hidden better, given you made me wait so long." He splashed her with water. His long tail appeared out of the water and caught Sam's attention. Seth had dark, almost black hair that against his bright eyes and bronzed complexion made him gorgeous to look at. It also didn't hurt that, being a merman, he had alluring attributes of a siren within him.

"Hey!" She laughed.

"How'd you get lost?" he asked with genuine curiosity in his voice.

"You will never believe what happened today. I finally confronted Sky and Derek in one of their fights over my future."

"Oh. Yeah, the typical day-to-day fights." Seth quipped.

"Well, it led to Sky taking me to meet the rest of my family on Earth. He took me to a huge mansion, and there were so many people there who are supposedly related to me. They gave me the penthouse. And it turns out that the house next to us is filled with another family from the magical realm," Sam rambled.

"Woah. Woah. Slow down. What?" He propped himself up on a rock. "My news was just that I found a way to get legs for a day, but you have me beat."

"You found what?" Sam nearly yelled. Her voice echoed in the cove. "How? Where? When? I mean, when are you going to use it? Is it only a one-time thing?"

"One time, but I think I can get more. I was hoping that, on my day at land, we could go on an adventure and maybe find the potion?" His eyes gleamed up at her. "I know that the water-to-land spell for mermen is a myth, but it wouldn't hurt to try and find it, right?"

"Of course, but where'd you find the one day spell?"

"So, it's actually a type of coral that I can eat. Someone I ran into gave me some, but it came with a price."

"You ran into someone? Is it safe? Corals can be extremely toxic."

"I think that is the price. He said that, long term, the coral can have negative side effects. It's all down to the person and how their body reacts to it. He also said that the coral is the main ingredient for the potion we'd have to make. I don't know if he's telling me the truth, but I want to at least find the potion before deciding," Seth said as he turned and had his tail flow in front of him in the water. "I don't know. I'm scared, but I don't think I can live in the water any longer. I'm all alone in this realm."

There was a moment of silence between them. Seth had been alone in the oceans of Earth for his whole life. They had no idea how or why he was in this realm. No mortals could see him if he wanted any chance to live. *No mortals. Who was this person that Seth had met?* Sam only saw him by chance while she was practicing controlling her fire by the ocean. He approached her thinking that she would be safe to talk to since she clearly wasn't human. They had bonded over their lack of knowledge of their parents and having powers they had to hide. In fact, Seth was the only person Sam had told about her gift outside her siblings. She knew she couldn't trust anyone with the secret, but she also knew Seth could relate to living in secret. *Who was he going to tell anyways?*

"Well, you won't be alone longer. I'm going to help you get the potion and then maybe we can finally escape."

Seth looked at Sam as she said these words and just smiled. He didn't say anything back, but they both knew that all they wanted was to have someplace where they weren't the odd ones out. Where they didn't have to run or hide because they had powers. "Well, the first thing I'm going to do with legs is walk on that sand over there." Seth pointed towards the sand covering the cave floor behind them. "Maybe lie on some grass. Climb a tree." He kept speaking, but Sam stopped listening. She looked at his face, bright with a large cheek-to-cheek grin. She liked seeing him like this.

"The first thing I want to do when you have legs is see if I can finally swim faster than you," she said laughing.

"As if." He laughed too. "Legs or not, I've still always lived in the ocean."

"We'll just have to wait and find out." Sam rolled her eyes. She couldn't wait for Seth to live on land. She hated that they could only meet a few times a month and always for short times, since she had to hide him from her family. *When he's on land, we can hang out without anyone finding out about his true identity. Although now, with having a whole family, sneaking off doesn't seem so likely.* "Where are you going to live once you get legs?" Sam looked towards her friend with a slight frown. "I don't think our beach shed idea is going to work out."

"Oh, right. Our very own personal shed by a secluded beach. Oh man, we can only dream."

"If I figure out my powers and get away from Derek and Sky, I'm ready to get that shed."

"So, never..." Seth laughed and looked at Sam with a smile. He scooted closer to her. "As for me, I don't know. I'll have to find a job or something. Maybe I'll become a magician." He laughed, but Sam's face dropped. She hadn't thought about whether they would still be anywhere near each other once he had legs. "Don't worry. I'll always be by the ocean, so we won't be far." He rested his hand on Sam's knee. "I can always do illusions in Hollywood." They both stared through the cave opening at the gorgeous pink and purple streaks in the sky above the glistening ocean. Seth lifted his hand towards the sun and changed its appearance to look like the moon. "Tourists would love this type of stuff." He giggled, and Sam looked in awe at how pretty the moon looked in the sunset colors.

"Yeah. Your powers were literally made for that," she teased. So far his powers of illusion were only good for hiding him from humans at sea. "Think about how much fun your illusions and my mind control could be if we went on quests together."

"That we'll definitely have to try." Seth looked up at her and smiled and then pointed at the sky as the moon disappeared and the sun returned. "It's getting late. You should head back before your new family comes searching for you."

"You're right. I'm probably not making a good impression right now. I just, well, I don't know what to say. They don't even know about my gift or at least haven't mentioned it."

"They don't?" He asked, surprised. "Maybe it's for the best, though, you know. The less people who know, the easier it'll be to hide." He shrugged.

"Yeah, but hey, before I go, can I ask you something?" Sam steadied herself on the wet rock.

"Of course."

"Who was the person you met? They couldn't have been human, right?"

"I don't know. I was a bit unnerved that someone had seen me at all, but he said he knew the land of sirens and other creatures, so, no, he wasn't a mortal."

Could it have been someone in her family or the house next door? "Be careful. It seems suspicious that someone magical was just ready with helpful information." She got up and waved at him. "See ya next week."

"Bye! Oh, and I expect a mansion tour once I can walk on land!" he exclaimed.

"I recently found out that Iris messaging is real, so, if I figure that out, you could get a tour even sooner." Sam nodded excitedly and then left.

Knowing the route better now, Sam made sure to avoid being visible to the window boy. She looked at the waves and could make out Travis and a girl on surfboards. *Mia! She's here and already friends with Travis, huh?* She waved them down, but they didn't notice. Instead, Sam saw a wave the size of a bus looming over them but remarkably staying still. Travis had his hand up in the air as if he was controlling the wave. *So Travis controls the ocean? Mia must love that, and maybe he's the one that found Seth. I have to find out who Seth met without exposing him.*

She continued watching in awe as the wave was about to come crashing down, but this time Mia moved her arm up and froze it. *Woah. Mia is definitely a lot better at controlling water than I am with fire.* Sam hated admitting it to herself, but she could barely start a flame, much less control it if it was rushing towards her.

She resumed walking, but this time with her head hanging low. She watched the sand as her feet kicked it around with every step. *Maybe you can finally train with other people here. Mia found someone to teach her. You can too.*

As she neared the mansion, she heard unfamiliar voices. *More family?* Sky was talking to some girl. "Maddi, I finally got them to move to the house!" he said. "Sam helped a bit, and Derek finally gave in."

"That's great. Where are they?"

"I don't know where Sam is, but the rest are here. Do you want to come inside and meet them?" Sky said with a little hesitation in his voice. Sam walked towards the side of the house near the door and peered over the corner.

"I'd love to, but I also have exciting news. Remember the Greens?" she asked as her face lit up.

"Yeah..."

"Well, I got their mum to let them come here for the summer! There are four boys and one girl. Unfortunately, the girl is too young to come without her parents, but the boys are waiting back at the house." She gestured towards the other mansion. "I'm going to go get them, and then we can all meet each other."

"Okay, see you soon!" Sky's voice went an octave higher almost cracking. Sam could hear his voice quiver. As he closed the door he palmed his forehead and muttered something under his breath.

I wonder if one of these boys was the one I saw through the window. She continued sneaking around the side wall of the house and entered through the side door Ashley had shown her. Sam was immediately hit with a sweet smell of baked goods and vanilla. *Are they making something special for us? A mansion filled with family means no more ordering pizza or eating out every night.*

Sam walked into view of her now huge family. "Hey! Sam! We missed you earlier," a guy said. She had no idea who he was or what her reply should be.

"Oh. Uh, sorry, I got lost exploring the house. It's huge," she said and then locked eyes with Ethan. She retreated beside him, trying to avoid questions about her whereabouts.

"No worries. We'll show you around more after dinner. We had an idea, actually. Oh, by the way, I'm Jake." He had an overall cheery look about him, with his ear-to-ear grin and large almond-shaped brown eyes, despite wearing dark clothing—a black tee-shirt over tight, dark ripped jeans that complimented his khaki skin tone.

I wonder how long they've all known we exist? "Hi. Thanks for letting us in," Sam replied rather shyly. Jake giggled along with the others.

"Guys, sorry to interrupt, but I have important news. Maddi is bringing over the newest members of their family, so I need everyone to be really polite, okay? Please…" Sky said as he scrunched up his shirt in his fists.

"Okay, Dad," Travis joked, rolling his eyes. He walked in along with Mia, both drenched and tracking in sand. He began snickering to Jake. Sky's eyebrow twitched at the sight.

"Please just get your jokes out now, okay." Sky sighed. "And clean up that sand, before the guests arrive."

"So, Maddi is coming over, huh. Are you sure you want to be wearing that?" Ashley teased as she looked at Sky's attire in disapproval. Sky looked down at his plain black shirt frantically.

"Is this not okay? Oh no! it's the camo pants, isn't it? What should I change into?" Sky asked. Everyone erupted into laughter. Sam couldn't help but smile. *Having a family seems like fun.* She hoped that she would get the chance to get close to all of them and join in on the banter next time. The idea of this house being safe seemed promising. *Staying here would be perfect. I can help Seth out and I have a feeling that living here means Derek will loosen up about using our powers.*

"Chill, Sky. You look fine, and Maddi likes you already. Don't worry so much," Derek assured him as he put his hand on Sky's shoulder. He quickly created a gust of wind to blow the sand away to the corner and smiled at Sky.

Hmm. Derek seems to know about Maddi. How often has he come here and left the rest of us in the dark about our family and this house?

Sam turned suddenly as she heard a knock on the door. *That must be the Green brothers and Maddi.* She was having to keep up with a lot of names right now. She surely wasn't going to remember anyone tomorrow.

"Okay. Here goes nothing." Sky walked over to the door as he muttered to himself.

He opened the rather large and grand oak doors to reveal the expected guests. Sam could see why Sky was so into Maddi. She had an aura of confidence and control around her. On top of that she was also stunning. Her dark blonde hair shone golden under the ray of sunlight now entering the home. She looked like a princess. But to Sam's surprise, Maddi wasn't the only eye-catching person at the door. The boys all looked like models. They were also strikingly similar in appearance, as if they were the real life representation of a person at different ages—well, except for one. *It's window boy!* His eyes were starkly different from his brothers' green ones, and he was the only one who didn't have golden brown locks. If Maddi looked like a princess, he definitely looked like a prince, especially in his navy blue sweater and white button-down shirt. She couldn't look away. He noticed her and smiled back, shyly. *Shoot. Sam! You can't stare at them.* She turned to her brother Ethan, who had noticed her eyeing the guests and held back a laugh. He gently nudged her shoulder and then looked back at the guests.

"Hey, everyone! These are the Green brothers. They're from...Sweden," Maddi declared.

Sam couldn't help but notice a slight hesitation in Maddi's voice when she said Sweden. *Maybe I'm not the only one riddled with secrets.* She looked back at the blue-eyed boy as Maddi introduced his name. *So his name is Logan, huh. He seems to be the youngest of the four.*

"Damn, Sweden? That's dope," Travis said but immediately got a look of disapproval from Sky. "Oh, uh, sorry. That's cool." He laughed awkwardly.

"Would you guys like to join us for dinner? We have more than we can possibly eat ourselves." Sky's voice became soft and almost reserved when he spoke. *Maddi really makes him nervous.* Sam projected her thoughts to Ethan and Mia.

"Yeah, actually. This is not the Sky I imagined from what you and Derek mentioned." Ethan struggled to not laugh as he whispered subtly to Sam and Mia. Sam loved seeing Sky like this because she had only ever seen the strict and slightly irritating side of him.

Maddi really kills his controlling side.

"Now we just got to find the person who gets Derek off of our backs," Mia whispered to the twins.

Does anyone like that exist? Sam laughed loudly. She made eye contact with Logan who was now staring at her in confusion.

"Sure, we would love to," Logan interjected in a thick European accent. His face lit up with a grin. *Is that what a Swedish accent sounds like?* Sam smiled back at him appreciating that he took the attention off of her and her siblings. She mouthed, "Thank you."

"Okay, that sounds nice." Maddi tried to be polite, but Sam noticed that she was also nervous. Sky and Maddi both kept looking at each other and then looking down as they spoke. *Okay, so they both like each other and are oblivious to it. Good to know.* Sam was trying to figure this family out to see if she even fit in here and more importantly, she wanted to learn everyone's little quirks. *I want to make this a home.*

CHAPTER 4

ANGEL POWERS MAKE BASKETBALL SCARY

Dinner smelled delicious. Sam's stomach growled. She had forgotten all about eating between the mansion, the people, and Seth. She was ready to devour everything in front of her. There was a large tempered glass dining table filled with food from different parts of the world. *I wonder if everyone here made a dish. Feeding over a dozen people every meal everyday must be hard.*

Sky walked over and opened the Olympic blue curtains to let the sunlight filter in. "Come. Sit. Let's start eating." He grinned and gestured to Maddi as he pulled a chair out for her. The rest of them started to find seats.

Sam pulled Ethan's arm and took him to the seats next to Logan. He turned towards her and smiled, but neither of them spoke a word. *Does he remember me? I wonder if he told anyone that he saw me.* She pushed off the awkward silence by focusing on the food.

"Could you pass the bread, Ethan?" she asked, waiting excitedly since she had been smelling it from the moment she walked in. He passed them to her, and she eagerly took a few pieces. Sam felt a breeze. *Did Sky open the windows too?* She looked up to find the windows closed but noticed that everyone was using their powers one way or another. Derek, across from her, was cooling off his soup by blowing frosty air from his mouth. *I can't believe Derek had us use our powers so secretively all these years, and now he has no problem using them for his simplest needs.* She looked towards Sky, who was trying to make the day sunnier. He had his hand up towards the sun and was shifting the sun's rays to create a golden hour appearance in their dining hall. *Wow, so Sky controls weather? I wonder what everyone else's special gifts from their parents are. Maybe I should be using mine to blend in?*

She looked at Ethan, who frowned in confusion. He began grabbing a plate of salad and turned to Sam. He shrugged as he raised his hand and instantly made his salad look more vibrant. *Shoot, it's my turn. These rolls could be warmer, I guess.* Sam held her hand under the table and tried to generate heat onto the plate in front of her. Warmth floated up to her face. *This seems to be working.* She was about to remove her hand when a small flame burst over the rolls. *Shoot. Shoot. Shoot. What am I going to do?* She lifted her hand and tried to focus on getting rid of the flame before it got big enough for anyone to notice. She closed her eyes and opened to see the flame gone. Her face lit up in a grin for a second until she realized Logan's napkin was in front of her. He had thrown it on the rolls to extinguish the fire. She pouted. *Oof, still can't control that.*

"So, fire, huh?" He smirked at her. "That's pretty dope," he said, mimicking Travis earlier. Sam laughed a bit loudly. His accent made California slang sound sillier than it already did. Everyone turned to look at Sam and Logan, who were both blushing. "I'll take a few warmed rolls as well." He tried to ease the awkwardness, but all Sam noticed was that he wasn't using his powers. *First Maddi hesitated about where they're from, then he acted like he hadn't seen me earlier, and now he's hiding his powers?* She passed him some of the rolls.

"I don't think we should risk warming them again." He smiled and began eating.

"Agreed," she whispered. "Thanks, though."

"No worries. Powers are hard." Logan sighed. "Is that tzatziki?" He pointed to a dish on the opposite end of the table.

"Yeah, here you go. Ash was trying to make something new for us today," Travis said, passing over the bowl.

Tza—what? How did he pronounce it? I guess, I'll try it too. She watched as Logan ate his bread with the dip and did the same. *And what are his powers?* Sam contemplated asking him directly. *No, just keep quiet. He might ask questions about where I was going if I ask him. Or maybe he really didn't see me? Okay, Sam, maybe just ask him.* Sam opened her mouth and nothing came out.

"So how's Sweden this time of the year? Pretty cold now, huh?" Sky asked Logan, cutting off any chance for Sam.

"It's fine. Not too cold."

"Isn't it still snowing there right now?" Travis asked, confused.

"Oh yeah. You know how it is. Once you live in the snow, it doesn't seem that bad." Logan's older brother chimed in and gave Logan a side-eye look of disapproval.

"Yes, that is what I meant. We are used to it now."

His answers are so vague and confusing. Sam watched his brothers, who seemed to fit in easily, unlike her or Logan. One of them was helping Nikki bring a few trays and almost dropped the pad thai. He quickly froze the food in midair and then raced to catch it.

"So, do you speak Swedish?" Sam asked Logan.

"Mostly English," he replied but kept staring straight at his food.

"Oh, interesting." Her voice wavered. *He seems more interested in holding secrets than a conversation.* Maybe it was Sam's need to protect her secret meeting with Seth, but she was definitely intrigued by Logan. He looked up at her with wide eyes.

"Um...my brothers and I went to boarding school in England for most of our lives, so we never picked it up." Logan immediately blurted out. He was nervously tapping the table with his fingers.

Something's off about him.

After everyone finished eating, Maddi helped Sky take all the dishes to the kitchen. The two of them began cleaning while the families watched. "I feel like we shouldn't be here anymore." Logan's eldest brother gestured to Maddi and Sky flirting and giggling.

"Welcome to our everyday life, Hayden." Jake reached his hand out to shake Hayden's. "Let's leave them to it and maybe go play basketball?"

"Sure, that sounds good," Hayden replied, looking at his brothers for agreement.

Wow. New family and new friends all in one day. Everybody left the two flirting teens and headed towards the beach. Sam didn't know how she had missed it on her way to Seth, but between the two houses was a shared basketball court. *No, volleyball? Tennis?* The court had the lines for nearly every major sport painted on the ground, but no other gear or hardware. Sam stood confused wondering how they were going to play with no hoops and no ball.

Ashley walked to one end and said a few words as her hand hovered over the now-glowing ground. "Kaláthi." Nikki quickly ran to the other side and repeated the same thing. Boards raised from the ground. Sam looked on in awe. Her mouth fell open. In a few seconds, a hoop and a long pole could be visible. *Well, that answers the basketball questions!* She looked shocked that nobody else seemed to think this was unnatural. Sam wondered what you had to say to make it a different type of court. *I don't think I've ever seen this much magic in one day or even a month.*

"We're ready," Ashley said, picking up the basketball that materialized in the middle of the court.

"Okay, in honor of our new friends, we'll have Hayden be one team captain and Travis can be the other." Jake declared as he eyed Travis.

They definitely have a plan to win this already. Sam hadn't played in a few years now. She had been on a little kids team when her parents were alive. It was a much different life. She didn't know how she would play with all the older kids, but it seemed like Ethan and Logan were joining in, so she had some support.

"We pick Derek." Hayden sure was playing to win. He had already started picking out the older athletic people.

"We'll take Ash," Travis said. Ashley went in, high-fiving Travis and Jake. Sam watched as everyone got divided up and she found herself on the opposite team to both Ethan and Logan. *So much for that support. At least I have Travis and Ashley.* She mustered up her courage and joined the court.

"Get ready to lose." Ashley winked at one of the middle brothers as they stepped up to the center for the jump ball.

"That confident, huh? By the way, it's Liam, in case you were wondering," he chimed, winking back at Ashley. He had a boyish smile that made Sam blush, but Ashley didn't seem phased. Before Liam could notice that the ball was thrown, Ashley flashed past everyone's eyes and tapped the ball to Travis. "Super speed? Two can play that game." He slowed the ball's speed and intercepted it before Travis had a chance to catch it.

"Finally, someone to make this game interesting!" Ashley grinned.

So powers here, too? All I know is how to make the ball disintegrate into ashes. Let's not try that today. Sam saw Logan run towards Jake to try to block him, but he was about a foot too short. He looked behind him to see where he was moving, but Jake disappeared. *Where'd he go?* Nobody was behind Logan, and Sam was dumbfounded. Looking around, Sam saw that Ethan and Mia were shocked too. "What just happened?" Laughter came from where Jake had been.

Travis, who now held the ball, threw it towards the seemingly empty air next to Logan, and to Sam's surprise it stopped and floated in midair. A faint silhouette shined against the sunrays. *Jake can become invisible?* Nikki ran towards him but as she got closer, Jake split into three people, each with the basketball. *Which one's real?* Sam was sure Nikki would stand no chance, but then she saw her turn into a shadow and race around all three Jakes until there was only one of him again.

"Brother, you always use the same tricks." Nikki smiled. She stole the ball easily from the now-dizzy Jake.

Everyone was using their powers to play the game. Sam was no longer playing a game of basketball, but some weird battle of angel children instead. She watched Travis make water materialize under Sky and then Sky retaliate by having the sun evaporate the puddle. *I really wish I could use my mind control powers here, but Derek would kill me if I even hinted towards having the gift.*

Ashley seemed to be guarding Liam heavily as they both tried to counteract each other's powers. It almost seemed unnecessary, since neither of them were getting possession of the ball. They definitely had a spark, but Sam was more interested in the conversation Ethan seemed to be having with Logan. They were laughing as they returned to their spots on the basketball court. *Maybe I can ask Ethan to scope out Logan for me?*

As the game progressed, Sam found herself more so just running back and forth and not really participating. She noticed Logan high-fiving Ethan and patting his back after they performed a smooth alley-oop. *Why do they have such good chemistry already? I wonder what they're talking about.* She ran towards Derek, who had the ball, but he easily took a shot past her and made a basket, having the wind guide the ball in when it was about to fall outside the hoop. She walked back to her side, her body hanging low. *Come on, Sam! Where is your competitive spirit?*

Jake started with the ball, and Sam ran to be open on the right-hand side of the court. "Pass to Sam! She can do it," Ashley yelled at Jake, who quickly pivoted and passed the ball to Sam. *Shoot. Sam. Shoot.* Sam turned to the hoop and noticed Ethan and Derek coming in to rush her. Her palms were getting sweatier. It would be easy to take the ball right out of her slippery grip. *Shoot.* Sam breathed heavily as she saw Ashley block Ethan, but Derek was making his way across the court. *Shoot.* The hoop blurred in front of her eyes. Her head felt like it was burning. *Shoot.* Sam pivoted towards Travis and passed him the ball. Her shoulders felt tight. She palmed her forehead thinking how dumb that was. *You could have tried.* She sulked.

The rest of the players hurried around her but seemed to continue the game without noticing her. *You're coming back here tomorrow and building some faith in yourself Sam.* She continued trying to get into the game for the rest of the hour as the sun set by the waves next to them.

***

The sunlight at the court had slowly dwindled down from bright orange to black. The game had ended about thirty minutes ago, but Sam was still on the court watching the waves crash. *I wish I had a bit more confidence in the game.* She was deep in thought about everything that had happened in just one day. *How can I have such an aggressive power like fire and be so timid? And how do I use my powers to my advantage without being too aggressive?* She laid down to look at the sky. She could see stars for once, which was surprising to her since Malibu was still a densely populated city. *At least after today I now have a huge family. And they all seem to get how annoying Sky can be.*

"Sam." Derek walked up behind her. "You're still out here?"

"Hey, yeah, needed time to think." She patted the ground next to her and Derek joined her to look at the stars.

"So. How's the house? Sky thought you deserved the penthouse," Derek asked.

"Deserved? Probably more like he can control me better there," Sam said. Derek laughed.

"I noticed you weren't quite on your A-game today, though. What happened? You used to love basketball." Sam didn't respond right away. She wasn't really listening to her brother's words.

"Huh, sorry, what?" Sam finally answered. Derek turned towards her with a concerned look.

"Are you okay?"

"Can I ask you something?"

"Of course."

"Can you train me? I want to be able to fight. I want to be able to use my powers like everyone today, not be limited by them." Sam made eye contact with Derek. He sighed, got up, and reached out his hand. Sam took it and got up. He looked at the waves crashing by the ocean in silence with his arms crossed. "You can't, because you and Sky have some weird plan. Okay, whatever. Forget I asked." Sam began to walk away.

"No, wait," Derek called out. Sam stopped and turned around. "Trust me, I want to train you. I think you need to be able to protect yourself. Life isn't easy for any of us, but Sam, life's really not going to be easy for you if anyone knows what power you have." Sam took a step back and looked down. *That's the first time he has been so honest with me. It's kind of scary, but I like it.*

She walked towards her brother again and put her arm on his shoulder. "Then teach me something. I know Dad trained you to fight with weapons and Mom wouldn't let you do anything before you passed her power tests."

"Sky won't allow it."

"Aren't you older? The way you've been running things, it seems like that should mean you have the final say." Derek looked back at her with a frown. Sam hoped that, if she pushed Derek enough, he'd succumb to her plan. He ran his fingers through his hair, looking away from her momentarily.

"Okay, let's do it. Starting tomorrow, we're going to work out and train for one-on-one combat. They have a great gym here."

"You really knew about this place all this time and never told us?" Sam asked. Derek's smile quickly turned into a panicked frown.

"Listen. I made some mistakes. I didn't know if being around everyone would be better or worse for you." He looked down. "Today seemed like a really impulsive decision, but I've been thinking a lot about it, and I think we can make this work. You know. Staying here. Having a full family. And your training."

"That sounds good." She gave Derek a hug. She didn't understand all of his decisions still, but she really did feel for him. *He did have to start taking care of all of us at the same time as grieving for our parents. I should be giving him some slack.* "Can you teach me any of the cool tricks you know, too?"

"How about I teach you one right now?" Derek smiled. Sam's face lit up as she nodded excitedly. "Okay, so the key to fighting well isn't always being the bigger or stronger person. A lot of the time, you're going to need to use your opponent's strength against them." He lifted her arm and bent it moving her elbow towards his nose. "Your elbow is the strongest part of your body. If someone is coming in behind you." Derek positioned himself behind Sam's left shoulder. "Swing your elbow back into their face. Any upward blow from your elbow to the face will likely push the opponent backwards giving you time to better position yourself." Sam looked back at him and smiled. *This is actually really cool. I didn't think I could overpower someone physically stronger.* She began trying to imagine different scenarios where someone was coming up behind her as she practiced the motion again.

"Hey! Derek! What are you two doing?" A voice yelled behind them. Derek turned quickly.

Shoot, Sky's here. Sam stopped practicing and faced Sky. "We were just..." Sam stuttered.

"You were training, weren't you?" Sky interrupted Sam.

"Yeah. We were. How long do you think we can protect her ourselves? Sooner or later she has to learn. Keith won't take much longer before finding out who has the gift." Derek took a firm stance in front of Sam as Sky approached them

"Not now. She's too young." Sky looked pissed. Lightning struck on the ocean and dark clouds quickly covered the moon. "This is only going to bring attention to her, and you know it."

"You don't want to mess with me, Sky." Derek blew some wind from his mouth, creating a gust that made Sky struggle to move forward.

"I think creating a freak storm will draw att—" Sam tried yelling over Derek and Sky's powers.

"You know I'm more powerful, Derek." Sky shouted, cutting off Sam. Thunder rolled in the background. Sky and Derek stood face to face glaring at each other.

I can't believe it. They're back to ignoring me in a conversation about my life. I guess the Maddi effect wore off already. "Guys, I'm done. If you won't teach me, I'll find someone who will." Sam ran off towards the side of the mansion. She kept running past the side yard and the fountain in front. *Every step I make forward with Derek, Sky takes us back five.* She turned towards the wooded area in between the two mansions and ran through the dense brush and trees, barely able to see anything. *They're so worried about my safety, but then too distracted to even notice that I left. It makes no sense. Nothing makes sense. Why would learning how to use my powers be dangerous? Can't it only help to have more knowledge?* The spongy grass bounced under her feet. She lit a small flame on her hand to create light. She didn't want to risk anything bigger that she may not be able to control.

Sam stopped after a while to catch her breath and placed her hands on her knees, getting rid of the flame. *I can't make the same mistake as with dinner.* As she stood back up and walked forward something hit her forehead. Sam looked up to see a weeping willow tree with several low-hanging branches. *When are they going to treat me like a person and not their personal project, fighting over how I should behave and what I should do?* She angrily swatted the branches and took a seat on the ground, starting a mini flame on the end of twig next to her.

"Sam?" A familiar husky voice spoke in front of her. She looked up and saw the same blue eyes that seemed to be catching her in the worst moments.

"Logan?"

"What are you doing here?" He walked closer and crouched down beside her. *Shoot. What do I say? He can't know about the gift or Derek and Sky's real reason for bringing me here. Divert the conversation. Divert! Divert!*

"Nothing. Just exploring." She looked at the flame in her hand and felt a bit self-conscious about the last time she used her powers in front of Logan. She let the flame disappear. The lack of light made it more awkward between them.

"Me too. That and avoiding the phone call my brothers are on with our mom. She wants me to come back, and I only just got here." Logan sighed, shaking his face as he looked down.

"Let me guess. She's making all the decisions about your life even though your siblings can do whatever they want?"

"Yup. She doesn't even care if my brothers stay the whole summer, but I have to come back as fast as possible. It's so frustrating being the youngest," Logan ranted.

"Do you ever feel like you had to grow up too fast, but everybody still treats you like the kid you used to be?" She looked down.

"Yeah, actually I've been feeling that for as long as I can remember," Logan said in a soft voice. Sam was surprised. She didn't think he would relate. "I'm the same age as when my brothers all got to travel and be their own people, yet somehow I don't actually have any of the control or autonomy that they have."

"Exactly. Hierarchy seems to matter more than maturity or experience." *Wow. He kind of gets me.* "We don't get a say in anything, but if we act like the children that they treat us like, then we're also wrong." Sam looked over at Logan to see him nodding.

"How can we act mature and be young and let others dictate our actions?" He stood up and walked towards a bench beside the tree. Sam hadn't noticed it before. "I just don't get it," he continued his thought. Sam joined him and suddenly realized how small the bench was and how close they were sitting next to each other. *Sam. Don't trust him too much. You still don't even know his powers.* She had her guard up, but she also felt a sense of security knowing she wasn't alone in how she felt. They sat in a comfortable silence—the kind that you could enjoy and not worry about the conversation dying down.

"I guess that's the life of the youngest kid." Sam laughed sarcastically.

"Yeah. Always having to sneak out and avoid the adults."

Logan looked at Sam. *Shoot. He saw me, didn't he?*

"I was afraid you were the person I saw in the window."

"Where were you even off to?" He laughed.

"Just finding a quiet place by the beach." *I don't think I can trust him to know about Seth. Not yet, at least.*

"Anywhere I should go?"

"Yeah. The beaches here are amazing. Between the caves and tide pools it would take years to explore everything." Sam finally met Logan's gaze. "Maybe we can go sometime. I'll show you the places I've found."

"I'd like that." He got up and then gestured to her to follow him. "Actually, since we're already hiding out from the older kids, why don't you show me some right now?

Sam sprung to her feet and they walked towards the clearing in the woods that led to the beach. "Let's do it!"

PART 2

SAM BLEU AND LOGAN GREEN

CHAPTER 5

DIRT BIKES AND DEMONS

———

LOGAN

The two fourteen-year-olds walked off the cement of the court onto the damp sand. It was colder than before from the night's breeze. *Thank the angels that Sam was willing to do something right now. I don't think I could have argued with mother any longer. I can't leave Malibu until I figure out my powers.*

Logan watched as Sam looked around the beach. "Hey, why don't we explore over there?" Sam proposed as she pointed at the dense forest to their left.

"I don't know, it's pretty dark out. We won't make it very far." Logan shuddered just looking at the forest. It was pitch black through the thick brush and trees.

"Let's find a way. I'm sure Sky keeps something in the garage."

I guess it's the forest or going back to the call with my mother. Forest wins. Logan gulped. They walked over to the small building near the mansion that had been repurposed as a garage. Thankfully, it hadn't been locked. Sam lifted the door and gasped.

"Woah," Logan mumbled. He walked through a row of dozens of dirt bikes. *Mother would never let me ride these.* His fingers ran over the cold metal as he examined all of them.

"We need to try these out." Sam quickly tried to climb onto one of the bikes but nearly fell.

"I don't know. Do you know how to ride one? This seems dangerous."

"I'm sure there are smaller ones." She dusted off her knees. Logan pursed his lips, trying hard not to laugh. *You're a prince. You're trained not to react impolitely. Don't laugh.* Sam looked at him and began laughing. "What?" he asked, blushing.

"You're just so serious." Sam ran to the back, and her face lit up when she saw a few smaller bikes. "Perfect. Let's try these."

"If you say so." Logan reluctantly tried carrying the bike out of the garage. *Too serious, that's a first. Maybe I do need to be more adventurous like her.* Both of them looked at each other and then mounted the bikes. "I didn't expect the amount of danger you were ready for when I agreed to exploring, Sam." He laughed, but his palms were sweaty, and his chest felt heavier. Sam turned her bike on and immediately it kicked a few inches in the air as she tried to get it under control. Sand flew behind her, making the air around Logan murky. "Shoot, Sam. You good?" He coughed, choking on the sand. *I don't think this plan is going to end well.*

"Woah, yeah sorry 'bout that." She regained her balance and sped towards the forest. Logan rushed to get his bike going and followed. "Let's see if we can find the next house over!" She yelled over the sound of their bikes.

"Do you think there are even more of us?" Logan caught up and was now next to Sam as they both entered the forest. *Father never mentioned Sam's family, so maybe the next house is like us, too.*

"Only one way to find out." Sam's voice rumbled as she drove over the fallen tree branches and uneven dirt patches. They both drove, winding through the trees nearly missing them several times. "I'm kind of proud of us for not falling yet."

"Why'd you take me on an adventure you expect us to fail at?" Logan laughed.

"I wasn't really thinking about what would happen after we started riding." Sam blushed.

I guess that's the perk of not being royal. You can start first and figure out later. Sam rushed in front of Logan, teasing him to speed up faster. He followed Sam and began accelerating. For a brief moment Logan was ahead, but she quickly passed him again and was happily surprised until she saw a light in front of them. There was a clearing coming up in the trees and someone or something was shining a bright light towards her.

"Logan! Slow down," she yelled trying to slow down her own bike. Unfortunately the clearing was coming up much faster than she could slow down her bike.

"I think there's a tractor ahead, Sam!" Logan yelled, reaching his hand out instinctively. *Oh no! She's going to crash.* Logan halted his bike.

SAM

Sam shielded her eyes from the light as she braced for impact. Fear paralyzed her body, but as she lost hope, she felt time suspend around her. Her bike slowed down at a faster rate than the world was moving around her. It halted right at the edge of the forest and the next house over. She let out a deep breath, realizing she had forgotten to breath. She squinted her eyes to try and see beyond the light. *What was I about to run into?*

"Thank goodness you're alright." Logan stopped his bike next to her and put his hand on her brakes. A tall and slender man sat on the tractor in front of them. He had extremely dark eyes that contrasted his milky white skin.

"What are you doing out here, children?" His voice croaked as he spoke. A shiver ran down Sam's spine at the way he uttered the word "children."

"We should really head back," Logan whispered.

"Not so soon, won't you come visit my home?" The man gestured back to his farm-like house. A red barn stood on a vast piece of land. The grass that spanned the property was all extremely fresh, but there seemed to be no animals anywhere. Sam could have sworn she saw more than ten fingers on the man, but he quickly tucked his hands behind him.

"No. We have to go," Logan answered. Sam stood there in fright. *Something is off about him. He isn't human, is he?* She looked at Logan, and they both started their bikes. They tried turning around, but a loud roar came from behind them. The ground cracked beneath them, and tree roots grew rapidly towards their bikes.

"Nobody leaves me without coming in to stay. I don't like such rude guests, reminds me of the time I invited Mr. Orwell to dinner." The man beamed his tractor's lights at them and began running over trees. *Orwell? As in George Orwell?*

"I thought George Orwell died in the 1950s?" Logan said, looking equally confused.

If he died in the 1950s, this man had to be way over fifty years old, but he doesn't look a day older than twenty-five. Sam was now sure this wasn't a human. *I know I asked Derek to go on a quest, but I didn't think I'd have to do this alone.* "What do we do?" She yelled towards Logan who looked at her with a blank face.

"Watch out!" Fright quickly took over Logan's face. Sam ducked as the tall man threw what looked like a knife over her head.

I really hope he doesn't have any more of those. "We need to get away from these roots." Sam yelled. They watched the plants around them grow to monstrous sizes. Their size wasn't the only thing that concerned Sam, though. They had started turning into oddly bright colors with spots on them. *Are those poisonous?*

Sam looked back and saw another knife heading towards Logan. *Shoot.* She closed her eyes for a second and concentrated on the knife. *If there's ever a time to be able to use your mind powers, Sam, it's now. Please work.* She imagined herself grabbing the knife and stopping it from hitting Logan. Sam opened her eyes, and the knife had changed directions. Unfortunately, only slightly. Sam watched as it headed straight into Logan's bike tire, which immediately deflated, and the bike went out of control whirling around. A tree nearly fell on Logan as he tried getting the bike in control. Finally, he hit the brakes, but before he could get off, he lost his balance toppled to his side with the bike falling on him.

LOGAN

"Sam! Help," he screamed. With Logan's bike on the forest floor, the tractor was the only light shining near Logan, and it quickly moved near him. *If I don't get out from under this bike, my mother will be the least of my worries.* Logan pushed the bike up and was able to inch out slightly until a tree branch fell directly onto the bike. *Man! How am I going to get out now?*

"You're a powerful one, aren't you?" The creepy man taunted as he headed towards Logan. "I don't mind taking you back to my house alone." Orange vines floated around the air next to Logan. His heart raced as he saw them get closer.

Alone? I don't want to be anywhere alone with this guy. He looked around and saw the knife in his bike's tire. Logan struggled to take the knife out with his sweaty hands. He managed to pull it out, but it fell to the ground as a vine sprung at him. *Magical powers, if you'd like to activate and reveal yourself now, please do.* Logan reached for the knife, closed his eyes, and began waving his hands around hacking at the vines.

SAM

No way I'm letting this creep take Logan anywhere. Sam ditched her bike and ran to get Logan out. She tripped over an overgrown tree root and nearly fell on one of the newly-changed plants. *Phew. Poison ivy looks like a treat compared to that.* She reached Logan, who was swatting vines away, and struggled to lift his bike. "Come on. We're going to have to make a run for it." She helped Logan up and they sprinted.

"Then—" Logan muttered but was cut off by another tree falling in front of them. This time neither of them could escape. "Sam, we need a plan. We can't outrun him." They both looked back at the tractor, but the large vehicle closing in on them was no longer their biggest worry. Instead of the horrifying human face that Sam already thought was going to give her nightmares, she saw a three-eyed blue face. At the forehead, the man had grown a third eye that stared deep into her own eyes. An icy feeling crashed over her body, and she felt her chest tighten. Her heart raced. She shivered as her hands sweat, but the cold rush continued.

Shoot, a plan. We need a plan. She had spent her whole life trying to figure out the plan Derek and Sky had for her, but she had never made many for herself. At least never alone. Of course, she had the plan to get a beach shed with Seth or the plan to train with Derek, but they had always been wishes she would daydream about that she didn't think would happen. Now she needed to make a plan she could actually execute, and she needed it fast.

"Give me that knife," Sam muttered, still trembling. The tractor ran through yet another tree, and more plants around them were turning bright colors. Sam closed her eyes and threw the knife at the creature, aiming for his forehead. She knew he was too far for the knife to reach and he was hidden behind the tractor screen, so she focused on the knife with her mind. She visualized herself running through the poisonous vines and stabbing his third eye. As she opened her eyes, she was surprised to see that it had worked. *I did it?* The knife had managed to reach the creature, and there was an enlarging hole where his eye used to be. A screeching yell filled the forest for a few seconds, and she saw the third eye glow and disappear. Within milliseconds, his figure completely dissipated into thin air. *I did it!*

"How'd you do that?" Logan asked, panting. His eyes were wide, and his mouth stood open as he watched the creature turn to dust.

"Do what?" Sam asked.

"That knife! You had to have done something for it to hit him like that," Logan said.

"I don't know what happened. My bike seemed to slow down on its own back there, too. I should have hit the man's tractor, but I didn't." She changed the topic to try to steer Logan away from her gift. There was some truth to her words, though. She didn't have any explanation for her not crashing. *Why didn't he try using his powers here? Sure, it was weird at dinner, but not using powers while you're being attacked?*

Logan shifted uncomfortably and looked away from her at the bike he had just ruined. Judging from his silence at her statement, she suspected he might be hiding something, too. Sam desperately wanted to ask him for answers. *Are you really from Sweden? What are your powers? Why don't you use them?* But she knew that, if she asked, she'd probably have to answer some questions about herself, and that was the one thing she couldn't do.

"Yeah, I don't know. Thanks for coming back for me, though." Logan faltered, shrugging as he looked down at his pants that were ripped and covered in dirt.

"Thanks for going on a stupid adventure with me." Sam was slightly embarrassed that she had gotten them in such a dangerous situation.

"I'm definitely making the plan next time." Logan laughed.

Next time. The words rang in her mind. *I'd like a next time. I can't believe he isn't more mad or concerned about what just happened, though. Maybe he isn't as serious as I thought he was. Definitely more fun than Derek and Sky.* She looked down, not knowing how to reply. Both of them walked quietly, carefully avoiding the overgrown tree roots on the forest floor. The greenery had stopped attacking them since the monster had died but were still shades of bright orange and red. *Will these plants ever return to normal?* "I never thought I'd look forward to getting sand in my shoes, but it beats walking around monster plants any day." Sam said, finally breaking the silence. *Shoot, that was such a lame thing to say.*

"I guess your wish has been granted." Logan laughed and pointed at the clearing of the forest where they could see the beach. "Want me to walk you back to your house?" He turned to her.

Sam's heart was still racing from making sense of what just happened in the forest—the encounter with the creature and the awkward conversation with Logan. She had this odd feeling of not knowing what to do with her hands, which were still shaking. "No. Thanks, though." She smiled and awkwardly stood still, unsure on how to say goodbye. The silence between them lasted a bit too long. Sam kept making awkward glances upwards and looking back down.

"Sam! There you are. Can you stop running away like that?" Derek yelled. *Oh, thank the angels! Get me out of this situation.* Sam had never felt more relieved to feel protected by her older brother. "Can we talk? Alone?"

"I'll take that as my cue to leave," Logan said and then turned to leave. Sam watched him walk away. *I really hope he comes back to the house and I can figure out his powers sometime.* She stood there dazed by her own thoughts. *Derek can't find out about this or I'll never be allowed to leave the mansion again.*

"Sam? Hello?" Derek snapped his fingers in front of her. "What happened back there? Did you figure out my life for me yet?" Sam let out a sarcastic laugh as she came back to reality. She walked leading the way into the house. "Okay, stop with the attitude. Stop and listen, Sam."

She halted in her tracks and folded her arms in front of her chest to hide her trembling hands. She wanted to show her brother she was ready to take control, but inside she was still scared from what she had just seen in the forest. *Sky said demons wouldn't dare come close to us, but that creature sure was far too close for comfort.*

"Sky and I see your safety first okay? We just see it in a different way."

Sam let out a reluctant laugh. "Yeah, I got that much."

"But we should be talking to you more about it. I agree," Derek said. Sam's frown softened. She looked her brother in the eye. "Sky hasn't exactly agreed to weapon training, but I'll work on him. Until then, let's continue with self-defense and your powers."

"Fine. But also, I want to be in on your meetings. I want to know what exactly is going on."

"Sam…" Derek ran his hand through his hair. "How about this: we train your powers and, once you can handle the flame and your mind control together, I'll fill you in."

"Deal." Sam held out her hand to shake. "But we're ramping up the training schedule on my terms. I'm sick of you dictating everything." Derek laughed and put his arm around Sam's shoulders. They walked into the house. "Tomorrow at 6 a.m. Derek, don't sleep in."

Sam ran to the elevator and made her way up to her floor. *I can't believe that just happened. Maybe I should have stayed to see Sky and Derek figure things out. But also, what just happened with Logan? What are his powers and why doesn't he use them like everyone else?* Thoughts raced through her mind. *Doors are finally opening for me.* The elevator door opened to her penthouse. Sam giggled to herself and got ready for bed.

LOGAN

I wonder what made Sam really run away? And how did she throw that knife perfectly at that creature? Logan kept going over the scene in his head, thinking about how the knife seemed to curve abnormally around the tractor frame until it was able to hit the creepy man. *What kind of fire power helps you with that?* He had to go find Sam again and ask her. Maybe she could help him figure out his powers, although he was still embarrassed that he couldn't do it on his own. *Maybe whatever my powers were could have helped me in the forest. Sam really carried us both out of that mess.*

Logan walked back into his house, hoping his brothers had already ended the call with their mother. He knew Hayden felt bad about their mother's rules and Kyle understood how overbearing she was, but Liam seemed to be taking their mother's side about Logan going back. *Why wouldn't he want me to stay and find out about my powers?*

"Bad news, brother." Hayden sighed. He was crouched over the kitchen counter with Liam, staring at the phone.

"She wants you to come back before summer ends. We have a few weeks." Liam scowled.

"We?" Logan replied. He looked around for Maddi or the other cousins but none of them were there. *Why is the house so empty?*

"Yeah, since you complained about Mom treating you unfairly, she's making us all come back. Thanks a lot." Liam scoffed.

"Okay. Take it easy, Liam. You don't know how hard it is for Logan to be so young and have so much responsibility."

Thank you, Hayden.

"But I'm afraid that leaves you very little time to figure out your powers, little brother. Mom might not let us use them again when we get back." Hayden frowned at his own words. Logan felt bad that, even though it was his fault that they had to return, Hayden was taking it with such grace.

I feel like everyone in this family has the qualities of a good king, but I'm stuck with the title and I'm not sure I'll appreciate it as much as the others. "Why did you all refuse the title, anyway?"

"No way was I going to go through our mom's training anymore once you were born." Liam shook his head violently. "The intense lessons in Greek, staying home for schooling, and mandatory visits to other kingdoms to meet princesses was *not* for me. I'd much rather be at boarding school in England, far away from anything royal."

Boarding school does sound like fun. I wish Mother wouldn't keep me home all the time. I stick out like a sore thumb everywhere I go. It was bad enough for Logan to be seen as serious all the time, but he was also the only one with such a thick accent. *I hope Sam doesn't think too much about the Sweden thing. I want her to like me as a friend and not a prince.*

"If only Mom would let Arabella take the throne. Little sis actually wants it and could do such wonders in the position. Then you'd be free, too." Hayden took a seat at the kitchen island.

"Yeah, if only. How can Mother think that women can't rule when she has been ruling with Father for so long?" Logan sulked. "Do you think he will ever let us come back? He has to, right? I mean he wouldn't let us come here to find out about our powers and then force us to live powerless again."

"I can only hope. I'd also like to get to know our cousins more. Mom's side of the family is so pretentious and boring compared to Dad's side, with all these angel children." Liam laughed.

"Are you sure it's the cousins that sparked your interest? Or is it the girl in the house next door?" Hayden teased.

"Yeah, you really seemed to enjoy that basketball game." Logan winked. He nudged Liam's arm lightly.

"Okay, okay, let's not forget that you just snuck off in the night to avoid Mom. Where did you go anyways? And who did you go with?" Liam stared at Logan.

Shoot, he's onto me.

PART 3

SAM BLEU

CHAPTER 6

DEMONS IN HER HEAD

———

KNOCK. KNOCK. Sam sat up frightened as she heard pounding on the door. She had been dreaming about the tall man from the day before. *KNOCK. KNOCK.* "Sam? You ready?" Sky asked from outside Sam's door. She scrambled through her clothes, rushing to get dressed.

Huh. I didn't think Sky would be joining us. "Ready!" She opened the door, and her face lit up with an ear-to-ear grin. "Are you training me today?"

"Derek and I are tag-teaming." Sky looked around. "Gotten used to your new place yet?"

"It's really nice. How exactly did we get such a big place for all of us?"

"My mom and Ashley's dad made some arrangements for us before they left. It's insane how they let us stay here as children. I'm convinced more magical beings were involved, but it's hard to figure out who isn't human around here."

"So none of us have parents?"

"Nope."

"Not even your human ones?" Sam wondered if Sky knew about where their magical parents went after they died. *Did they all actually die? Or do they just not exist on Earth anymore?*

"Nope. It's a long story, but our parents married people who already knew about the different realms and magic. They would all go out and fight together. Even your mom, before she met your dad." Sky looked down. "One of their adventures didn't end so well. The few that survived decided to leave Earth for good. Well, except for your parents." Sky's voice faltered as he said the last sentence.

"They just left you?" Sam asked. She played with her fingers, thinking about her own parents. *Why'd they stay long enough to have us and then just leave?*

"It's more complicated than that," Sky said quietly. Sam realized she had probably just struck a nerve. "We don't know exactly what type of beings they are or what they were doing on Earth in the first place, but they needed to reunite with the others who died here."

"So death on Earth isn't the end?" Sam asked. *I hope that doesn't apply to whatever Logan and I met yesterday. Never seeing that creepy man is definitely the goal.*

"To be honest, I'm just as confused as you are. They left when I was around ten and Ash was much younger. We don't remember much, just that for a few years we stayed with random caretakers, but, now that I'm older, we live alone." He quickly laid out the details of his life as if they had no impact on him.

"That must have been tough." Sam sighed. *I didn't realize how little control Sky had in his own life. It seemed like he knows about everything, but I guess not. We really do have a lot in common.* "Thankfully we don't live alone. We have each other," she said as they made their way to the kitchen for breakfast.

"Yeah." Sky smiled and laughed.

"Why is that funny?" Sam couldn't help but join in with his nonsensical laughter.

"You just usually aren't so sweet to me," Sky chuckled. He pointed to the counter full of food. "Okay, but hurry. Grab something. Derek's waiting outside." Sam made her way out with Sky. She couldn't stop thinking about what he had said. Even he didn't know anything about what they were doing on Earth. *Why doesn't he let us help out more? I wonder, if Mom's alive in another realm, then where is she?*

***

Sam stuffed the rest of her breakfast in her mouth as she put on her combat boots to train. Sky and Derek were waiting outside, but Sam felt hesitant going anywhere near the woods again. She sighed, letting a deep breath out, and walked outside.

"Hey. You're finally here. Okay, so the first thing we need to do is train your mind and your body to be in sync. Your mental powers are only as powerful as your ability to control your own mind. And your fire. It's you. You can't separate it from yourself, so if at any time you let your emotions take over you, it'll reflect in your powers." Sam wondered how Derek knew so much about the gift. *Mom died pretty early on in all of our lives and she never mentioned her gift until right before she left. Maybe Keith knows. Is that why Derek still talks to him?*

"Okay. So. Um." Sam lifted her hand up and envisioned a flame growing on her fingertips. *Come on. Come on. I need them to see I can do this.* Nothing appeared. "Uh. I'll try again."

"Take your time, Sam." Sky reassured her by placing his hand on her shoulder. Sam closed her eyes, and suddenly a flame appeared. *Yes! Nice, Sam!* It began growing over her whole hand. *Wait.* Images of the forest encounter flashed in her eyes. Sam tensed as she tried to regain focus. She felt as if she was back in front of the demon. Her hands got sweaty, but the flame had nothing to do with it. All she could think of was being in the forest trying to help Logan. *You controlled your powers yesterday, Sam. Today's no different.* She straightened her posture and attempted to clear her mind.

"Uh. Okay, yeah, keep it there," Derek said as he stood at a distance.

Shoot. Why is it growing larger still? Stop!

"Sam?" Wrinkles appeared on Derek's face as he backed up further. The fire had spread around Sam in a ring formation.

"I can't control it." Sam didn't know what to do. Derek had just said that she was fire. *If I can't control the flame, does that mean I can't control myself?* Sam's eyes became watery. *Sam! Stop. You have to focus.* She closed her eyes but, instead of focusing more, she felt wind and water. She opened her eyes to find Derek creating an oxygen-deprived environment while Sky started to make it rain right above her. She coughed on the empty air as her lungs burned and an icy chill fell over her. The flame was gone, and she fell to her knees, drenched and cold. "Were both of your powers necessary?" Sam asked, feeling a bit hurt after seeing how well they were able to use their powers to counteract her own lack of control. It made her failure doubly hard to digest. *Shoot.* She pounded her fist against the ground.

"It's okay, Sam. We all struggled at first. Fire's just a bit more dangerous than the rest of our powers," Sky said, taking off his jacket and handing it to her. *More dangerous.* His words rang through her mind. *Of course. Of course she was more dangerous. Add that to her inability to control the gift.* She began feeling like maybe she should just let Derek and Sky make decisions for her. She didn't feel too secure about her capabilities anymore.

"I'm going to go dry off. Let's talk later," Sam muttered before Sky or Derek could add anything else. Sam needed to leave. She couldn't face the disappointment her cousin and brother felt, and she definitely couldn't face the embarrassment she felt. *Really, Sam? You couldn't even create a small flame. You've done that a million times before. What happened out there? Are you really that out of control?*

"Maybe she isn't ready, Derek," Sky whispered but Sam could still hear him. "Let's just get her settled here first."

Ha! Settled in a penthouse! Sit here unable to use my powers. I'll fit right in. Sam couldn't help but imagine all the people she had just met using their powers as she watched alone from the side.

"Wait," Derek called out, running after her. Derek grabbed Sam's arm as she was walking away. "You want to know the truth about things, right? You made a deal. First you would control your powers. Then we would tell you." Sam looked into his serious eyes. "You can't run away at the first sign of fear, Sam. You have to do the things that scare you."

Sam looked down at her soaked clothes and then looked up at her brother. Her body wanted to give up, but Derek was right. If she ran today, then she would never get her answers. Sam looked down at her soaked clothes and then looked up at her brother. "Okay. You're right." She had to get out of her own head. *Chill, Sam. Derek and Sky won't let anything happen to anyone if your powers get out of control.*

"Alright, so how about you dry your clothes with some fire?" Sky said, winking at her. *Okay. Fire. Warmth. You can do this, Sam.* She closed her eyes and envisioned the flame around her. *Clear your head, Sam.* She felt warmth growing and spreading—in front of her, behind her, then all around her. A knot formed in her stomach. She opened her eyes and there was a ring of flames. She could see Derek and Sky's figure through a blur of red and orange. "Okay, Sam. That's good. Now focus on keeping it at this height. Don't let the flames spread."

"Remember, you are the flame, Sam. It's not a separate entity you have to control; it's you," Derek said. Sam felt the fire warming up her clothes. The water began evaporating and Sam's vision became foggy. She closed her eyes again and began to focus. *Control me. Why does the fire seem so separate and distant?* "Sam, you're doing it." Derek's voice was filled with enthusiasm.

"Now comes the harder part. Can you get rid of the fire?" Sky shouted.

Shoot. This is the part that I can never do. Come on, Sam. Focus and maybe this time it will work. She began to try to reel in the flames. *I need to make them disappear. Right? Is that how you go about it? This whole the-fire-is-you talk Derek keeps bringing up is very confusing.* Through the multiple thoughts racing through her head, Sam started to lose focus. Her eyes were closed again, but she could feel the flame grow outwards in an unpredictable manner.

"Uh…Sam? You can do it. Focus!" Derek yelled, his voice shaky.

Sam, maybe the idea wasn't to get rid of the flame. Did that mean she was getting rid of herself? She was so confused. All the instructions from the boys were just clouding her mind further. She felt herself tensing up. She couldn't get rid of the knot in her stomach. "Derek, Sky, I don't think I can." Sam opened her eyes and immediately saw how widespread the fire had gotten. "Do something, please!" She looked around her and couldn't figure out what to do next. Suddenly a very familiar sensation hit her again. The air escaped her lungs as she fell into a puddle created by Sky's rain. She coughed as she rested on the ground, her hands and knees trembling on the cold cement. The flames were out. Derek and Sky rushed to her and helped her up.

"Don't worry. At least we know you can control starting the flame now."

"Yeah, Sam, that's progress," Sky congratulated as Sam looked down at the jacket she had borrowed which was now drenched. "Don't worry about the jacket. It's just rain." He laughed.

"Alright, tomorrow, same time?" Sam said abruptly and then made her way inside to get changed. *Well, that was a mess. But still. This is a step in the right direction. I'm finally getting the training that I've been asking for. Derek was right. I can't get scared and back out now.*

CHAPTER 7

I AM FIRE?

———

As the next few days passed, Sam continued her training. Every day, 6 a.m. sharp, Sky and Derek woke her up. Nobody else was up yet, so they could help her practice all of her powers. Then, once the rest were up, they would all disperse and practice their own powers. Travis and Mia would hit the waves. Ethan would join their older cousin who could shapeshift in the forest. Derek and Sky always made some weather phenomenon occur. Sam wondered when they would tell the others about the gift, if at all.

Do I just hide these powers forever? Never use them? She would sometimes get distracted thinking about Logan and his lack of powers too. *Maybe, Logan is also hiding his powers? What could he have?*

It had been almost a week since the forest attack incident. The whole other house had basically been silent except for the occasional visits from Maddi. *I wonder if Maddi knows about my powers? She's behind closed doors whispering with Sky all the time. But whatever, focus, Sam.*

She had finally controlled the flame enough to both conjure it and make it disappear. The third time really was the charm. At the last session, Sam had tried to get rid of the flame again, but Sky and Derek had gotten distracted when Jake woke up earlier than usual. They went on an elaborate ruse to get him away from Sam's training, leaving her struggling alone. She had almost completely turned into a flame herself, a thought that scared Sam more than anything else. *If I turn into a flame, can I figure out how to turn back?* Her fear had helped her absorb the flame entirely. *That was the key. Absorb it—not get rid of it.*

Now they were going to focus on trying to use her other powers. *Today's the day! You get to finally practice this gift that seems impossible to use. And Seth said he had news for tonight's meeting, so you just have to make it through the day of training alive.*

Sam walked into the kitchen and grabbed her usual breakfast. Derek and Sky weren't there yet. *Huh. Did I actually beat them down here?* She walked outside to where they usually trained to see if anyone was there. *Nobody? Where'd they go? Sky at least has to be up. He woke me up.* Suddenly, there was a bright orange blur in front of Sam. "Woah!" she screamed as she fell backwards. Another blast came from her right side but this time, Sam was ready and raised her hand absorbing the fireball as it barreled towards her.

"Nice. A little slow on that first one, but that was good, Sam." Sky came in extending a hand to help Sam up.

"What? How did you…"

"We found a magical flame thrower in the library," Derek interjected. "This thing is really fun. Kind of jealous of your powers now, Sam."

"I was so confused." Sam laughed. She pushed Derek's shoulder playfully. "What's the plan for today's training, or are you two just going to play with your new toy?" Sky and

Derek looked at each other. They both grinned. "Come on. No more of these secrets. You guys promised."

"Okay. Okay. You're going to start trying to use your gift to enhance your fire powers." Derek put down the flame thrower. "Mixing powers together is the best way to defeat people who have stronger powers or more experience using their powers."

"And if you ever come into contact with Keith, you're going to need this training. He has the power to control time, and years of practice. By now, he can probably separate time within the same room." Sky said, sounding a bit scared.

"What do you mean?"

"He can mess with his opponents by making time faster for him and slower for you. Or he can control how fast a single object or being goes through time while everything else continues at a regular pace."

Is that what happened to my dirt bike in the woods? "How would my powers fit into that?" *Do I stand a chance if he can just freeze time for me and do whatever he wants? Can I get immunity from his powers?*

"That's the thing. He may be able to manipulate fire, especially if you conjure some up yourself, but if you're controlling the fire with your mind, his ability to also control the time of the fire will be weakened."

"So multiple forces weaken each other?" *I guess that makes sense.* Sam was unsure on how she would be able to battle Keith, though. She had finally gotten the basics down with fire, but she hadn't even practiced the gift for a while. She almost ignored it, since using the gift would expose her and her fire was hard enough. She never felt motivated to explore the other set of powers she had except for when her life depended on it in the forest.

"Yup, there's a lot we need to all learn about how your powers work. Tomorrow's training is going to be more reading than actually using your powers. We're going to give you some books that talk about his powers and your gift." Derek ran his fingers through his hair. "But today, we want you to get a taste of how powers can mix. That way you have something to go off of when you read about it later."

"We're going to have you use your mind to control an orb of fire."

"Isn't that kind of useless, though? Shouldn't I use my mind to control something about fire that I can't control myself, you know, seeing that I *am* fire?" Sam conjured a flame in her hands. "I can handle it fine now without my mind actively getting involved." Sam was always reluctant using her gift. It was for good reason, though, since she had been told so often to be very cautious about letting anyone know she had it. *Hopefully Logan isn't still suspicious about what happened to the creature in the forest.*

"The point of this is to make sure you know how to do everything in multiple ways. Keith and everyone else after your powers know exactly what fire can and cannot do. They will know how to beat you if you rely solely on it. That's what makes the gift so alluring to people. Besides the fact that it's so powerful, barely anyone knows exactly what you can do with it. When they block you on the fire front, you'll have to make up for it with the gift." Sky went on ranting a bit more, but Sam got distracted. *What books are out there if nobody really knows what the gift entails? Have all the previous people who were given these powers kept them that secret? Why would we be given such a strong power if we can't reveal it to anyone and thus not use it?*

"What exactly can the gift do? You've thrown around mind control, and I know I can read people's thoughts and project my own to others, but what else?" Sam blurted out. *Should I even have this much power? How am I going to know if what I'm doing is good?* Sky's face was puzzled by her interjection. She realized she had interrupted whatever Sky had been saying and felt a bit bad. "Sorry. I just want to know what exactly I'm working with."

"We don't fully know yet, Sam," Derek answered.

"We're hoping our parents have some books in the library that will have some clues. A lot of the training we're going to do for the next few weeks, maybe months, will be research. When Keith finally finds us here, we'll have no choice but to battle him off." Sky ruffled a hand through his thick, long blond hair.

Few months? I wonder what the timeline is. Am I expected to have some battle with Keith? If he's after my powers, I doubt he'll give me time to train and get better at using them. Sam hoped she wasn't right, but she had an odd feeling about how this plan was going to work out. "Won't he just keep coming back until he has my powers?" Sam asked. The Keith that Derek met didn't seem like her brother anymore. *He isn't someone I'd want to meet, yet alone fight. Ever.*

"So…" Derek looked at Sky, who nodded. "There are some myths about banishing people from certain realms. Our hope is that, by the time he finds out about you, we can figure out how to banish him from Earth."

"Is that what happened to our parents? You said they had to leave and Mom didn't. Was dying her punishment for breaking the rules?" Sam's face drained in color.

"We don't fully know. It's just a myth, so those books are our only hope for answers." Sky sighed. He looked disappointed in himself.

"Okay, but now, we want you to try to dissociate yourself from the fire training we've been doing. Take the fireball you have and make it move using your mind rather than the fact that you are fire," Derek repeated. Sam focused on the fire. She had almost forgotten that she had conjured it and had been balancing it on her hand. It was becoming more of a second nature to her, which made sense, since she was supposed to be the element itself rather than someone who merely controlled it.

"Okay. So I have to passively control it. How am I supposed to stop myself from controlling a part of me and instead try to actively control it with a different part of myself?" Sam began confusing herself with her own words. This whole being the element, fire, was confusing in itself. She didn't understand how her siblings were all elements but also had human forms. *How are we people and elements? What happens to our respective elements if something happens to one of us?* Sensing the confusion her brother and cousin had on their faces, she clarified. "I guess what I mean is how do I know when I'm controlling the fire with the gift rather than the fact that the fire is me and I'm controlling a part of me?"

"Think about how you feel when you use your gift to levitate an object. Try to emulate that feeling with fire," Derek said and then nervously glanced at Sky.

Levitate? Besides the knife in the forest, I've only really used the gift to read minds. The concerned looks on Sky and Derek's faces weren't helping with Sam's nerves. She tried to hide her jittery hands behind her.

"The truth is, we can only speculate about your other powers, since we've never had the gift ourselves. We're hoping to learn about them with you in training," Sky added.

"Okay. I can try that." Sam made her fire disappear and then looked around for a heavy object. She spotted a large potted plant next to the house door and focused on it, trying to lift the plant and move it next to her. *How exactly does it feel to levitate an object?* All she could think about was how it felt to attack the forest creature. *Are there more like those creatures out there, and does Sky know how close they are to us?* Sam shook her head trying to focus again. *Maybe Mia will have some answers later, but you have to focus now. Everyone will be awake soon.* She tried to emulate the feeling she had when she threw the knife at the creature. *Imagine yourself carrying it, Sam.* Slowly the plant lifted up and, although it seemed to rock to the side a bit, the pot made it over to Sam in one piece. *Phew.*

"Nice! Now I'm going to throw a fireball at you." Derek lifted the thrower. "Try and get the same feeling when you levitate the fire." He launched the fire upward giving Sam time to get a hold of it before it reached the ground. Sam felt herself struggling to envision herself catching the flame. She wanted to desperately just control its essence, but she focused harder trying to trick her mind into thinking the fire was another object like a ball. She levitated it in front of Derek, moved it past Sky, and brought it towards her.

"I think I got it!" Sam was clearly excited. *Maybe you can use all of your powers. Then you can use your gift in secret.*

"Good, but we're just getting started. Now try to control it through these obstacles." Sky raised his hand, and the sky turned dark. Rain clouds appeared, and a lightning bolt struck in the middle of the three of them. The sound of thunder roared. Sam was taken aback and it showed, as the fireball dropped a bit before Sam gained control again. "Don't let anything distract you, Sam." Sky made a trail of rain flow towards the fireball.

"Don't let anything take out your fire, Sam," Derek yelled over the thunder. Sam walked back and the fireball followed. She willed her mind to move it lower towards the ground and zoom past Sky. Derek created a gust of wind that blew the fireball towards the rain. Sam fought for control of the fire. She closed her eyes and concentrated on splitting apart the fire. Her eyes opened to two flames nearing the rain. She used her mind to take control of them both back from Derek and willed them to go towards both of the boys.

"Take *this*, guys!" She teased them by having the flames circle them. A smile appeared on her face but was quickly replaced with fright as Sky created another lightning bolt that smashed one of the fireballs to the ground creating a small brushfire. Sam was taken off guard and, in an attempt to save the other fireball from getting struck, she lost control of the fire around Sky. He quickly wiped it out with some rain.

"Sam. Never get cocky," Sky quipped.

Sam was getting frustrated. She had to think quickly. *Maybe if I control the lightning and not the fire, he won't know what to do. Catching him off guard is my best bet to save the flame.* She focused her attention on the fireball first. She raised it up above Sky and Derek, making it look like an easy target. Then she waited. *Sky has to strike this. It's too easy a target to not.* Just as planned, Sky tried striking the flame, but Sam was ready. She extended her frustration through her gift and redirected the lightning bolt away from the flame. She was ecstatic for a second, realizing her plan worked, but that didn't last long as she heard Sky wail out in pain.

"Ow!" Sky fell back. The lightning had struck right at the plant Sam had placed next to them, shattering the glass pot. A piece had flown up, striking Sky's arm.

"Shoot. I'm so sorry." Sam rushed to Sky, her head suddenly burning. "I thought controlling the lightning would have been a better way to save the flame. I didn't think it would..."

"It's okay, Sam. I'm fine. I just need to get this glass out." Sky winced in pain as Derek examined his arm.

"I'm going to take the piece out. Let me go get some first aid stuff, okay?" Derek reassured Sky. He glared at Sam. "Stay with him."

"Thanks," Sky croaked out as Derek left. "Don't worry about it. That was a really good technique and when you're actually going against someone; a glass shard in their arm will be a good thing." They both let out a chuckle. "Until then, though, let's figure out how to control the gift more." Sam gave Sky a hug from the side, trying to be careful of his arm.

"Thanks for all of this. I really appreciate what you and Derek are doing for me."

"Of course." Sky looked relieved. Derek hurried back with supplies.

"Okay. Um. Hold onto this with your teeth." Derek rolled up a towel and placed it in front of Sky's mouth. "On three, I'm going to take out the glass." Sky looked away. "One. Two."

The towel fell out of Sky's mouth as he let out a silent scream trying to act brave. "Damn, Derek. What happened to three?" Derek handed Sam the piece of glass in a towel.

"It's the oldest trick in the book, dude. You never hurt someone when they expect it. You can thank me later." Derek looked at Sam. "That's good advice for you, too. Don't go after someone when they expect it. Seems obvious, but you'd be surprised what your brain justifies during a battle."

"Okay, so that's definitely the end of practice for today." Sky snatched the roll of gauze from Derek's hand. "I'll take it from here." Sky looked at him, his trust clearly lost.

"Today was good, though. Glad to see that you're finding alternate ways to use your powers, Sam. Tomorrow, we hit the library."

Sam hoped that Derek and Sky's plan to read about their powers was a good one. Keith's time control magic was so new to Sam. *Changing time around objects in the same room? How does one win against that? Mom, wherever you are, I've never asked you for anything, but please do me one favor. Please have at least one book in this library about your gift.*

CHAPTER 8

SCARY DEMON, SCARIER BROTHER

———

Tired from the morning training, Sam headed back into the kitchen and found Ethan and Mia eating. "Sam! How's the secretive training going?" Mia asked, gesturing for Sam to join them. "Why did Derek look so panicked a few minutes ago? He came racing in and left in such a hurry."

"I accidentally shattered a glass pot, and uh…" Sam looked away from her siblings. "The glass may have gotten stuck in Sky's arm." Sam put a hand above her eyes, trying to hide her shame.

"Oh, wow. Derek seemed so scared." Mia laughed. Ethan and Sam looked at their older sister confused. "What? This can't be that big of a deal to you guys."

"Um. Well, Sky seemed pretty hurt, so…" Sam waited to see why her sister was so unaffected by what she had just said.

"The first time Derek and I trained together, I almost drowned him. It comes with the whole having magical powers and no parents territory." She laughed. "I'll go check up on Sky. Make sure he wraps it up properly." She continued to chuckle as she left.

"That was not what I expected." Ethan looked at Sam. "From either of you. How was training with the gift otherwise?"

"I don't know, man. I want to be excited, but it's all so confusing. Do you understand what Derek means when he tells us we are the four elements? And why are there people like Travis who can control parts of water too?" *Are there partial fire or mind controllers too?*

"I wish I knew, dude. I wish I did." Ethan shook his head as he lathered jam on his toast, generously.

"And the other thing is that Derek and Sky told me today that their plan involves maybe months of training. Do we really think Keith is going to let us have months before he comes back to see who has the gift?"

"I guess we'll just have to trust that they have a backup plan if Keith shows up earlier." Ethan shrugged, but Sam still felt uneasy. She had thought that the knot in her stomach was from her powers, but she wasn't training now, and it still hadn't disappeared.

"Hey, have you all been to the shed out back? We're missing my old dirt bikes!" Sky came in looking panicked. His arm was half-wrapped, and blood had already stained the bandages.

"No, we have dirt bikes here?" Ethan nearly jumped in excitement. He turned to Sam. "Did you know that?"

"No. Woah, that's cool." Sam shook her head rapidly. *Shoot, I had forgotten that we left them in the forest. Sky's not going to be happy when he finds one with the tire punctured.* "Maybe ask Derek? He's probably the only one of us who knows how to drive them." She shrugged, acting innocent. Sky ran out calling for Derek.

"Seriously, Sam? What do you know?" Mia tilted her head and glared at her.

How does she always know when I'm lying? "Let's go outside. I'll explain there." Sam led the others outside and walked towards the forest. "So, a while back, when I was running away from Derek and Sky—"

"That's an everyday thing for you, sis," Ethan remarked.

"Well, I ran into Logan." Sam sighed.

"Ooh. He's super nice. A bit mysterious, but sweet," Ethan said.

"His brother Kyle is too." Mia smiled.

"Can you guys focus?" Sam stared at her siblings. "We kind of stole the dirt bikes and rode to the next house over." Sam's voice faltered as she saw Mia's eyes grow large. "And I wanted to actually ask you about it too, Mia. We saw someone, or rather something."

"Sam, how could you be so reckless!" Mia shouted. Ethan seemed rather pleased in comparison. He looked at Sam, his eyes keen for more details. "Derek and I don't take you on quests for a reason."

"I know. Trust me, I get it now," Sam said in a soft voice. She looked down, her body shrinking. *I never thought I'd understand why Derek and Mia kept me away for this long.* She hid her face in her hands, resting her elbows on the counter. "Logan and I were not prepared for what we saw."

"How did you get away?" Ethan asked excitedly.

"I threw one of its own knives, which went through its head. It kind of just dissipated then."

"That was definitely a demon, but I wonder how it got so close to us. They wouldn't dare come alone to a place with so many of us," Mia said, confused. "Can you take us back to where you met it?"

"S-sure," Sam stuttered.

"I finally get to go on a quest! Nice! Thanks, Sam." Ethan looked at her happily. Sam gave a blank stare back. She was reluctant to go back, but she needed answers.

They walked towards the forest, which felt darker than before. Sam's whole body was on edge as she walked past the familiar trees. She kept fidgeting with her jacket strings. Her and Logan's footprints were still fresh in the muddy dirt, but Sam couldn't find the knives the demon had thrown. As they walked through the forestry, Ethan cured the off-colored poisonous plants. They reverted to green and shrank back down to their normal sizes.

There they are! The dirt bikes. Sam ran towards the bikes that were left untouched, but there was no sign of the tractor. "Wait, the demon who attacked us had a tractor. It was right here." Sam pointed at the farm. In daylight, Sam could make out the barn much more clearly. There were still no animals or workers to be seen, but the land looked perfectly maintained.

"What did the demon look like?" Mia asked, examining the broken tree branches and flat tire.

"It was really tall and pale-skinned. It also had really weird nimble fingers, and its voice was very hoarse. Oh, and it had really wild, bushy dark hair," Sam said.

"This is not good." Mia's voice was filled with worry. "That means another demon or someone working with the demon came back and cleaned up. I need you to take me to the other house. I want to see what the demon left behind. And we're going to need to take these bikes back to Sky and tell him, Sam." Mia looked at her and Sam knew she was about to get into major trouble.

"Do you think we can even take the bikes back?" Sam asked, avoiding the mention of telling Sky.

"Maybe. I think Ethan and I could try patching the hole in this tire." Mia pulled out a twig and then found a few soft leaves. "Ethan, I need you to make a patch out of these leaves." She stood up and let Ethan use his magic to place the leaves over the tire. Then she raised her hand and closed her eyes. Sam could see the leaves tighten around the tire as they dried out. The rubber started steaming.

"Woah. Did you just—" Sam said. *Travis has been a really good mentor for her.*

"It's only a temporary fix, so we can carry it back, but first I need you to show me the other house," Mia said sternly. They continued walking past the area where the demon had found them.

Sam hadn't realized it before, but the building was distinctly small. The red barn-like structure sitting in the middle of a couple of acres had a small apartment next to it. She pushed the barn doors open and immediately a rank smell rushed outwards. "Oh. Disgusting! What is that?" Sam retched.

"That's really not good!" Mia exclaimed as light filled into the barn. They could see pieces of flesh hanging from the ceiling and random animals slaughtered on the ground.

Wait, no. Are these humans? Sam tried not to step on the blood or skin on the ground. "Mia, what is this place?" she asked in fear. Sam tip-toed around the floor with her arms closed. The knot in her stomach felt like it had been undone and folded back tighter.

"I think I liked it better before we went on quests, Sam," Ethan said, grabbing and clinging onto her arm. She wrapped her arm around her brother and they both stared at Mia for answers.

Please tell me why we're standing in human flesh and you look like you're completely fine, Mia. "This has Oni written all over it. It's a Japanese demon that spreads diseases and skins mortals. It looks like this one was running a meat business selling diseased human flesh off as food," Mia informed, crouched next to a certain piece of skin. "Humans will eat anything if it's guised as chicken." Sam looked at Ethan and furrowed her brows. A shiver ran down her spine. "To be honest, I'm kind of proud you beat an Oni on your own, sis."

"Thanks," Sam replied, not knowing if she should feel happy or disturbed. "Can we head back now?" She stepped to the side but accidentally stepped on a piece of skin covered in dried blood. "Ugh, please!"

"Sure, but promise me you won't go venturing out again. I'm going to talk to Derek and Sky about this. If there was a demon out here, then we need you to stay at home even more so than usual." Mia looked at Sam and then back at the ground. Sam followed her gaze and saw that she was staring at two horns on a pile of hay. "I'm surprised that the Oni died so easily. It's almost as if he was sent here as prey and not the predator." Mia's face finally showed hints of worry. Sam felt uneasy hearing her sister's words.

What does that mean for me? Do I have these months Derek and Sky have planned for research? Sam stayed silent and followed Mia and Ethan out of the barn. They headed back to the mansion.

***

Thankfully, Sky wasn't at the shed when they made it back. Mia looked at Ethan and gestured for him to help her put the bikes they had carried back into the shed. "Thanks, Ethan. I'm going to go talk to Sky right now, Sam. You might want to hurry upstairs or somewhere out of sight when I do. I don't think Sky will be pleased with you when he finds out." Mia spoke softly. Sam nodded and watched her older sister leave.

"You're screwed, Sam." Ethan sat in the sand and dragged her down by her arm to join him.

"Yeah, but I'd rather be in trouble with Sky than another demon."

"You must be really good with your powers if you defeated one, though," Ethan remarked, his eyes shining with hope but sadness at the same time.

"Nowhere near as good as you or Mia. You casually fixed the forest and the bike tire. Mia didn't even have a hint of fear in her eyes when we saw the barn. I barely made it out of that demon encounter."

"You have a lot more to deal with than either of us. We all have different paths, Sam. You've defeated your first demon. I've cleaned up my first ecosystem. I think we can both celebrate." Ethan reassured her by putting his arm around her shoulders.

What would I do without you, brother? She smiled back at him, glad that she always had him to cheer her up. "You're right. Next time, though, I want you by my side in the fight."

"Of course. I'm kind of scared after today, but I also really want to see a demon dissipate into dust. That sounds so cool." Ethan gestured his hands to mimic something exploding. They both laughed, and Sam leaned her head on his shoulder. "But also, I wanted to ask you. Are you still seeing Seth today?" Ethan's eyes lit up again.

"What is your obsession with Seth?" Sam continued laughing. "And yes."

"It's just so cool that you have a secret friend. And this secret friend just so happens to be a siren. How are you not more obsessed?"

"Okay, whatever, Ethan." Sam brushed his excitement aside. "I'm going to head out to see my 'secret friend' now. I don't want to be here for Sky's lecture and Seth has some surprise for me," she said, glad that Ethan had reminded her to meet him. *With this whole Oni situation, I almost forgot that Seth promised to tell me something exciting today.* "Bye."

"Bye! Be safe," Ethan said. His words echoed through Sam's head. *Everything about today feels off. It's almost like a heaviness in the air. Hopefully whatever Seth has will distract me.*

***

Seth? Where are you? Sam stood in the cave and looked around. She turned around towards the entrance to see if she was in the right place.

"Right behind you!" Sam felt something grab her ankle and she fell backwards into the water.

"Seth!" she said as she scrambled to the surface. Seth grabbed her arm.

"Easy there. You know how to swim, don't you?" he teased.

"You're so dead." Sam laughed and splashed Seth. "You're lucky I can use fire to dry off easily. Otherwise I'd be *so* mad."

"Hey, it was all a part of the plan. I want to see what you can do now. You've been telling me about this training every night now. You really know how to keep up the suspense," Seth joked. Sam got out of the water.

"Okay, watch." She laughed. Sam held her arms to her side and concentrated. Heat radiated off of her nearly instantly.

The water evaporated out of her clothing creating a cloud of steam. "Here you go!" Sam said as she stepped out of the steam.

"Wow. That's pretty cool." Seth clapped as Sam took a bow. "Thank you. Thank you very much."

"But now get back in the water," Seth said, taking a serious tone.

"What?" Sam looked surprised.

"The thing I wanted to tell you about. It's a place a short swim away from here. It's gorgeous; I promise."

"Why didn't you tell me this before I dried my clothes?" Sam whined.

"It's fun making you frustrated," he teased. "Plus, it's more practice for you. You're welcome." Seth laughed as Sam reluctantly jumped in.

"And it's an easy swim for people who aren't sirens?" She eyed him.

"Yup. Thirty seconds underwater."

"Alright, lead the way," she said. Seth took Sam's hand, and they both went underwater. Sam could see Seth's shimmering, deep teal tail speed off a bit ahead of her. She followed. They seemed to be going through an underwater tunnel. Sam felt pressure building up on her lungs, so she picked up the pace and eventually saw some light. She broke through the surface of the water gasping for air. Cliffs circled all around her. Leaves glistened in the sunlight as they dangled around the edge of the rocky mountain edges. It looked like they were inside of a volcano, but that couldn't be right. They were in southern California. "Woah. What is this place?"

"Over here!" Seth swam towards a rock jutting out from one of the cliffs. "You can rest here. I have no idea how this swimming hole came to be. It's literally like someone took a cylindrical chunk out of a mountain and filled it with water."

"It's amazing." Sam was at a loss for words. She stared up at the golden rays shining on the ocean water, creating dancing blue shadows on the cliff walls. The bright turquoise water was clear enough to see a few feet below them and Sam felt as if she had stepped foot into a fairytale world.

"Anyway, I thought you could show me more of your powers here 'cause, you know, I doubt anyone would find us here."

"Sounds like a plan. I feel like, with both of our powers, we could do some interesting things here."

"Yeah. 'Interesting things' is how I always describe illusions to people." Seth let out a sarcastic laugh. "It's such a passive power, though. I can trick people into seeing things, but Sam, with your gift, you can make things actually happen."

"Yeah, maybe if I can actually use them." Sam climbed a rock jutting out of the water. "I either can't use them at all, or when I do, I end up hurting people, like today."

"Hurting people?"

"I tried to use my mind to move lightning, and well, let's just say it ended up with glass shards in Sky's arm."

"Woah, woah, woah. Tell me more." Seth leaned on the rock and Sam explained the day's events. She conveniently left out the demon hunting since the whole idea of one being so close to them still scared her. Seth sat next to her with his eyes wide and ready to hear more.

"I'm not exactly sure why the gift even exists. It seems like a burden, not a present." Sam crossed her arms and buried her head in them.

"Well, I guess that depends on how you look at it, right?" Seth pulled himself up on the rock with his tail splashing in the water. He put one hand on Sam's shoulder. "On one hand, it's dangerous if anyone knows you have the powers, but on the other hand, what if you really mastered the powers? Imagine how much good you could do and how much better the powers are in your hands rather than someone with bad intentions."

"Yeah, I want to think like that, but the fact is that the powers only seem to be hurting people." *Keep on training, Sam. It would be cool if I could use them to help people.* "But you're right, it would be nice if I could control them." They sat in silence for a while as they both took in the words. *Maybe they'll help Seth get his legs.* "Enough about me, though. What about you? Did you find anything else about getting legs or the coral?"

"Actually, I made quite a discovery a few days ago," Seth said.

"Well then why are you holding out?" Sam playfully nudged Seth. "Spill!"

"So I found another magical being wandering out by these cliffs the other day," Seth continued.

"Wait, really?" *Who could that be?* "Please tell me you didn't talk to them." Sam's face scrunched up in concern.

"Well. I thought about it for a while, but I had to take my chances." Seth smiled profusely. "Turns out he was from another realm where a bunch of magical creatures live."

"Another realm?" Sam had only heard about realms a few times before. Derek had told her that many magical realms existed, but she had no idea how one would get to them or what life there would be like in these different places. "How'd he get here?" she asked.

"He didn't say, but that's not the point. He told me he could help me out. Figure out if I had any non-siren blood in me. He said if I was part human or part angel/demon, then he could help me get legs by getting rid of my siren half using some magical device or something. And, well, I told him about my powers, and they must have come from an angel or a demon, right?"

"Is that what you want? You want to get rid of all of your siren abilities?" Sam looked shocked.

Seth put his head down and muttered in an almost inaudible volume. "It may be my only option to not live alone in the ocean forever."

"Do you think this guy is legit? It seems awfully convenient that you found him and he would know how to help you." Sam turned to be face to face with Seth. "Like come on, really? Was he even shocked to see you here? Sirens aren't usually found on Earth. He doesn't seem very trustworthy. Why would he just be right here with all the answers to your very unique problems?"

"Okay, sheesh, stop. I just wanted some answers, okay? I get it," Seth snapped. Sam took the cue and stopped talking. "I get it, okay." He ran both of his hands through his hair. "It's just that there doesn't seem to be anyone with any knowledge of my past. I know it was dangerous, but it's all I could do. We don't all get to live with a bunch of people like us." Sam looked up, her eyes wide. She looked away quickly, avoiding eye contact. *He's right. Shoot, Sam. He was so supportive even when you told him you ended up hurting your own cousin. Could you not be a little more empathetic?*

"Sorry. I didn't mean to…"

"It's fine. You're right. I shouldn't be exposing myself to strangers."

"Can you at least promise that if you meet him again, you'll call me over? I don't want you seeing him alone."

"Sure," he said rather unconvincingly. "I doubt I'll see him, though. He said he would make his way back here sometime. But that's it. He just gave me 'sometime.'"

"Maybe that's for the best. I mean, he already told you that you could possibly separate yourself from your siren half." Sam put her hand on top of Seth's. "We can figure out the rest. We don't need him."

Seth gave her a half smile. "Let's hope."

"My training for the next few weeks is going to be a lot of reading. I'll finally have access to the library in the mansion. I'll research this."

"Thanks, Sam. I would really appreciate that."

"I'm sorry for not being so understanding before. I just worry about you being here alone and all." Sam motioned around the cave.

"Yeah, it's lonely only having dolphins for friends, but I'll be okay. I promise." Seth looked down and back up rather fast. "Okay, now hurry. We have to get back so you can head out in the sunlight," Seth replied. The two of them left the rock pool and headed back to the cave. Sam got out of the water and dried herself again.

"Maybe we won't wait another week? I can come by more often now that I'm staying so close by and not moving around."

"Sounds good." Seth gave Sam his first real smile since they talked about the strange man he had met. "Just shoot me a thought." He winked and went under the water to swim away. Sam began to climb out of the rocky cave and walked back towards her house. *I really hope that man doesn't come back.* She had an eerie feeling that this man was dangerous. *Why would a person be lurking so close to two mansions of magical kids trying to "help" people if he didn't have his own*

agenda? Is he connected to the demon's tractor disappearing?
She kept walking and made it to Maddi and Logan's house.
I wonder if Logan's still here. Did he go back to wherever in Europe he's really from?

"Sammy!" A familiar voice echoed behind her. Sam turned around in fright. "I haven't seen you since you were this tall." Keith stood in front of her, motioning to a few feet above the ground. A shiver ran down her spine. She walked backwards carefully. She covered her mouth with her hand while the other one trembled by her side. Sam couldn't help but notice a scar down the side of his nose that, on top of his tall dark presence, made her brace herself.

Should I run? Should I stay and listen to him? I mean, I know he's supposedly after my powers, but he doesn't know that I'm the one with them yet, right? Maybe I should hear him out.

"Oh. Don't be afraid. I just had a few questions for you." His voice was very hoarse and insincere. "I mean. I just overheard you and your cute little fish friend talking about sending thoughts. That wouldn't be more than a little joke between you, right?" He laughed. "Not like you can send thoughts to people?" He walked closer to Sam as she continued to back up slowly.

"I don't know what you're talking about."

"Well. Unless you had, say, telepathic powers?" Keith said, disregarding Sam's response. "It's you. You have the gift."

Okay. Um. So he knows. Shoot. Run, Sam. Run! Sam started sprinting towards her own house, but time seemed to slow down, and no matter how long she ran, she didn't seem to get any closer. It was as if gravity's pull was stronger on her than anything else on Earth. She tried stopping, but as she came to a halt, time sped up and she fell. Sam got on her knees that were now badly scraped and turned around, resting on her hands.

"What are you going to do even if I do? How would you get them?" Sam tried sounding intimidating.

"Oh, Sam. How cute. I could always just take you. Then I'll have you and your powers." Keith was at Sam's feet now looking down at her. "Lucky for you, today's not the day that I do that. Where are our precious siblings? Ethan's not attached to your hip like usual?"

"Sam!" Travis' voice trailed behind her.

"Yes, please help!" Sam shouted. *Maybe he can get me out of this mess. Keith wouldn't follow us home, right?* Before she could figure out what to do, Keith raised his hand, and Sam couldn't hear Travis' voice anymore. She turned around to find him frozen in his tracks. *There goes that plan.*

"Poor guy. Does he even know who I am?" Keith snickered.

"I don't even know who you are anymore," Sam muttered under her breath. *What are you going to do, Sam? He'll freeze anyone trying to help you. You're on your own. Think!*

CHAPTER 9

NOT EVERYONE FREEZES UNDER PRESSURE

———

Keith towered above her. He was wearing a long black coat on top of a gray vest and white button-up shirt. A pocket watch hung on the side of his dark jeans on a silver chain that shined bright in Sam's eyes. She got up, shielding her eyes, and said her words louder. "I don't even know who you are anymore." She walked towards him. "What happened to you when Mom and Dad died? You abandoned us."

"Sammy, I…" Keith took his chain and spun the pocket watch around.

"Stop calling me Sammy." Sam was too flustered to keep listening to Keith's insults. "You know that's not my real name." She snapped.

"Fine. Sameera. Happy?" He laughed at the sudden rage inside of Sam. "It's not my responsibility to take care of all of you. Mom and Dad would never have made it on Earth anyways. They have duties elsewhere. You were all too weak to understand that."

"You're disgusting!" Sam yelled. She hadn't realized just how much anger she had towards Keith.

"I'm honest," he said. Sam scoffed hearing his words. *Honest. Nobody has been honest here.* "Then what's your real plan, Keith?" She got up, trying to seem more intimidating. "Seems like Derek's already turned you against me. You'll know my plan soon, little sister. Besides, you only have the gift by accident. When Mom left Earth, she was supposed to give those powers to me!" He towered over her. "I'm the oldest." His voice roared in her ears. Sam didn't know what to say next. *Is that possible? Am I not supposed to have these powers? I mean, even if Mom knew Keith would turn out to be a jerk, why not Derek or Mia or even Ethan? They're all older. Why me?* Her thoughts were interrupted as she saw someone exit the backdoor of the neighboring house. Out came Logan, holding a trash bag. *Shoot. Keith will freeze him too.* She wanted to warn him, but it was too late. Keith had already noticed him.

"Another witness." Keith laughed. He raised his palm towards Logan's face, the watch chain dangling out of his fingers. Logan made eye contact with Sam, giving her a look of concern. Sam's eyes opened wide in anticipation for Keith to freeze him, but, instead, Logan continued walking towards them. Keith put his hand down and raised it again with more force, furrowing his eyebrows when nothing happened.

"Everything alright? Won't your arm get tired?" Logan joked. Keith's face clouded with confusion and anger. He crinkled his nose, showing off his scar more.

How is he still moving? Sam looked at Keith whose face was wrinkled in concern. "Yeah—" Sam could barely get her words out.

"Don't worry, child, just having a talk with my sweet sister," Keith interjected. He pulled his hand down and raised it again. Logan looked up at him confused.

"Sam, did you forget? We had plans tonight. You and Ethan were coming over. Ethan's already inside. Come on," Logan said as he took Sam's wrist and began walking her inside. Keith didn't object. Instead he looked at Logan with a death glare.

"I'll see you another time, Sam. And next time I'll find you alone," Keith threatened. He turned around and disappeared into thin air.

"Thanks." Sam took her hand out of Logan's. "You couldn't have come at a better time." *Why didn't Keith's magic work on him?*

"Yeah, I sensed that. Who was that?" he asked. Logan put his hands in his pockets. He stared intently at her, but she didn't meet his gaze.

"Uh. Don't worry about that." Sam looked towards Travis, who was unfrozen but dazed. "I have to go. Sorry."

"Wait, at least promise me that we can talk soon? I'm still a bit freaked out about that forest creature, and now this guy. Was he really your brother?" he whispered.

"Yeah, he is," she said looking down embarrassed. "And sure." Sam ran off towards Travis to help him up. She didn't really have plans to talk to Logan about this again. He kept getting too close to finding out about her gift.

***

"You saw who?" Derek yelled. Travis and Sky sat next to Sam at the kitchen table. "He was here? Did you tell him anything?"

"No…" Sam replied hesitantly, knowing that wasn't really what he was asking.

"Phew. Good. Then he may not know," Sky interrupted.

"But I didn't have to say anything to him. He figured it out." Sam could see the anger building up in Derek as he balled his hands into fists and then released them. Sky stood up. "What? How?" Derek finally answered. Both him and Sky towered above Sam, waiting for a response. *How do I tell them that I've been sneaking out to see a friend and that I told him about my gift. Wow. Sam. Even thinking about it makes it sound like a stupid thing to do.*

"I was talking to someone else, and he told me to send him thoughts." Sam held her legs in close to her chest. "And, well, Keith put two and two together."

"You told someone about your gift? Sam! We trusted you with training, and you've been lying and sneaking out this whole time?" Sky was yelling.

"Who is this someone?" Derek put his hand on Sky's chest, trying to get him to calm down.

"His name is Seth. He's a siren." Sam's voice was barely audible now.

"A siren? On Earth?" Travis looked at Sam confused.

"We don't know why or how he got here. He doesn't remember who his parents are or anything about his past," Sam answered. She didn't know what they were going to say next. An awkwardly long silence fell in the room. She couldn't help but think about how Keith said that he was coming back and how Logan wasn't affected by Keith's powers.

"Okay, guys. I don't know what powers you're talking about or what this whole sending thought issue is, but what's done is done. Can we focus on getting away from that dude?" Travis blurted out, ending the silence. He still looked dazed and scared from being frozen. "Seriously. Who was that? A demon?" Sky and Derek looked at each other.

"That's our older brother," Derek said. "He's after us because he wants the powers our mom passed down to Sam."

"To Sam? As in a singular child?" Travis asked, seemingly more confused now. "I thought angels left all of their children some powers, and you guys got the elements, right?"

"Okay. Travis, we need you to keep this to yourself," Sky said and looked at Derek.

"Our dad gave us the elemental powers," Derek chimed in.

"Wait, you guys are the children of two angels? That's so cool!" Travis's eyes lit up.

"Not exactly. Our dad is the devil." Derek sighed. He ran his fingers through his hair. Travis frowned almost as quickly as he had lit up about two magical parents. "Our mom was different from most angels. Her powers were known as 'the gift.' She gave that gift to Sam, and now Keith, who took after our father, is after her powers." Sam couldn't help but think that the way Derek had said that last sentence made him sound mad at mom for not giving him her powers.

"The gift?" Travis said, looking at Sam. "So you get extra powers? That's a sweet deal. What can you do?"

"Control the mind, I think, and other things. We don't really know too much about them," Sam said shyly.

Sky turned to Derek and whispered, "Did he really have to be here?"

"Sky, I'm right here!" Travis looked up, offended.

"Yes. He did. We can't have him telling everyone else in the house what he saw," Derek said, trying to calm Sky down.

"Still here!" Travis chimed in.

"Get used to it. They think nobody else can hear them when they get into their planning mode," Sam snarked.

"We need a new game plan," Sky said to Derek.

"See. Completely ignoring us." Sam laughed and looked at Travis, who smiled. "But I agree for once. Your months-long plan ain't going to cut it. I need access to the library now. I have a few ideas I want to research."

"Like what?" Derek was intrigued.

"Well, Seth..." Sam sensed the tension in the room when she said his name. "He told me that he met some guy who was talking about splitting powers with some device. Wouldn't that solve everything?" Derek came closer to Sam and took a seat. "I mean. If we split the gift among us all, someone would have to steal the powers from all of us to get the gift back. That would be a lot harder and not as worth it right?"

"How do we know this guy was telling the truth?" Sky stood behind Derek still.

"Yeah, and why was he talking about this to a siren? Plus, it might be Keith. I wouldn't put this past him. Luring us in through your friend."

Derek was right. This man could have been Keith. He was lurking in the area just now. "It could be a trap, but it's our only idea as of now. And, *Seth*..." Sam emphasized, getting slightly irritated that her brother kept referring to him as "the siren" rather than his name, "needs it too. If he can split away his siren side, he might be able to get legs and live on land."

"Sam, we can't risk wasting time on ideas just because you want to help out your little friend," Sky commanded. Sam was getting angry with the two boys. They kept talking about Seth as if he wasn't also a person.

"He isn't my 'little friend.' And besides, the only other thing I can think of would involve putting Maddi's precious family at risk. You wouldn't want that, now would you, Sky?"

Sam was bitter now. *Shoot. I'm going to have to tell them about Logan now.*

"What are you talking about?" Sky asked. Sam had succeeded in getting his attention, but she had screwed herself over in the process.

"When Keith was talking to me, Logan walked out. I was sure he was going to end up frozen like Travis, but Keith's magic didn't affect him at all." Sam's voice wavered. "I don't know why, but that's the only other lead I have against Keith."

"No, that's not possible. Is it? Logan? He's so young. Keith must have let you both go on purpose," Sky said, trying to grasp what Sam was saying.

"Okay, Sam. You're right. We can't involve Logan or anyone from the other house, so power splitting is our only idea right now. We'll go with it," Derek said. He was clearly trying to recenter the conversation while Sky was spiraling. He had his hands running through his hair and he was breathing heavily.

Yup. Bringing up Maddi really did mess with him. Sam watched as Sky took a deep breath and then joined back into the conversation.

"So we're going to go with the idea that we think Keith planted in our heads?" Sky's voice was full of disbelief. "I agree we can't involve Maddi, but isn't this the worst way forward?"

"Maybe, but it's the only stepping stone we have, and seeing that we have no time, we have to go with it. Keith could be back anytime and now he knows Sam has the gift." Derek leaned forward and placed his hands on Sam's knees. "We have to double your training. We're going to bring in Ethan and Mia in the mornings to train using your powers. Then after, we're all going to go read up anything we can find on the gift, time control, and splitting powers, okay?"

"Okay," Sam agreed, nodding.

"What should I do?" Travis looked at Derek.

"Just take care of everyone else. We're most probably going to have to leave to find this device if Sam is right, and you're going to be one of the oldest ones left." Derek said. Travis nodded at his instructions.

"And don't tell them about anything. Not a word about the devil, the gift, or Keith. Okay?" Sky eyed Travis.

"Chill, dude. My lips are sealed." Travis motioned around his mouth as if he was zipping it up. Sam laughed. "What?" Travis asked, laughing.

"Nothing," Sam replied. *Travis is such a stereotypical surfer dude. It's almost funny.* Knowing that Travis was more lost than her gave her comfort. She was finally not the only one completely out of the loop.

"Okay, off to bed, guys. We start the new plan tomorrow," Sky said, clearly tired of Sam and Travis' jokes.

"Bed? It's barely 8 p.m.," Travis protested.

"Okay, well, just get out of here and do whatever. I need time alone with Derek."

"Fine," Travis said, walking off.

"Okay, sure, but remember our deal. No more secrets," Sam said before heading up. She didn't mind falling asleep so early. She was going to need it. *Derek was right about Keith. He really is evil now. I hope this new plan works. After seeing the lack of remorse in him today, I don't want to find out what he would do if he got a hold of both time and the gift.*

CHAPTER 10

HOW DO YOU DEAL WITH CHECKMATE?

———

After getting to the middle of the third edition of *The History of Magical Devices*, Sam's head was going to explode. It had been a week of scouring their family library for information, and she hadn't even read a single word on magic splitting devices yet. At this point, she was confusing herself by reading more. *Does this device even exist? And do I want to use it?* She couldn't help but think about how she had asked Seth if he wanted to get rid of a part of himself. *Am I doing the same thing? Stop, no, Sam. You can't have second thoughts now. It would be better for everyone if no one person had all this power.*

She put her book down and walked outside the library. "I'm just going to grab a snack," she muttered, but the boys were too busy doing their own research. Travis and some of the others were making food in the kitchen, so she slipped out the side of the house and walked to the basketball courts again. *Someone must have forgotten to transform the court back to normal.* After checking that no one else was around, Sam picked up the basketball on the ground and took a shot at the basket. It was about to fall out, but she quickly got a hold of it with her mind and pushed it in. *It almost feels good to be using magic again after all this reading. Maybe I can fight Keith. Wait. Who am I kidding? One basket doesn't make you strong, Sam.*

She straightened her posture and stretched out her arms. Her mind was a swarm of frustrated thoughts and all she wanted was a moment of silence. Sam looked around her again and still nobody was nearby, so she closed her eyes and stood still. She scrunched her face and let her hands light up on fire. *You are fire, Sam.* She let the flames envelop her until she felt lighter. *Keith wouldn't want your powers if he wasn't threatened by them.* Warmth rushed through her. She felt a sense of control for the first time. As she felt warmer, her mind felt more relaxed. No longer was the flame just merely surrounding her. She was the flame.

Then, as suddenly as she had sparked the fire, she absorbed the flames and fell onto her knees. *You did it!* Sam had finally mustered the courage to let herself fully become a flame. The prison of her self-doubt thoughts felt like it had been burned down. She got up and, with more energy than before, she ran back towards the library.

"I think I found something!" Derek said, rushing over to greet her. His face had lit up and the dreariness he'd had in his voice all morning disappeared. "There was supposedly a kid of an angel a couple hundred years ago who created a ritual to get rid of or give away partial powers. It involved one of the main magical devices." He pointed excitedly at a page in the book. Sam took a look.

Seryphia, the child of the angel of weather, felt burdened by the responsibilities her powers came with. Unable to constantly control the powers and ward off people after them, she researched the separation of powers. Sam's eyes widened. Seryphia's situation was almost identical to hers. "I guess they're right. History does repeat itself." She looked at Sky and Derek. "Where would this device exist?" Sam's voice echoed off the high ceilings.

"Athanasía?" Sky looked up with worry on his face. "We need to go to Athanasía," Sky affirmed. Derek looked back at his younger cousin with a wrinkled forehead.

"Isn't that the realm where magic began?" Sam asked. By now she had learned a lot about how multiple realms existed, each with its own structure and purpose. Earth was in a fully mortal realm, and Athanasía was home to all the immortal beings.

"Yes, it's where Keith lives. You were born there, Sam," Sky said. He started walking around the library, pulling books related to Athanasía off the shelves.

"What? I always thought we were all born on Earth."

"The rest of us were, but you and Ethan weren't. Maybe that's why Mom gave you the gift," Derek said with a hint of sadness in his voice.

"Well, I kind of wish she hadn't," Sam blurted out, realizing this was the first time she had outwardly said those words. She didn't know if she felt liberated or ashamed for wanting to give up the gift. "Anyway, where in this realm would we look for it?"

"Let's find out. There has to be something in one of these books that talks about where they left ancient magical devices," Sky said as he took the book from Derek. Sam scoured through some others. "It says here that most of the devices were given to different museums of angel families."

"Do you think Keith has the power-splitting device, then? Our mom was an angel, and he probably was the one to tell

Seth about it," Sam said and looked at Derek. He looked up and to the left and then down, avoiding eye contact with Sam. "What?"

"Our house in Athanasía used to be a museum that they closed off when someone tried to steal some artifacts. With him showing up here and someone planting the idea in Seth's mind, I'm almost certain he has it."

"Now it all makes sense," Sky ranted. "Of course. This is why he just left Sam to come back to us and why he didn't try attacking us sooner. He knew we would end up coming to him." Sky paced back and forth. "So then we don't go. We're going to stay and figure out a better plan."

"You know we don't have a chance if we stay here, right?" Derek grabbed Sky's arm to stop him from pacing more. "He's using us like pawns on a chessboard, knowing that he's a step away from checkmate no matter what we do."

"What do you mean?" Sam closed the book in her hand and looked up at her brother.

"If we don't go, he'll just come to us, and this time he won't just let you get away. Plus, I'd rather not see what havoc he will create on Earth. I'm sure he won't mind revealing magic to humans."

Sam hadn't thought of that before. She always thought even demons wanted to keep magic a secret, but Derek had a point. *When you're trying to gain more power, you usually don't care to hide the power you already have.*

"If we do go, he'll be ready for us knowing we need the device," Derek continued talking. "We should go, but we need to figure out how to get the device from him. Sam," Derek looked directly back into her eyes, "you're probably going to have to face him with your powers."

Sam knew he was right, but her heart still sank as he said the words. With Keith's time powers, she was going to have to try really hard to gain control in a situation with him. She nodded, trying to stand straight and appear confident in herself.

You already overcame your fear of giving into the flame. You can do this too. "Okay, let's go," she said and looked at her older brother and cousin.

"Wait." Sky wriggled his arm out of Derek's hand. "You think we can just show up at his door like this? She isn't ready." Sky spoke to Derek as if Sam wasn't in the room.

Damn. Thanks for the support, Sky. Sam slouched again. Any confidence she had tried to have quickly left her. She knew he was right. *We aren't ready, and Keith knows it. He'll definitely use it to his advantage.*

"What are we going to do here? He's just going to come back. We don't have time to train anymore. Sam can do it. We just need to believe in her," Derek said.

"Guys—" Sam tried to speak up.

"This is going to be a mistake." Sky looked at Derek, ignoring Sam.

"Well. We're going, so are you coming or not?" Derek stopped leaning on the chair near him and looked straight at Sky.

"Fine. We'll make a plan and leave tonight." They both turned to Sam. "Go get Ethan and Mia and get some stuff to go."

"What about creating a plan?"

"Derek and I got it," he said and then walked her out, not giving Sam a chance to say anything else. The last thing Sam saw was the door to the library closing in on her face. She pounded her fists against the door. *Again? So much for being kept in the loop.* She continued to knock and scream at them to open the door, but nobody answered. Travis and Mia walked in behind her. "It's no use. Sky's too stubborn, and that door's soundproof." Travis laughed.

"Oh, great. I've just been yelling at nothing, then." Sam buried her head in her hands and crouched down to the floor. "Do you know where Ethan is?"

"Haven't seen him," Mia replied. Travis waved them goodbye as Mia joined Sam on the floor. "What are you so stressed about?" She looked at her with concern.

"We have to face Keith, and they're making a plan without me again." Sam threw her hands in the air and sighed. Mia's eyes grew wide, but she quickly focused them on Sam again.

"Don't worry too much. The odds may not look favorable but worrying won't help. We just have to act now."

"Do you feel ready?" Sam looked into her older sister's eyes. *She's been training with Travis a lot and has been on quests already. She has to feel ready, right?*

"I don't think you're ever ready to go fight your own brother." She took Sam's hand. "But I'm glad I have you by my side as we do it." Mia looked back at the door they were leaning on. "Now, as for Derek and Sky, I can't believe they didn't even tell me that we're leaving."

"Welcome to my world," Sam teased. Mia rolled her eyes and laughed.

"Let's go find Ethan." She gave Sam a reassuring smile, lifting her up to leave.

***

Sam walked downstairs with Ethan and Mia. *I wonder if Sky and Derek will let us in on the plan before we get there.* It frustrated Sam. After all the training and promises to keep her in the loop, they had gone back to ground zero—no communication. And now Ethan and Mia were being dragged along to go on a dangerous mission, and Sam couldn't even tell them what they were going to do once they arrived.

"Derek, what's the plan?" Mia dropped her bag in front of him. "We just got here and we're leaving again? I thought you said this was going to be permanent." She pouted with her arms folded across her chest.

"It will be. We just have to get the splitting device. Sam filled you two in, right?" Derek stared into Mia's and Ethan's blank faces.

"I didn't know what to say. I don't even know what's happening," Sam said, realizing it sounded childish since she at least knew about the device, but she needed to take a stand.

"Fine. I'll fill you in. Come with me. Sam, stay here. You and Sky are going to train more before we head out." Sam took a seat and waited for Sky to say something as the others left. Sky continued reading and said nothing for a while, so she finally spoke up.

"So are we going to do anything?" Her voice came out harshly. Sky looked up and, without closing his book, tossed another one to Sam.

"Read as much as you can. Knowledge and strength go hand in hand." *Has he already given up on this plan enough to not even prepare me more? We haven't even begun the mission.* Sam took the book, but immediately put it down next to her.

"Mia told you about the demon, right? You know Derek's right about Keith just coming back if we don't go," she said forcefully.

"Yeah, she did. That was incredibly stupid, Sam." Sky sighed. "We don't have a choice, but that doesn't make it easier for me to willfully walk you into a dangerous situation."

"I turned into the flame today, fully. I know you said I could do it, but I didn't have the courage to do it until today," Sam said. *I really need him to tell me he thinks I have a chance. I need someone to tell me I do.*

"That's great, Sam." Sky's voice was still soft and broken. "I really hope Keith has even an ounce of a soul left in him. I don't know what I'd do if any of you get hurt on this trip."

"I don't know, either." *He definitely doesn't believe we can win. After all these years of trying to be in on the game plan, I really thought they would have come up with something better.*

***

The others finally returned. Derek held out a compass and placed it on the ground. "Thankfully, Ashley's dad was kind enough to leave us one portal to access the other worlds." Sam vaguely remembered how her parents would mysteriously take her older siblings to different dimensions when they were younger, but she hadn't travelled to any other realm herself.

I still can't believe that Keith used to play imaginary wars with Ethan and me, and now we're going to fight him for real. He used to be so careful in using his powers against us, pretending to let us win with our barely existent magic back then. I wish we could say he'd go easy on us tonight too.

"Okay, here we go," Derek mumbled. He pressed the center, and a portal opened up. "Think of your full name!" He yelled. "Raiden, Skyra, Miara, Ethren, and Sameera Bleu."

Sam looked at Derek as he said these words. She was so used to the names they used to blend in that she had almost forgotten what they sounded like. They all stepped in and the world went white for a second. Sam opened her eyes as they adjusted to the light in the new realm. The skies were purple and gray.

"Are those other planets?" Sam asked as she stared at gorgeous celestial bodies around her.

"Yeah. They're all home to different magical beings. Your friend Seth is probably from that teal one." Derek pointed at a beautiful teal sphere covered in bluish-white fog. Sam's mouth dropped. It was truly surreal seeing planets this close to the planet she was currently on. And the current planet itself was a lot to take in. Unlike Earth's blue-and-green natural appearance, Athanasía was very mauve and midnight blue. The ground itself was a deep wine color. "You'll get used to the look soon. It's always a shock after Earth."

A shock? She felt like a little child, looking at the world and taking an interest in every little detail. *I can't believe I was born here, and yet this place seems so foreign.*

"Okay, but how do we get to Keith's, and what's the plan when we do?" Ethan muttered.

Is he not mesmerized by this place? Sam had a hard time focusing.

"It's not far from here." Derek pointed at a castle in the distance. It was covered in fog, but even then it looked immense.

"Sky, Mia, and I will try to find Keith and get information. You and Sam are going to go find the device." Derek turned to Sam. "When you find it, just project your thoughts to us.

We won't transfer your powers until we get back to Earth. We want to be as far from Keith as possible when we do so. He can't get his hands on any of the powers."

So that's the plan? Split up? Sounds like the beginning of every bad plan, but I guess I have to trust them. "Alright." She looked at Ethan and gave him a reassuring look. "We got this." They all walked towards the castle. Sam continued staring at the world around her. There was magic everywhere, except it didn't look foreign here. It looked naturally blended into everyone's lives. Sam could see some shops next to her. There were objects floating around, being set in place and purchased all with no human interaction. *This is amazing.* It was truly a shock at how different society had developed where magic existed.

For an hour or two, they continued towards the castle and only stopped once to get food. *Even eating here involves powers.* Sam felt like magic had replaced what humans called science on Earth.

"Sam!" Sky waved his hand in her face.

"Huh? Sorry." She looked up to see that everyone was up and done with their food.

"I know this is a lot of new information, but the stakes are high tonight, Sam."

"Yeah. Sorry. I know. Let's go."

***

They were finally at the castle. It was a series of stone buildings that spanned the whole mountainside. For the last thirty minutes of traveling, no civilization could be seen. Some were shaped like domes, while others took more traditional castle shapes of cylindrical towers and parapets. It had a marble-like glossy finish, but it looked stronger and almost glowed in the dark through the fog. Nobody was around them. It was almost as if everyone steered clear of the castle. *Was I really born here? This place makes our mansions look poor.*

"How do we get in?" Sam asked Sky. She walked around the perimeter, still shocked at how close the other planets could be seen from behind the castle. Now that they were closer, she could make out that there was a glass dome greenhouse structure within the castle gates. *I wonder what it would be like to look at all these planets and the purple fog from there.*

"We have to make sure we don't let Keith find out that we're here," Sky said, bringing Sam back to reality. He looked around the gate in front of them to find an opening. Sam laughed.

How could anyone tell? This place is massive. The castle extended to the peak and all around the base. She wondered what transportation system someone would need just to get across it.

"Can we just climb the gate? I bet Keith wouldn't even notice," Mia said, walking towards the rose gold colored bars of the gate.

"Wait!" Derek yelled. "We don't know what defense system this castle has." Mia jumped back at hearing Derek scream so frantically. Derek turned to Ethan. "Can you create a system of vines to climb or something?" *Wow, I guess Sky and Derek really had thought a lot about this. I don't think I would've thought of a plant to lead us into the castle.*

"Sure. I'll try." Ethan nodded. Sam watched as the ground parted slightly and vines came out of the dark purple dirt. *Are those lily pads at the end of those vines?* Sam looked confused as Ethan raised his arm above his head and the vines grew large leaves. "Climb on top," he commanded everyone. Sam hopped on, trying to balance, and Ethan led them all to the other side of the gate touching no edge of the castle.

"Where'd you learn to do that?" Sam looked surprised.

"You're not the only one who's been training. Our other cousins showed me some new tricks," Ethan replied. Sam realized she hadn't really checked in on her siblings' lives. *Was I being selfish in taking all of Derek's and Sky's attention?* Sam snapped back into focus as Derek began talking.

"Let's head this way before we split up. I believe this building should be the armory." Derek pointed at a rectangular building with cylindrical towers on all four edges. They could see an arrow slit above the door. "We can stock up on some gear in case we need it." His voice stuttered as he said "in case," which didn't make Sam feel any better.

Sky opened the heavy wooden door of the building which creaked loudly, scaring all five of them. *Why is this castle so architecturally inconsistent? Half of it looks like it's from the future. Half of it is old wood from the medieval times.* As they walked in, Sam coughed on the dust the door had unsettled. Derek handed her a torch and Sam created a flame to light up the room. Immediately everyone gasped.

There were gems and scrolls sprawled across the floor. "Keith never won best organized in class, did he?" Mia muttered. Armor had been thrown to the edges of the room and was covered in mud and dirt. Sam picked up a shield and dropped it instantly, jumping back as she saw blood stains.

"What is this?" Sky lifted a scroll and began reading it out loud. "Katastrofí ka mool?" He struggled to pronounce the words.

"Wait, there's another paper stuck to the back!" Ethan jumped towards Sky and grabbed the sticky note. "It says 'Core of Destruction.'" His narrowed eyes grew wide as he read the words.

"I knew it," Derek declared. "Keith has been stealing spells and powers from different planets in this realm." He ran his fingers through his hair. "If he gets Sam's powers, there will be nothing stopping him from gaining control of all of the realms, even the mortal realm and Earth."

I can't let him do that. Sam imagined Earth filled with demons like the one she fought in the forest. She had barely escaped, and she seemingly had the powers everyone else wanted. *Mortals won't stand a chance against them.*

"What made Keith so evil? Why does he want even more power?" Ethan yelped.

"Why did Mom have to marry the devil?" Derek groused.

It's a good question. I never understood that dynamic.

"Listen, everyone. Take whatever gear you think will help you here. We need to get this device before Keith gets a hold of Sam's powers," Sky asserted. Sam picked up a few vests and eyed them to find labels or some indication of what they were for. "Those are anti-inflammatory protection pads, Sam. You won't need that," Sky said and Sam dropped them. A pair of tall boots in the room's corner caught her eye.

Are those Mom's? She rushed to put them on, and they fit. She slid a few scrolls that she had folded up into them. *Maybe these will be useful later.* All five of them headed back outside towards the castle gate entrance.

"Okay. Sam, Ethan, we're going to go find Keith. We'll keep him distracted and away from the museum side of the castle." Derek pointed to the dome-shaped building that had caught Sam's eye before due to its futuristic greenhouse appearance. "That's where the device would be if Keith has it. Everything should be labelled, so you'll know when you find it." He walked toward Sam. "I need you to forget any doubts you've had about your powers and just focus on the mission. Nobody is ever one hundred percent prepared for what life throws at them, but we all get through it." Derek had serious but soft, kind eyes. Sam gave her older brother a hug. She tried to take in all of his warmth.

"Okay, sure, that sounds great, Derek, but we have to be realistic, too," Sky quipped.

"Yeah, realistic is we're here and we have no more time, so shut it," Derek snapped. Sam appreciated that Derek had her back and wanted to bolster her spirits. "Be safe, everyone. And, Ethan, stick with Sam. We're relying on her thought-sending powers to communicate here." With that, Sam saw the three of them leave, took Ethan's hand, and headed for the peak.

I don't know how I'm going to win, but Keith has to lose.

CHAPTER 11

FULL OF POWERS, BUT POWERLESS

—

Sam and Ethan scoured the musty room, looking for the device. The glass surroundings proved to make the dome building scary rather than cool. Anyone could be watching them go through the museum's items. *Where could it be?* Sam coughed from the dust flying off the metal shelf she was searching. None of the labeled plaques matched a device for splitting powers. She was trying to stay positive, but one thought kept popping up in her head. *What if Keith has it, since he knew we would come for it?* She tried to push it out of her mind and continued looking.

"Did you check behind that wooden armoire?" Ethan pointed to the opposite corner of the room.

"Yeah, I checked everywhere." Sam stretched her hands up and behind her head in frustration. "I think we need to start checking the rest of the castle."

"Derek told us to stay here," Ethan replied.

"Yeah, but what are they going to do? Distract Keith forever? We need to get this device."

"Fine." Ethan put the books he had moved back into place and picked up his stuff. "By the way, what exactly are we doing with your powers? Are we all getting some part of it?" He looked a bit excited about the idea as he rushed towards her.

"I don't know. I'm keeping thought projection and mind reading though," she teased him as they left the building. Ethan laughed and put his arm around Sam's shoulder.

"As long as you're safe after this, I don't care about the powers," he whispered in her ear. They were back out on the purple ground and could see half of the castle below them, while the rest was hidden below the fog layer. The peak of the mountain felt strangely isolated. Even though Sam knew the gates were a long way down, the fog created the illusion that they were on a small hill overlooking other planets. The air around them felt humid. The sky seemed to be getting darker at the peak too. "Is it night here? Or daytime?" Ethan looked puzzled.

"I have no idea," Sam said, trying to look for the next building to search.

"Night, if you go by Earth time. Here the sky always looks like this," a deep voice spoke behind Sam and Ethan. They turned around and froze as they saw Keith standing in front of them. *So much for distracting him.* Sam stepped closer to Ethan and took his hand in her own. *Guys, Keith found us.* She projected her thoughts to Derek, but she got too distracted by Keith's words to listen in on her brother's thoughts for a response. "Ah, how cute! You two were inseparable as children, too. I missed seeing both of you, so innocent and young." He laughed.

"And you were nice when we were children," Ethan yelled back. Sam's stomach was doing flips. She could feel Ethan's hand getting sweaty. Her heart wanted to jump out of her chest and run away.

"Okay, you know why we're here," Sam yelled. "What do you want from me?" *Ethan, we need to buy time until Derek finds us.* Sam looked at Ethan and sent her thoughts. *That could take hours. Have you seen this place?* Ethan thought back as Sam read his mind.

"I want you, Sam," Keith said, shuffling through something in his pocket. "And you want this, right?" He held up a ring of metal, maybe the size of Sam's palm. *How does that split powers?* "If you can get it from me, then you can have it and leave, but if—" A sinister smile grew on Keith's face. "If you can't get it from me, well, then you stay."

"Stay?" Sam didn't mean to say the word out loud, but she always thought Keith would just take her powers and leave her.

"With me. Here. After all, you were born here, and this was always supposed to be your home."

"Fine," Sam challenged her eldest brother. *If I can hold him off for a while, then the others will be able to find us and together we can take on Keith.* "Ethan, we can do this." She gave him a reassuring look and tried to force a smile on her lips. He nodded reluctantly and looked back at Keith.

"This will be amusing." Keith laughed as he waved the ring in the air. "Come and get it," he teased. Ethan began to grow roots through the ground that travelled towards Keith. They shook the ground beneath them, almost making Sam fall. She hoped they would make Keith drop the device. As the roots got close to their brother though, they began moving slower and slower, until they almost didn't move at all. "Is that your best?" Keith snarled.

"No!" Sam said, shouting despite not standing too far from Keith. She raised her hand up and created a few fireballs that she threw all around Keith. "You might cause us to move slower, but you can't get rid of the fire completely." She smirked. The fire started moving inwards and Keith looked at it playfully. He raised his hand towards the fire and cupped his chin with the other hand.

"No, but I can—" He didn't finish his sentence. Suddenly, Sam saw the flames start growing faster towards her and Ethan.

"Sam, make sure it grows away from us!" Ethan exclaimed. Sam nodded but as she tried to move the fire, time seemed to slow down on her powers but quickened around the fire. She watched as the flames grew towards Ethan, with her powers having a severely delayed effect on stopping them.

"Ethan, move!" she shouted. Ethan jumped across a line of fire in front of him and now stood much closer to Keith. Sam watched Keith's smile grow bigger and bigger. She could hear him cackle and the combined noise of his laughter and her fire cracking in the humid wind made her dizzy. She tried to focus on controlling the fire with her mind. *Derek said that if I could control it with my mind, his time powers would be weakened. Where is he anyways?* Sam tried to tap into her mind control powers and managed to make the fire back off of her and Ethan. *Now just make it vanish.* She looked up at Keith, who was still laughing and enjoying himself. She closed her eyes and tried to absorb the fire. As she opened her eyes, she could see the fire slowly disappearing. *Did he let go of his hold on me?* She looked up and noticed Keith was distracted.

"Sam! I got it!" Ethan was running towards her with the ring. *Did he actually get it while Keith was trying to control me?* She couldn't believe it. Keith had promised to let them go if they got it. She started running towards them, trying to get to Ethan and the device.

"Not so fast." Keith's voice was lower than before. He looked taller and scarier now, too. "We're not done yet." He raised both his hands, one facing each twin. Sam felt her legs moving slower and slower. She looked down to see she was barely moving. Even the dirt around her was shuffling slowly. She could feel it hit her leg and fall as she tried to move. Sam looked up to find Ethan completely frozen and Keith walking towards him. "Did you think it would be that easy?" He took a hold of Ethan's shirt and unfroze him. Sam could see Ethan flailing his arms and legs as if he was running, but Keith wouldn't let go of him.

I'm out of ideas. She projected to Ethan's mind.

We have to be sneaky. Anything he sees, he'll slow down or speed up to his advantage. Ethan thought back. *I'm going to try to create vines behind him and grab him by surprise. Can you try to light them on fire before he realizes they're there?* Sam tried to go through the training she had received to think of anything she could use.

How will you get away from the flames if I do that?

I'm hoping he'll let go of me when he is caught off guard. Ethan's face was pale from trying to get out of Keith's grasp.

And if he doesn't?

"We have to try," Ethan said, looking in her eyes and nodding.

"Trying to figure something out, Sammy?" Keith mocked her. That name made Sam's blood boil. She knew he was saying her name wrong to irritate her, but with everything going on, she couldn't help the rage building inside.

Go. I got you, Ethan. Everything Keith had done over the years started coming back to her. She was furious at him. He had left them when they needed family the most. He didn't reach out to her once. Then she found out that he still called Derek and only because he wanted her powers. *But he isn't even taking my powers. He's playing games with us instead. What does he want?* "Why are you doing this? Even Dad wasn't this cruel, and he's the devil, for angel's sake," Sam screamed.

"Sam, you have no idea who you're talking to. I'm the reason Mom is gone. She had a while left before she had to leave, but I knew she wouldn't be able to give her powers to everyone if I killed her," Keith roared. Sam's heart dropped. She knew he was bad, but hearing him say that he had killed their mom confirmed that every doubt she had ever had was wrong. It confirmed that the worst case scenario, what she hoped was wrong, was in fact true.

"Does power really mean more to you than anything else? What will you get with all this power?" Sam asked, wanting to believe that some ounce of humanity was left in him.

"Mom was selfish. She knew she'd leave us behind, so I knew that it was my chance. She should've never had children. If she was going to abandon us, I decided I was going to take advantage of her magic." Keith laughed. His grip tightened on Ethan who let out a squeal. "Still trying to escape, little brother?"

Sam saw the vines forming behind Keith, who was smirking as he saw Ethan struggle. She closed her eyes and let out a grunt. Before she could conjure fire, the ground below her began trembling. Rock cracked under her feet, letting out a roar. She looked at Ethan, who seemed furious with Keith's latest revelations. A crack grew from where Sam stood towards Keith. In a matter of milliseconds, it split apart, creating a canyon and Sam could see the rock under her. There was a golden aura coming from below that seemed to shock Keith too.

"Nice trick," Keith said as he lifted Ethan above the hole he had created. "What are you going to do now, Sammy?" More fury built up inside her. She could feel the fire taking over like it had on the basketball court. It started at the tips of her fingers but then grew throughout her arms and legs. She focused on the rocks in the crevice, slowly warming them.

"I never wanted these powers, but, if it means you can't have them, then I'll keep them forever," Sam fumed, trying to buy time. She could feel the ground in the pit liquifying. *Keith can't know what I'm doing. The one thing he can't control is my mind.*

Ethan's forehead was covered in wrinkles. Sam could see the vines he was growing in the crevice. They were covered in thorns and were now as tall as Keith. As they hovered above his head, Sam looked at her twin brother and nodded. "Now, Ethan!" Sam yelled at the top of her lungs. Vines slowly moved towards Keith. Before he could realize that something was happening, Sam turned into a flame and, as she had hoped, Keith started slowing her down.

Sam took advantage of being Keith's focus. She used her gift to make the molten rock below Keith explode, creating a wall of lava. *Ethan, did he let go? Run, now!* Sam saw a blur of fiery red and green through the lava. *Ethan?* Sam tried projecting her thoughts to see if Ethan was okay. Her heart raced faster as she tried to read his mind but got nothing.

She heard a shriek that she desperately hoped was Keith's, but as the lava wall fell, she could only see her twin brother falling into the crevice. Keith had seemingly disappeared.

"Ethan!" she screamed, crying. She felt a knot form in her stomach as she tried her hardest to absorb the fire and lava below Ethan to save him.

"Miss me?" Keith's voice rang in her ears. She turned to see him materialize behind her. *Shoot! How'd he do that?* Sam turned back to the fire that burned near Ethan. She saw a hand reach up out of the flame and heard a cry.

"Sam! Run!" he yelped.

"Ethan!" She jumped in the crevice and ran through the fire trying to extinguish it, but Keith had a hold on her again. The smell of charred rock rushed her as she saw Ethan struggle to escape. She began moving faster than she could control, and her powers seemed to slow down. She tried controlling the fire with her mind and as a part of herself, but both seemed to have a delayed effect. She tried to stop running and look around for objects to take out the fire manually. As she turned to the left, the world flew past her. She looked to the right and the world moved at a snail's pace. Time started blurring together and Sam felt nauseous. Her ears began ringing as her vision blurred out, nearly drowning out Ethan's screams.

"I love you, Sam," Ethan said, crying in pain. It was the last thing she heard before silence swept in. She crouched down towards the ground toward her twin, but as she looked down, her vision went black, and she fell.

CHAPTER 12

NOBODY ESCAPES TIME

———

Sam's eyes slowly adjusted to the barely lit room. Above her was a dark mauve sky. It looked like she was outside, but there was no breeze. This didn't feel like Earth anymore. *Oh, shoot. Athanasía!* Memories of the battle came rushing back to Sam. She felt her palms get sweaty as she thought about Ethan. *Maybe he's also here somewhere?*

Sam felt a hard surface underneath her. *Cement, maybe?* She tried getting up but felt weak. Her arms trembled as they supported her. She pushed her legs off the side of whatever she woke up on. Then she pulled herself in an upright position slowly. As Sam looked up, she began realizing she was in a circular room with a tall, transparent ceiling. There were archways leading outside on all sides of her. Fog rolled in from them so that Sam could only make out a faint outline of the castle buildings outside. She was instantly startled when she realized that there was a person on the couch. "Sammy! You're awake. Finally."

"Keith?" Sam said, even more startled than when she was unaware of his identity. "Where are the others?" She looked around and jumped off the platform. Her legs felt like jelly, even weaker than her arms had been. She mustered her strength, hiding her weakness from her older brother.

"They're mostly fine and back home." Keith's voice was deep.

Mostly fine? No! He means Ethan. Sam's brain rushed to the last thing she had seen before finding herself in this room. Ethan had been drowning in flames. "Do you have Ethan somewhere, too? You have me. Let him go," she snarled.

"Oh, Sameera. So young and naïve. He died. Remember?" Keith laughed. Sam knew he was right, but she wanted to believe he was lying so badly. She wanted her twin brother to be back home with the rest. A sunken feeling hit her. She felt numb to her emotions, knowing that she should be sad, but also as if she couldn't understand what Keith was telling her.

"What happened to you? You were so sweet. We used to get along. Then Mom and Dad died, and you completely changed." She sobbed. Sam hadn't seen her parents since she was seven. Keith had basically become the devil haunting Sam's life when they left.

"I grew up. I had to," he thundered. His eyes flashed black for a second as he smirked at her.

"What happened to Dad? And how could you kill Mom?" Sam had always wanted to ask her older brother more about their mom. He was the one who had known her longest, since the rest of them were so young when she died. Tears formed in Sam's eyes. *Of course Ethan is actually dead. If Keith didn't hesitate to kill his own mother, he wouldn't care to save his younger brother.* Keith walked towards her with a large, menacing grin on his face. She wanted to drop to the ground and bawl her eyes out, but she needed to stay grounded in case Keith was going to attack again.

"Dad was smarter than you think, but that's in the past now. Both of them are gone. You have the gift. And I have you." Keith gloated as he stepped closer to Sam and lifted her chin. "Baby sister, you have no idea what the gift is, do you?"

"My family will come and get me. They aren't going to leave me here." Sam trembled as she wriggled her face out of Keith's grip and stepped back.

"They would if they knew you were alive and here. Plus, they won't be able to. You'll see in time. You and I have a long life ahead of us," Keith taunted. He turned around and went to the bookshelf behind the couch. He grabbed an old, dark maroon hardbound book and tossed it to Sam. She barely caught it, falling slightly because of its weight. *Fighting Without Magic.* "There are some clothes in the armoire behind you. Change and meet me in twenty minutes. We're starting your training. If you keep fighting the way you did last night, we're both in trouble." Keith left through one arch, disappearing behind the fog. His eyes and voice had softened as he said his last sentence. It was almost as if, in a split second, he had actually started to care about her.

Training? Is he helping me or taking my powers? Sam went to the armoire and took out the clothes. There were some tight black leggings and a loose gray shirt. In a small compartment, she found some protective gear. She changed and put on the arm and elbow pads. *I wonder how much Keith will actually show me. If he's anything like Derek or Sky, I'm not actually going to learn much.*

She slipped on the same boots as before but noticed the scrolls she had hidden were gone. Sam turned around and walked towards the bookcase. She ran her fingers across the books. *How Prophecies Fit in the Current World. Living*

Alongside Humans. Creatures and Equality. How Athanasía Compares to Other Realms. Sam picked out the last book. *Is he right? Does everyone think I'm dead too and now I'm stuck in Athanasía?* She opened the book and looked at the table of contents. Her eyes landed on four words: *Realm of the Dead.* All the numbness she felt from her fear of Keith evaporated.

Ethan's death suddenly hit her. Her eyes began tearing up. *Could he be lying to hurt me?* Sam stepped away from the bookcase and threw the book onto the couch as she fell to the floor. *No. It wouldn't make sense. What would his motivation be? Plus, I saw it with my own eyes.*

Their game plan had failed, and her inability to control her powers had caused Ethan to die in the process. She hugged her legs and wept on the floor. Her own twin brother was gone, and she was to blame. It should've been her. It was her fault. *Why is Keith training me now? Is that what he meant by me fighting last night? Wouldn't he want me to not be able to defend myself so he can take the gift?* She felt confused and heartbroken. The fact that she had no idea how to get home, or if she would ever see her family, was settling in.

Scenes she had never envisioned before rushed to her. *Graduations, birthdays, weddings. Vacations, family dinners, just joking around.* She would never have those again with Ethan. He was the one who understood her. He was her other half and now he was gone.

Keith walked in and saw her on the floor. "Didn't I tell you twenty minutes? What's wrong with you, child?" He saw her weeping. "Oh, Sam. Don't worry, you'll be stronger soon." Sam looked up, confused, seeing Keith's eyes opened wide in concern for her. His grin was gone and replaced by a slight frown. It was like Keith hadn't figured out what he wanted with her yet. One second he was yelling at her, and the other he was helping her. He knelt down, hugged her, then reached out a hand. "Let's go now." His voice was stern but sweet. "Listen to me and we won't have many problems. I'll train you to be stronger and better equipped to deal with your powers." *Better equipped? Is he going to let me keep my powers?* "I don't want this anymore. I don't want these powers, not when they got Ethan killed," Sam lamented.

"Well, it's too bad then that you have them, little sister. You might as well learn to control them," Keith exclaimed, his voice almost apologetic towards Sam.

"Why aren't you just taking them from me? I thought that's what you wanted?" Sam stared into Keith's watery eyes. *Is he also sad about Ethan? Why would he get him killed and then be sad?* Just as Sam began to wonder her brother's intentions, Keith's face transformed. His evil grin returned and he arched his eyebrows.

"You succeeded in breaking the splitting device, but I have you now instead, child. It's much better than just your powers," he jeered. Any ounce of compassion on his face was replaced with anger, with his eyes darkening again. "Now I told you to get ready. Stop wasting my time with your crying. Ethan is gone, and you have to deal with it," Keith scolded. Sam felt a shiver go down her spine. She held her hands and flinched as Keith abruptly got up. He left through the arch. Sam could hear him mumbling outside, but she couldn't make out the words. She crawled to the edge of the room and cupped her ears to figure out who he was talking to.

"You have to be more gentle. She's only so young. Listen to me," a voice that sounded like Keith chastised. *Is he talking to himself?* Then, within a few seconds, Keith returned through another arch.

"I'm sorry. I know you're hurting," Keith said, his voice sweeter. He walked in slowly and this time wore a small smile. His face was relaxed, and his voice almost seemed kind. Sam scooched backwards in fear.

Why does he keep changing attitudes? Does he care about me or does he want to hurt me? "Stop! Stop all of this. I just want to go home. If you're really sorry, you'll take me home," she shrieked.

"Now I can't do that, but I promise I'll make you stronger. You won't ever lose control of your powers again after I've trained you."

"What's the point of my powers? I can't use the gift unless I want to hold the whole world's moral obligations on my shoulders. I can't use fire because people are going to be afraid. Even *I'm* afraid of my fire. I'm the reason Ethan died." Sam's face was covered in tears. She wanted to go back to the naivety that Derek and Sky had kept her in. *At least back when I had no say, Ethan was alive.* "What do I do? How do I fit in when everyone uses their powers so freely? I don't belong here."

"You think you need powers to fit in?" he heckled. "You lived on Earth. Humans don't even know magic exists, but you thought openly using your powers would make you normal?" Sam began to see the irony in his words. "You know. It's funny how a person's environment can brainwash them to want to fit in so badly. You hold the two strongest and most influential powers. Everyone wants them. But you, you want to be like everyone else. What even *is* normal, Sameera? Did you ever think that normal is only what the masses currently want? Stop trying to be normal." He pounded his fist on a table. His face momentarily shifted to his wicked glare, but then softened again. "Embrace your differences. Use your powers wisely. You never know who might take them away from you when you're distracted worrying about others approval. The only approval you need is the one you give yourself to start living."

"And how do I give myself approval while Ethan stays dead?"

"You just do. I'm giving you an option to learn to control your powers. Are you going to take it?"

"Doesn't seem much like an option." Sam sniffled. Keith's face tightened.

"She's wasting too much of my time. You aren't doing it right!" Keith punched the wall by the arch. "Wait." He shook his head ferociously. "Wait!" Then he looked up and smiled again. "Just meet me outside to train." His eyes were watery. "The pain will go away soon, Sam. Soon, I promise." He left again, but this time he didn't return.

Sam tried hard to get ready to go outside, but every few seconds she remembered another memory of Ethan and started crying all over again. "I love you, too," she voiced, knowing he wasn't there to hear it.

Ethan knew our plan was dangerous, but he went with it for me anyway. I should never have let him. We were supposed to grow up together. He always had my back, and the one moment he needed me to have his, I failed. Sam tried to imagine what he would say to her if he was here. *He'd probably be mad at me for giving in to Keith and not trying to escape.*

Sam knew Keith was right about her needing to figure out her powers. She would never be normal, but she didn't have to stay with him to do it, did she? She wiped the tears off of her face and tightened the straps on her elbow and knee pads.

As she walked outside the room, she looked around her to see if Keith was nearby. She couldn't make out much through the misty air. She could, however, see the gate entrance on the bottom of the mountainside where they had entered before the battle. *Maybe if I sneak out now, I can find Derek, Sky, and Mia. Maybe they haven't left yet.*

Sam instantly sprinted down the mountainside. The gate glowed rose gold in the distance amidst the fog. Large brick and stone buildings rushed past her. The ground was uneven, but her adrenaline motivated her to keep moving. She couldn't see the lily pad vines that Ethan had created by the gate. *Did it die with him?* She continued to cry, but she kept moving towards the entrance.

Sam climbed the edge. She saw a man in a deep wine red cloak wandering by the exterior edge of the castle. "Help! Help!" she yelled. He noticed her, but instead of helping, he just looked up. His face was mostly hidden behind a hood, but Sam made out a creepy smile. "Please! Help." When he said nothing, she jumped from the top of the gate and ran as far away from the castle as she could, only looking back at the man who stood and laughed at her.

Within a few seconds, a bright white light flashed, and then she felt metal hit her forehead. *No! How can that be?* She was back within the castle gates.

"I told you, little sister," Keith uttered as he materialized behind her. He put a hand on her shoulder and looked suspiciously at the man outside. "You and I are going to be together for a long time."

PART 4

LOGAN GREEN

CHAPTER 13

SORRY 'BOUT THAT

———

Logan breathed in the salty ocean air as his toes curled in the damp sand. He was going to miss his cousins and having so much magic around him. *I wish mother wouldn't force the royal life on us so much. I don't want to go back yet.* He kept thinking of the day they had left Aiónios in Greece to come to Malibu. *I had such high hopes about finding my powers. Now all I know is that weird, creepy guy with Sam couldn't freeze me.* He remembered how Sam had left so abruptly and how he had seen Travis frozen. *Did that guy have time control powers? Why didn't they work on me? Why was he talking to Sam?*

Thoughts of all the weird interactions he'd had with Sam these past few weeks came racing through his head. *That girl has so many secrets. I swear she has answers. I need to find her.* Logan hadn't seen her for a few days now. She usually snuck off to the caves by their houses every once in a while, but the whole neighboring house had been silent. Even Maddi hadn't gone over there in a while. *I wonder if everything is alright.* Logan looked at the ocean waves crashing in front of him as he continued thinking about Sam and the other house. *It was nice meeting someone my age. I've been around adults for too long. They all expect me to be at their level, but I don't even know what I want to do with my life yet. I don't even know who I am yet.*

Suddenly, Logan saw a figure appear out of the waves. He stood up, accidentally kicking sand through the air. "Hello?" he yelled.

A boy around his age was struggling to make it out of the riptides in the water. Logan ran towards the water and took a hold of the boy's arm. He was breathing heavily and only wearing shorts made of seaweed. "Are you okay?" Logan asked, dragging the boy to dry sand and sat down next to him as he coughed out the saltwater. "What's your name?"

"Seth," he choked. "I'm looking for someone. A girl. She lives close by." Seth tried to stand up, but as soon as he got onto his feet, his legs gave way and he fell.

"Are you injured?" Logan was concerned as he caught the boy.

"Um. Kind of." He looked at Logan. "Sure, yes." Seth sat up on his knees.

"Wait here, I'll get some real clothes." Logan ran into the house and to his room to grab a pair of shorts. *Can I even ask why he's wearing seaweed, or is that rude?* He came back outside to see the boy trying to stand but miserably failing. "Here."

"Thanks." Seth took the shorts and eyed them, furrowing his eyebrows.

"You can have them, don't worry," Logan reassured. Seth slowly passed his legs through the shorts, trying to sit and put them on at the same time. *Should I help him?*

Before he could do anything, Seth raised his hand to Logan's shoulder. "May I?"

"Oh. Yeah, sure." Logan put his arm around Seth's waist as he pulled the shorts up. He helped Seth walk toward the houses. "So which girl are you looking for?"

"Her name is Sam. Sam Bleu." Seth continued putting his weight on Logan.

"Sam?" Logan hesitated in shock. *I should have known. Of course there's a seaweed-wearing boy walking out of the ocean trying to find her. What is it about her that creates these absurd situations?* "She lives in this house. I'll take you." They walked over to the back door of Sam's house. Logan knocked loudly on the door. They waited for a minute, but nobody came. Logan peered through the glass panel next to the door to see Travis sulking at the dining table. "Travis, can you open the door?" He knocked again. Travis' face shot up and he reluctantly walked over to the door.

"Sorry. This isn't a great time, Logan."

"This is kind of urgent. This boy," Logan looked at Seth, "is looking for Sam. He's injured too." Seth looked up and forced a smile on his face, although he didn't think Sam's family would have been happy to find out about him.

"Yeah. About that. Here, just come in. I'll get Sky." Logan and Seth followed Travis in, and took seats at the table.

"Are you okay?" Logan asked Travis. "You didn't seem like yourself sitting at that table."

Just then, Sky and Derek walked in together with bruises all over their arms and legs and their hair all messy, covered in dirt.

"Logan!" Sky looked startled. "What are you doing here?"

"We're looking for Sam. Is everything okay?"

"Sam's not here now." Derek fretted and looked towards the floor. He seemed to be hiding his face. "She won't be here for a while," he added. Sky gave him a confused look, wrinkling his forehead and raising his eyebrows.

Not here? Has she snuck off to those caves again?

"Wait. Is she okay? Did you guys go get the device? Is that what this is about?" Seth blurted out. Derek, Sky, and Travis all looked up in shock. *What are they talking about? A device?* Logan didn't think that Seth would know more about Sam than he did. After all, he had just materialized out of the ocean.

"How do you know about all of this?" Derek asked.

"Are you Seth?" Travis nearly jumped out of his chair. "You have legs! Did you get the device? I thought it was destroyed."

"Destroyed?" Seth's face fell. "Also, how do you know who I am?"

How did Travis know who he was? I guess I know nothing about Sam. Logan couldn't explain why he was hurt. He had only met her a handful of times. It made sense that he didn't know her, but for some reason he trusted her. "Okay. Wait. What device, and where is Sam, really?" Logan said, his voice more assertive than usual. Travis put his hand on Sky's shoulder.

"The truth is that Sam and Ethan didn't make it back from the trip," Sky answered. Logan could see Derek looking away to hide tears in his eyes. Seth, who already had been putting all of his weight on Logan, suddenly felt heavier to hold.

"What?" Logan didn't know what to say. *She died? How is that possible?*

"No. That can't be. What happened?" Seth's voice was fragile, breaking. "We had—" He stopped mid-sentence. Logan could see tears streaming down his face.

"We never found them, and Keith told us they were gone," Mia said in a solemn voice as she walked into the kitchen. She didn't look much better than Derek or Sky. Logan could see dried blood on her knees and a giant bruise on her arm. Her knuckles were covered in open wounds as if she had punched a wall, and her eyes were swollen and red as if she had been crying. She went over to Derek and held her older brother.

There has to be more to the story. "Is Keith the time controller?" Logan asked. He needed to confirm who that person he had run into before was.

"Yeah. Sam told me he was dangerous." Seth looked up. "He even came to me. He was the one who told me about the device. A few hours ago he came again and—"

"What did he say?" Derek rushed to Seth and Sky tried to hold him back. "Why are you in contact with him?" Derek's eyes were enormous. His pupils were dilated so wide they hid the whites of his eyes.

"He's the one who found the coral I needed to get legs," Seth revealed.

"Why would he do that? Derek asked, placing his hands on Seth's shoulders and slightly shaking him. "If you know anything, tell me." Mia came forward and pulled Derek back.

"I don't think she's dead. That wouldn't make sense. Keith needed her powers," Seth muttered. Derek looked at him intently.

Could he be right? This whole thing seems so weird. I saw what Sam did in the forest. Logan thought about the creature that was attacking them and how Sam was able to kill it with her powers. *She couldn't have been defeated that easily, right?*

"You think so?" Derek looked up abruptly. His eyes had a shine to them momentarily but were quickly replaced by more tears. "We were there. Keith even showed me what was left of Ethan's shirt." Derek wept. He fell to his knees and let his fists hit the table.

"I think you need to take a break from this, Derek," Mia said gently. She took his arm and started taking him away from the kitchen. "We'll talk about this later." She eyed Sky and Travis. "I don't know if it's a good idea to give Derek false hope right now. I was there, and it didn't look good. We just need some time to figure life out," Sky sighed, slipping his hands in his pockets and trying to force a smile.

"Yeah, we'll get going," Seth replied and pulled on Logan to help him out.

***

Logan and Seth walked towards the cabin in front of Logan's house. "I have to leave tonight to go back home, but you can stay here. My cousin gave me keys to this cabin and said they never really use it, so it's all yours." Logan pulled out his key ring and handed it to Seth.

"Listen." Seth placed his hand on Logan's arm to stop him. "I think Sam is still alive. Keith told me just today that he was giving me the coral because Sam wants him to."

"So?" Logan hoped he was right but failed to see the suspicious behavior he was claiming.

"So, he said *wants*, not *wanted*." Seth stumbled, putting pressure on Logan's arm. He looked up, his eyes sparkling.

"That could have just been a slipup, but I hope you're right." Logan turned away from Seth. *He and Sam seem to be really close. I hope he's right about her.* He opened the door and walked inside the one-bedroom cabin. His suitcases were packed and ready for him to leave. He checked his watch. "I have two hours before I have to leave, but let's think this through."

"What if he just has her up there? I know Sky said it wasn't likely, but he couldn't have killed her so fast, right? He needed her powers. He'd have to take them before. And at that point, why kill her?" Seth took the opportunity to sit down. He wiped the tears drying on his face. Logan could feel some forming in his own eyes, too. He didn't know how to feel. Seeing Sam's family try to be strong but then breaking down was getting to him. "And wait, if they were right about the device being destroyed, then he definitely needs her alive while he figures out what to do." Seth's face lit up with a smile.

"Do you know where she could be? Where did they take her for the mission?" *Why would Keith want her fire power if he already has time control? That seems so much more powerful, but I guess I don't really know anything.*

"She said they were going to the realm of Athanasía. It's apparently the central realm of magic."

"Immortality," Logan mumbled underneath his breath.

"What?" Seth looked up, confused.

"Athanasía is Greek for immortality."

"Let's hope that's a sign that she's alive." Seth laughed a bit.

"I have an idea." Logan took a seat on the bed next to Seth. "Maddi, my cousin, and Sky both have great libraries filled with information about the magical world. I have to leave soon, but take this phone." Logan pulled out a Side-kick phone. "I'll get a new one and contact you. You can research here, and I'll speak to my father back home about the situation."

"Thanks. I really can't give up on Sam. She never gave up on me." Seth smiled as he took the phone. For an unexplainable reason, Logan didn't want to give up on Sam either. He couldn't get her out of his head since their encounter in the forest.

"I don't want to, either." Logan trailed off. He looked up and a smile came to his face. "Okay, but can we discuss the elephant in the room?" Seth looked at him, confused. "What do you mean Keith helped you get legs? And how do you know Sam?"

"I saw her practicing with her powers one day, and I knew she wouldn't expose me to humans since she had magical abilities herself. And I was born a siren. So, yeah, I didn't exactly know how to walk when you found me back there." Seth blushed in embarrassment.

"Your injury was that you didn't know how to walk on legs?" Logan laughed, but quickly realized laughing may have been inappropriate. *Don't be mean, Logan.* "Sorry about that, I joke when I'm anxious."

"It's fine. I didn't know how to walk. I still don't understand legs that well." Seth wiggled his legs in the air and stared at them blankly.

"Do you also have powers?" Logan was curious to know about Seth and why he was so close to Sam.

"I have the power of illusions. What about you?" Seth asked.

"Immunity to Keith? I don't really know." Logan sighed, shrugging.

"Keith's powers don't work on you?" Seth jumped up, but his new legs gave out beneath him. Logan rushed to his aid.

What is it about Keith that everyone's afraid of? "Yeah, he tried to freeze me, but I don't know. Nothing happened."

"Well, whatever your powers are, they must be powerful." Seth gathered himself and fixed his hair.

"Maybe, but they're useless to all of us until I find out what they are."

"Maybe going back to your encounter with Keith will help us figure out your powers or what happened to Sam?" Seth exclaimed and took a hold of Logan's hand. Before Logan could react, the cabin walls slowly started melting into the ground, and Logan could feel the ocean's breeze. The ground rumbled as the two mansions appeared, towering above him. Suddenly, Logan found himself back on sand.

"Woah. What are you doing?" Logan jumped back as he saw Keith in front of him again. He walked closer to see Sam on the ground, yelling at Keith. The two of them didn't notice Logan—as if he didn't really exist.

"Focus. Listen in carefully. What really happened?" Seth specified but wasn't visible. Logan leaned in next to Keith, who turned quickly as the mansion door opened. *It's me? Wait, no, it's me in the past?* Logan watched as his past self pulled Sam away from Keith.

"I'll see you another time, Sam. And next time, I'll find you alone," Keith's voice roared in Logan's ears, but his face didn't match its tone. Logan hadn't noticed it before, but Keith's hand was trembling. His forehead had signs of sweat, and he definitely was eyeing Logan's past self with worry. *Keith was scared of me?* Rapidly, all the figures disappeared, and the cabin walls climbed back up to their original height. Seth's silhouette appeared in front of Logan, and soon he was back in the cabin as normal.

"What did you see?" Seth inquired. "Anything helpful? Did Keith's powers really not work?"

Seth's voice rattled in Logan's ears, but he couldn't focus. *Am I immune to being frozen because my brothers control time? Do I need them to beat Keith?* "What the hell was that?" Logan asked as he snapped back into reality. "How did you do that? Was that real?"

"It was an illusion of the memory in your brain. I just unlocked it." Seth smiled, clearly pleased with himself.

Great. Even the siren is good with his powers. "You're right, Seth. Keith was scared of me and he really emphasized wanting to find Sam alone," Logan confided.

"Then I'm sure he has her. I mean, it's perfect, right? Get everyone to believe she's dead and then have her to himself."

"Maybe so, but what does this mean about my powers? How am I supposed to help Sam if I can't figure them out?"

"You will, don't worry. This is a good thing. If you're really immune to him, you might be the only hope to beat Keith's plan." Seth's voice was gentle, trying to comfort.

I hope Father has answers. I could really use some. Logan tried to hide the shame in his face and looked at his suitcases instead of Seth. "I think I should head out and find my brothers. Our mother expects us to make an appearance at this gala tomorrow so I can't miss my flight." *Stop giving him so many details. Nobody can know about your family obligations.* Logan knew he rambled a lot when he was nervous or hiding his emotions.

"Huh. 'Gala' sounds like a royal event," Seth joked, mocking Logan's accent as he said the word. Logan laughed awkwardly, hoping that Seth didn't catch onto him actually being a member of a royal family.

CHAPTER 14

KINGS AND LORDS

___

Logan took out his boarding pass and handed it to the lady at the gate. "Last call to board Flight 2033 to Aiónios, Greece." The overhead speaker rang through their ears. His older brothers, Hayden, Liam, and Kyle all followed behind Logan as they climbed onto the flight. *I can't believe Father convinced Mother to let us all come, and I didn't even figure out my powers. Did she know we were going to live with more kids with powers? Well, I guess she got what she wanted. The son taking the throne is as far away from magic as possible. Maybe I really don't have powers, and Mother actually forced my brothers to pass up the primary heir title because of that.*

Logan couldn't help but feel disappointed in himself for coming back not knowing what type of powers he had. His brothers had all figured theirs out almost immediately upon coming to Malibu. Kyle could freeze time. Liam could change the speed of time on objects. Hayden could see visions of the past and future. Logan had hoped that seeing his older cousins would help him figure out his powers, and they had for everyone else but him. *Should I be concerned that I didn't? Or maybe being immune to other people's powers is my power?*

"Welcome aboard. We will provide lunch and dinner on this flight. In approximately twelve hours, we'll land in Aiónios, Greece. Wave goodbye to Los Angeles through your windows!" the pilot cheered as they began to take off.

"Here's to our powers and a new family." Liam held his hand out for his brothers to high-five.

Your powers, and a family I won't be able to have. Logan unenthusiastically high fived his brother.

"Listen, Logan. It'll be fine. We'll learn everything we need to know about our powers in time, okay? There's no way Dad is going to let you live a powerless life. Mom doesn't have that kind of influence over him." Liam patted Logan's back.

"Okay, I'm going to crash. You should, too." Liam adjusted his blanket and rested his head on the window. Logan, however, sat in the middle seat, too jittery and nervous to fall fully asleep. He took out a notebook from his carry-on and wrote:

```
Things to ask Father:
- Why couldn't Keith freeze me?
- Who is Keith?
- How do I get to Athanasía?
- Is it possible to not have powers?
```

***

Logan looked out the airport windows. He could see the beach behind the airplanes. *It's good to be home. I think.* Being home was a conflicting feeling. On one hand, he would finally get to ask his dad about his powers and sleep in his own bed again. On the other hand, he hated leaving California knowing something was wrong with Sam. *I wonder if Father will let us discuss magic at home or if we are back to Mother's zero-tolerance policy.*

"Hayden!" Their younger sister, Arabella, ran towards them.

"Bel!" Hayden lifted her in the air and spun her. She giggled. "How've you been? We missed you."

"And I missed not being Mom's center of attention. She wouldn't let me do *anything.*" She pouted. Logan walked over to his sister and grabbed her hand, which seemed tiny against his.

"Don't worry. I'm back." He winked. Even though Logan knew he was going to take on the most responsibility as the next king, he also knew that he would never rule in the same way his mother did. He couldn't deal with his mother's rules and restrictions. He wanted to be king, but he knew his sister wanted to rule more and in all honesty would be better at it. But of course his mother would never let a girl rule. It disgusted him that his own blood could be so closed-minded. *Wow. Five minutes back and already frustrated by your royal duties, huh.* Logan looked around for his parents. He needed to get his mind off of the work he had to do for the gala tonight, and he also couldn't wait to talk to his father. *He will know what to do about Sam...and my powers.*

"Mummy and Daddy are waiting just around the corner. They were fighting over something and told me to come get all of you." Arabella sulked as she laid her head on Hayden's chest.

"I'm sure it's nothing, Bel," Hayden said, trying to cheer up their sister.

I wonder if Mother really didn't know about the powers and the real reason Father sent us over to our family. "Yeah, don't worry. We're back and all together," Logan chimed in, faking a smile. *Okay, time to get Father alone and ask him about Sam. Maybe he knew her parents and can tell me why Keith, whoever he is, is after Sam.* Logan felt more conviction towards helping Sam than finding out about his own powers at this point. He had finally found a friend who understood him, and now she was gone.

"Sons! How great it is to have all of you back." Their mother came in to hug them. "Bella, get down. Your brothers are already tired," she scolded. Arabella frowned and looked away.

"Oh, it's no problem, Mother," Hayden said. "I've missed Bel."

"Anyway, how have you all been? Remember our family's honor. Did all of you offer to help out? You didn't act like a burden? And hopefully none of you got into any trouble." Their mother turned to the boys.

"Powers aren't trouble, Iris," their father muttered.

"Nikolas, did you say something?" Iris gave him a death stare.

"No. No trouble," Logan interjected. He couldn't help but sulk as he said those words. *Even if magic is trouble, I didn't get into any.*

"Dad, let's start putting the bags into the car?" Liam nodded towards the exit. "I think we all could get some rest today."

***

They drove through the island in their private car. People waved from outside with smiles and wide eyes. Logan missed the normalcy of being a non-royal in Malibu. He was happy his family had agreed to keep his prince status a secret while in California. In fact, Sam was the first friend he had made who had zero knowledge of his royal status.

After a few minutes, they arrived at their summer home. Their main castle was under restoration from recent earthquakes that had made their home unstable, but Logan didn't mind too much. They were currently staying in a villa which had a much more relaxing environment and fewer guards all around. Stone pillars held up a beautiful white marble building. An infinity pool stretched around three sides of the house and overlooked the island's villages spanning across the hill below them. Stone pavement spiraled down the hillside, leading to a quiet beach. *I can't wait for the private beach access again. Something about the ocean just makes it easier to think clearly.*

As soon as the driver parked, Logan and his brothers rushed to their main dining hall with their father. "Alright, sons. Your mother is putting Bel to bed, so I only have a few minutes to ask. Did you all enjoy the magic?" Their father stood at the head of the table and gestured for his sons to take a seat. They sat down at his approval, everyone nodding eagerly except for Logan.

Huh. I wish. Logan looked up to see his brothers' eyes on him.

"It was amazing to see how everyone there used magic in their daily lives, but we didn't all get to…" Kyle faltered.

"I couldn't figure out my powers," Logan blurted out.

"No signs?" Nikolas raised his eyebrow in surprise. "You really noticed nothing, not even with your brother's powers?"

"Well, this weird guy named Keith couldn't freeze him," Kyle exclaimed to their dad. "Do you know what that's about?"

"Kyle, how do you know about that?" Logan asked in astonishment. He was slightly relieved he didn't have to bring it up on his own, but he was sure his brothers hadn't seen him with Keith.

"If you fall asleep with your journal open on an airplane, make sure you don't have any secrets in it, Logan," he laughed. Logan looked at his brother dumbstruck and swatted his arm.

"Don't read my journal again, brother!" He clenched his fists.

"Boys! That's not the point. I have something to discuss with all of you, especially if you have already met Keith." Their father walked to the other end of the dinner table and grabbed a book from the armoire. The boys followed. "I haven't been very honest with you all. I do know about each and every one of your powers."

Logan's face fell. *How could he hide this?*

"I used to be a time lord before I decided to stay on Earth."

"A time lord?" Hayden snatched the book and started skimming pages. "Does that mean you were a god?"

"That's quite funny, son." Their father closed the book and pulled it away from Hayden. "There is no God per se. We all live among angels and demons. There are humans. There are magical beings. There is no God." King Nikolas took a stern tone in his voice and looked straight at Logan. "However, lords of different powers exist. They get their powers from angels and demons. For instance, there are lords for fire, earth, water, and air. There are lords of life and the mind, who are very often mistaken by the human world for Gods. And there are time lords."

"Time lord, as in Keith?" Logan inquired. His hands were sweaty thinking about how a time lord was scared of him. *What does that make me?*

"Yes, I'm afraid so," their father replied. He pursed his lips as if he was holding back from saying more.

What type of powers would scare a time lord? What powers would be able to defeat a time lord? Logan's mind immediately raced back to worrying about Sam. *She must be fine. Seth made sense when he said Keith needed her and with what Sam did in the forest, she seems tough enough to stand her ground.*

"So we've been wrong this whole time about God?" Liam interjected, ignoring the seriousness of their dad's answer. He took a seat at the table and grabbed his head. "Why didn't you tell us all of this before? Why wait until now? I mean, we could have skipped Mom's Sunday church mandates," he joked but looked distressed at the same time.

"Son, we live a very unusual life by even the magical world's standards. I am not supposed to give you access to your powers while I am here. It messes with the life lord's balance of powers. I could not tell you about all of this until I was ready to leave."

"You're leaving?" Logan took a seat next to Liam.

"I should not have stayed here this long. I was supposed to give you all your powers and leave the human world. I'm paying for that now."

"What—"

"Boys! Off to bed. I need to speak to your father. Leave now." Their mother rushed into the dining room, cutting off Hayden.

"Son." Their father made eye contact with Logan. "Your brothers may get their time powers from me, but you," he paused, having a coughing fit. "What I said about the lords. I was one, and now, Logan, you are one," their father whispered to Logan as their mother dragged him out of the room. His brothers all rushed to him to see what their father had said but Logan ignored them.

I'm a lord? Lord of what? Logan stood there in shock, watching his parents leave. His mother yelled at him in Greek and his father coughed loudly, but they were both drowned out by the words ringing in Logan's ears. *You are one.*

PART 5

SAM BLEU

HOW SETH GOT HIS LEGS

CHAPTER 15

STIRRING THE MIND

———

"You're a mind lord, and I'm a time lord, Sameera." Keith's voice was gentle as he spoke. They both stood in one of the many courtyards surrounding the palace's main hall. Sam still wasn't used to seeing plants coming out of a purple ground, and the very sight of them made her remember Ethan.

He'd be so fascinated with how the plants grow here, especially that denim blue rose bush. Her eyes were teary, and her shoulders drooped low as she held the silver sword Keith had handed to her.

"Hello? Athanasía to Sameera?" Keith slashed the bush, cutting a few roses of their stems with his sword. His pupils grew in size making the whites of his eyes no longer visible.

Demon eyes!

"Sadness is a weakness, child. The Mind Lord cannot be weak," Keith roared.

Mind Lord? "That's what we're calling the gift now?" Sam was mad that Keith would kill a plant in front of her. *One second he acts nice and tries to teach me something and then the next he's flaunting our brother's death?*

Keith took a deep breath, and his eyes returned to normal. "Put that feistiness into your fighting, Sameera." He raised his sword. "I know you can do better than this. You had no problem killing the Oni I sent to you."

"So it was you!" Sam raged. Flames flashed in her eyes. She swung her sword at him with a fiery anger.

Keith dodged Sam's strike by sidestepping. "Of course! I had to make sure you had the gift and that you could handle yourself." He spun, trying to strike her at the waist. "Derek and Sky were holding you back so much during your training. I couldn't tell what you could do, so I decided to take it under my control."

She ducked, nearly letting Keith's sword cut the edges of her hair off. "How could you send a demon, hoping it would die?" Sam knew it was foolish to ask this, knowing Keith was responsible for both their mom and Ethan's death. *Demons are on his side though, right?* She clenched her fist and then gripped her own sword tighter. It was slipping from her sweaty grasp.

"It was a demon. What do you care?" Keith brushed off her question.

Oh, my angels. Shouldn't I care? Or is he right and I just killed evil? It still feels wrong to send someone to their death, though. Keith threw the sword at Sam, who jumped to the side at the last second. She pressed her hand on her chest, gasping for air. "Were you trying to kill me?"

"You didn't die, though. I need you to see how strong you are. Stop holding yourself back," Keith provoked.

"Why do you care so much? You want to hurt me, but you also want me to be stronger. How does that make any sense?"

"In this universe, hurting you will make you stronger, little sister." Keith dusted off his knees and walked inside the main hall. "Come inside." Sam walked into the hall, which had the same mauve glow as the castle gates. A large, metallic steel dining table spanned the room, decorated in small silver knickknacks. One figurine of a soldier holding his sword up was placed next to one of a soldier holding a wand. "Who will win? Magic or weaponry, Sam?" Keith inquired as he walked behind her. His breath was warm as he hovered above her.

"Magic, probably," Sam replied timidly.

"That's where you're wrong." He tipped over the figure with the wand. "You seem to think that the person at a disadvantage cannot win. You can always win, Sameera."

"How?" *Does that mean I can find a way to escape Keith's curse that binds me here?*

"Life is just a game. If you make the right plan, you can always win." A large grin grew on his face. Sam stepped away from him, afraid he was going to switch to his evil side again. *Was he like this when I was younger, too? I don't remember him flipping between acting good and evil.*

Keith pounded his fists on the table, making the other figure fall as well. Sam pulled her sword back out and positioned it in front of her to be ready for his attack.

"Very funny, little sis. You're catching on." Keith's face relaxed again, and he laughed. "I think you're ready for a mission."

"A mission?" Sam put her sword back in its sheath. "To where?" *Maybe this is my chance to escape.*

"To another planet in this realm. It's where your friend Seth is from," Keith replied.

Seth! Maybe I can find him some answers. Keith placed his sword on the table and opened a cupboard next to him. He took out some protective gear.

"Take this and put it on." He handed her some matching greaves and vambraces for her legs and arms. It looked like he had deconstructed a blue and white iron robot and handed her the remains.

She put them on, nearly cutting herself on the metal edges. "And these are supposed to help me?" Sam lifted her arms but found the gear limited her movement.

"You'll need them to fight the demon we're going to visit." Keith had a rather calm tone that confused Sam. She followed him back to the courtyard. Her body hung low from the weight of the armor. Keith pulled out a compass and said some words Sam couldn't make sense of, and then a familiar warm white light filled the air. She felt a tightness in her stomach and then felt moist ground materialize under her feet. *Woah. What is this place?* Slowly, water rose next to her and she realized they were in an ocean. Keith pointed to his head, mouthing "read me."

How are we going to breathe? Sam sent her thoughts to him.

Look at your armor. Slide that white strip back. Keith thought back to her and pulled his own armor's strips. Immediately, both of their armor released a green gas-like substance and an air bubble formed around them. They floated to the top.

"This armor turns into a floaty?" Sam gasped as she poked the air bubbles around her arms and legs.

"Focus, Sameera. Look up." Sam's eyes grew wide as she saw the floating city. Large stone buildings soared above them on either side. They rested on oak and pine wooden planks where Sam could see sirens resting. The sky was a permanent sunset pattern of iris, periwinkle, and wisteria blue.

Seth would've loved to see this. Looking straight ahead, Sam saw a large mountain peak coming out of the ocean. The milky water ran straight between the buildings to an opening of random islands surrounding the mountain. "This looks like a magical version of Venice," she said, mesmerized. The once-heavy armor was actually quite light with the air bubbles helping her stay afloat.

"That's because the people who built Venice used this place as inspiration," Keith replied. "Follow me this way. We have a long way to swim."

"What? Weren't they humans?" Sam swam behind Keith.

"Occasionally, people traveling to different realms accidentally bring humans along. The humans can't comprehend the new environments, so as we send them back, we manipulate their memories to make them think it's all a dream."

"So they think they dreamt up these ideas?"

"Exactly. It's almost amusing seeing how different humans interpret things." Keith pointed to the mountain. "That mountain is where the ancient Indian myth of churning the ocean of milk came from. These buildings inspired Venice. And the sirens here inspired all the pirates searching for immortality," Keith said enthusiastically.

How much of Earth has been borrowed from different realms? Maybe every mythology has some truth to it. Sam kept looking around. Her mind was filled with conflicting thoughts racing and she couldn't believe just how much of the world she had known could have been taken from somewhere else.

"You're really going to have to put into effect all of the training we've done. This next demon won't be easy to defeat," Keith said, bringing Sam's attention back to the mission. "You're going to need to focus with your gift."

Sam and Keith reached the bottom of the island next to the mountain. It was made of blue sand that sparkled despite the lack of a visible moon or sun in the sky. They climbed up to it, and Keith transformed their gear back into regular armor.

"Get ready. I can already sense the demon's presence," Keith cautioned. Sam could feel a dark presence too. A ringing had formed in her ear, and the further inland they walked, the louder it got. "There it is!"

"Wait, what?" Sam stood frozen as a ten feet tall, headless figure walked towards her. It had charcoal skin and was adorned in golden riches. Sparkling sand reflected light off of the creature's large golden necklace, which, on top of the ringing in Sam's ears, was giving her a headache. The heaviness of her armor sunk in again.

Sam looked towards Keith, but instead of her brother, she saw the figure's missing head. It rested on top of a rock. "What do I do?" she yelled. Her voice echoed off the mountain, but the ringing in her ears was still louder. The figure made its way closer to Sam and pointed its scepter at her.

Sam's mouth suddenly felt dry. Her heart began racing and her hands trembled. Her joints stiffened as the ringing in her ears grew even louder. Suddenly Keith stood next to her again, with his forehead wrinkled. "You control the mind, Sameera. Push through it." She looked up to avoid looking at the creature. Pinks and purples in the sky blurred together as her vision fogged.

"Any helpful suggestions?" she screamed. Sam cupped her ears and fell to her knees.

"I'm not as soft as Derek or Sky. If you want to be stronger, you're going to have to learn to deal with things on your own."

What is this demon doing to me? And why isn't he doing anything to Keith? Sam focused her energy on her own mind. She needed to cure the grating ring in her ears. If it stayed, it would drive her mad. She screamed, her voice echoing off the mountain. As she heard her own voice, she focused her mind on it instead of the ringing. *That's it. Think about your own voice.*

The demon pulled its scepter back and then pointed it at her again. Sam clutched her stomach. She had a hard time breathing and her body felt nauseous. *Think, Sam! What can you do?*

"Little sister, sometimes the trick is to appease the enemy. And to motivate you, I'll help out your friend Seth if you pass this training test," Keith snarled. He looked at the watch on his wrist casually, as if everything happening to Sam was just an everyday occurrence. This enraged Sam, but the idea of helping Seth was energizing. She clenched her fists and looked at the demon's head again, thinking. It looked like another boulder on top of the rock, but with eyelids and an eerie open mouth smile. It sent shivers down Sam's back.

Appease the enemy? Sam closed her eyes and envisioned levitating the head. She felt as if her own arm was stretching to the head and carrying it. Her weak joints felt the immense weight, but she pushed through the pain. As she opened her eyes, she saw the head hovering above the demon's body. It found its way back to its original position and spun as if it was screwing itself back on. A golden glow emitted off of the demon, and Sam's body returned to normal. She stood up, dusted the sand off of her knees, and wiped her sweaty palms on her shorts.

"Good, Sameera. You're finally learning." Keith applauded. He nodded at the demon, whose smile grew larger. It walked towards the stone and sat down, closing its eyes.

I hate that he's right. As much as I want to leave, everything he has trained me in has made me a better fighter. "Do you control it too, or?" Sam asked her brother, confused.

"We are the children of the devil. Demons of all kinds have to respect us. If they don't, we make them." Keith's words made Sam feel uncomfortable. She had an ill feeling about what Keith had done to make anyone respect him.

"Okay, now how are you going to help Seth? The device was destroyed," Sam inquired.

"The myth about the coral is real. All we need to do is what the Devas and Asuras did ages ago."

"Huh?" *Is he referring to Hindu mythology?*

"Spin that mountain to churn this ocean. I promise you, it will give you what Seth needs." Keith laughed at Sam's lack of knowledge. She rolled her eyes and leaned back, crossing her arms.

"How do you want me to spin an entire mountain?" *Is there another reason Keith brought me to Seth's planet? He wouldn't be willing to help Seth without an ulterior motive.*

"The same way you levitated the head. This one's going to hurt, but we have time." Keith took a seat and continued laughing.

Just once, if he could teach me in a less irritating manner. Sam focused on the mountain and again she felt as if an extension of her body moved around the mountain. Her arms tried to turn it, but the mountain was too heavy. "Agh," she grunted as she focused harder. The mountain moved an inch and Sam unfocused. She rested her hands on her knees and panted. "You're right. This does hurt."

"Perspective, sister. The bottom of the mountain is much larger and harder to grasp. Even your mind knows that." Keith pointed to the peak.

Sam closed her eyes and imagined her hands holding the top of the mountain. She felt herself existing at the mountaintop and spinning the peak in her hands. The milky white and blue ocean churned. Small whirlpools formed next to the sandy edge of the island.

"Perfect. You did it!" Keith yelled over the waves crashing in the once calm ocean. "There it is." Several items floated out of the whirlpools to the surface of the ocean. They glowed in bright orange and golden hues.

"That's it? That looks like something you'd find in a reef on Earth," Sam said as she watched Keith pull out a coral.

"Yes, but could Earth coral do this?" He tilted a stem until it broke off. Glowing orange cream flowed out. "I'll return us to the castle and then deliver this to Seth."

"Let me come. I want to see him," Sam pleaded. *This is my chance to escape. If he takes me to Earth, maybe I can project my thoughts to Derek or Sky.* Sam's hands were getting sweaty as she watched Keith ponder her request.

"Funny, sis, but sadly I can't risk taking you back," Keith replied. Sam swallowed the lump in her throat. Keith picked up another one of the items from the ocean. It looked like a circular wooden board.

What's that? Is that also for Seth?

Before she could get a better look, Keith pulled out his compass and opened their portal to Athanasía. "Hurry, before I change my mind about helping Seth," Keith threatened. Sam begrudgingly followed him into the portal.

How am I going to get away?

CHAPTER 16

BITTERSWEET VICTORIES

———

"You won't always have me around and sometimes the demon won't respect you. It'll want to do more than just hurt you. In these cases, I need to know you'll be fine," Keith stressed as he placed his palms on the table. They were back in the main hall by the dining table. "Look at this figure." He pointed at a tall warrior surrounded by smaller elf-like figures.

"What about it?" Sam asked, confused. She walked closer and picked up one of the smaller figurines that was smiling. "This one looks sweet."

"What does the warrior look like?"

"He seems scared." Sam furrowed her brows. "But why? He seems to be the only one troubled here."

"This is another lesson, Sameera. The small figures know that they can beat someone who looks stronger because they're smarter." Keith picked up the larger figure. "This warrior knows that he's stronger, but he's still timid because he's outnumbered. His biggest weakness is unrealizing his strength." Keith pointed the figure at Sam's chest, pressing it into her shirt. "You're that figure."

"How?" Sam stepped back from her brother. Even though he was currently helping her, she never could tell when he would switch to being cruel again.

"You have the only power in the world that nobody else has, and yet you're so afraid to use it."

Shouldn't I be? If I mess up, nobody knows how to fix it. "That's easy for you to say. You don't mind hurting people, so the consequences of my powers mean nothing to you," Sam yelled back.

"What consequences are you so worried about?" Keith smirked. "You already killed your brother. Don't you think it's time you just learn to control yourself?"

Sam's heart sunk. She clenched her fists. Everything in her wanted to scream or cry or both, but Keith was right. *If I could've controlled myself back there, I wouldn't be in this situation.* She wiped the tears forming in her eyes and stepped forward.

"Well, the first thing I'm taking in my control is your word. You promised to help Seth. When are you going to do that?"

"Ah. Good. Courage is the most important step." Keith laughed. "You have to choose confidence in the face of your enemy."

"Well, you're my enemy. And I'm asking you again. When are you going to help him?" Sam felt small on the inside, but she desperately wanted Seth to be okay. She felt bad leaving him right as he was getting closer to his dream. *Even if I'm stuck here, Seth can still be free. Nobody else needs to suffer because of me.*

Keith shook his head and grabbed his ears. "Not yet!" he screamed.

"Um. Why not?" Sam inquired. She had a feeling Keith wasn't responding to her, though. He slammed his hands on the armoire next to him. She flinched and grabbed a dining table chair to guard herself.

"Give me more time." His voice echoed in the hall. "You can't help her friend." His face turned into a creepy grin again as he looked up at Sam. The strength she had used to force herself to stand up to Keith was slowly waning. She hunched over and backed away.

"Please. You promised." She gulped.

"Let me do it. It'll gain her trust. You don't understand the benefits," Keith screamed. His face was soft again. He scrunched his face tight as he covered his eyes with his own hands.

Why is he talking about me as if I'm not right here? Is this just a common older brother thing? "Yes. You need me to trust you if you want me to stay here," Sam declared. She was confused, but she was willing to do or say anything to help her friend.

"Fine. But make sure Sameera can't leave." Keith pulled his hands back down to his sides, revealing pitch black eyes. He glared at Sam with his menacing smile, as if he was looking right through her. Sam tried moving backwards again, but she hit the wall. She covered her face with her arm as she cowered in front of Keith.

Please switch to being nice again!

"You're in luck. I'll go right now to help Seth out." Keith was still smiling wickedly, but his eyes were back to normal. "As I said before, I need to know that you'll be fine if I'm not at your next battle, so I'm leaving these creatures here as I go." Keith incited some inaudible words and a few large wolf-like creatures appeared in front of Sam. She immediately ran and jumped on the dining table.

"How am I supposed to deal with them?"

"You'll figure it out. You're now the tall warrior, and these are your small elves, Sameera." Keith laughed and walked out of the room. The wolves looked towards his shadow as he left, but quickly refocused on Sam. She moved closer to the middle of the table.

One of them jumped onto a chair with its front two paws and growled, slobbering over the white table runner. Its nails were sharp and protruded at least an inch outside its grey fur. *Sam, remember you have powers nobody else knows about. Nobody can limit you but you. Just think!*

She looked around the room for a weapon. Keith's sword was still resting on top of the armoire. Sam jumped onto another chair and then leapt towards the top of the armoire. She grasped the top edge as her feet kicked around under her.

The wolves gathered around, waiting for her to fall. She kicked one in the mouth as she tried to release one hand to grab the sword. Instead of grabbing it, she accidentally pushed one of the armoire doors open and it smacked her in the face. *Shoot.* Sam scrambled to get a hold of the top edge with both hands again.

She closed her eyes and imagined the sword moving closer. She felt the hilt hit her knuckles. Another wolf growled under her, but this time she pointed the sword down and sliced its head off. The creature immediately turned into dark silver ash.

Sam ran outside before the others could bite her. There was a boulder in the distance. *If I can climb that, I'll have an advantage over the wolves.* The ground felt moist under her feet. Her breath was shaky as she panted.

A few more feet to the boulder. She practically leapt to the base of the rock. Then she pulled herself up using a small slit that she found at the top. *Keith's physical training is really paying off.* Sam stood on top of the boulder and tried to locate all the wolves. Her palms were sweaty, and she nearly tripped off the rock as she noticed the crevice Ethan had created. A tear slid down her cheek. *Shoot, there they are!*

The blurry sight of the creatures snapped her back to reality. She wiped her tears away, trying to focus her vision. The wolves were moving quickly to her. A few already circled around the boulder below her. She let out a groan and then began swatting her sword at them from above. *This isn't working. I need to switch to magic.*

Sam raised her hands towards the crevice and focused on the rocks at the bottom. The familiarity of the situation clouded her thoughts, but she had to push through to survive. *Keith said that pain makes you stronger.* She could hear magma boiling at the bottom of the crevice as anger and confusion towards Keith filled her.

Then she opened her eyes and glared at the wolves. *This is for Ethan.* She imagined her legs extending, kicking the wolves into the crevice. One by one, the wolves screeched as they unwillingly catapulted towards the opening in the ground. Sam somersaulted backwards and landed on one knee. This was slowly becoming her favorite fighting move, making her feel powerful. *Maybe, if I'm forced to stay here and learn from Keith, I can learn to defeat him.*

Sam felt a sense of victory for once in her life. She had defeated the wolf creatures on her own. She needed a better memory to associate with the crevice in the castle grounds, and now she had one. Bitterness was fueling a strength in her that should've scared her, but it didn't.

***

Days had passed since Keith left to give Seth the coral. *Is he even going to give it to him? How do I get proof that he kept his word?* Sam walked back to the rock where she had killed the wolves. At this point, she had seen every inch of the castle and all signs pointed to not trusting Keith.

His armory already had more scrolls and magical artifacts than before. She couldn't find the wooden artifact he had picked up at Seth's planet, though. *Where'd it go? I wonder what good a piece of wood could do.* Her only hope was that one day she could find a device or book that would help her find a way out of this castle. She conjured a flame in her hand and soaked in the warmth it emitted. Once again she jumped off the rock, flipped in the air and landed on the ground. She felt power surge through her. She needed to leave Keith behind for good.

Ring! Ring! Ring! Sam looked towards the castle gates. *Huh, is Keith back again?* She saw a figure, but the misty glow of the gate prevented her from making out any recognizable features. *Is that the same figure that laughed at me for trying to escape?*

PART 6

LOGAN GREEN

CHAPTER 17

FROM ONE CASTLE
TO ANOTHER

———

Logan ran downstairs, forgetting to change or brush his teeth. He had to find his father. He had barely slept the night before. *I'm a lord? What does that even mean? And father's leaving? What about the kingdom?* He ran past the grand library, making a mental note to head in there soon and find any magic related books.

"Father!" Logan panted as he placed his hands on his knees. "What do you mean I'm a lord? And where are you going?"

"Son, you're up early. Have the maids prepared your suit for tonight?" the king was sipping on tea and had a blanket draped over him, which was unusual—the weather outside was quite warm.

"Answer me, Father. Am I the lord of time? Is that why Keith's powers didn't work on me?"

"I'm afraid, yes. Yes, you are the time lord." his father sat up straighter.

"You're afraid?" *Great, he's leaving me with both the throne and powers he is scared of.*

"Don't get me wrong. This is a great gift to have. It's just you are the youngest son, and I hate to leave you so unaware. They make us leave our children to fend for themselves. It's honestly a very bad system, if you ask me."

Why is he acting so delirious? He usually isn't so wishy-washy. "Who is making you leave? And where are you going? Is it Athanasía?" *Maybe he can help me find Sam.*

"How do you know about Athanasía?" his father spilled some tea on his blanket, looking shocked at his son. Logan rushed over to clean it.

"Let me help."

"No, stop!" he swatted his hand away and carefully cleaned the blanket without letting it off of him.

"Are you okay, Father?"

"Yes. Never mind that. What do you know about Athanasía?"

"My friend, um. She went there to see someone named Keith?" Logan took a seat. "She never came back."

"Logan, there's a lot you don't know. We don't have much time, but I want to teach you everything I can. You and your brothers." King Nikolas hesitated. "As for Keith. I know him. He's a dangerous man, and someone you'll meet again soon, unfortunately."

"And my, um, friend?" Logan gulped, trying to hide his fear. He didn't want to show his father any weakness, but he was terrified to face Keith again knowing Sam was gone because of him. "Her name is Sam Bleu."

"Sam?" his father immediately set down the cup of tea. He looked at Logan with wide eyes and then looked down. "I knew her mother. I would hate for anything to happen to her."

"Can we find out? I need to know if she's okay," Logan blurted out. "People in California are depending on it." Logan could tell that his father knew more than he was letting on.

Why is he hiding so much information and what happened to Sam's mother?

"Go get your brothers, and I will tell you more." his hands trembled as he grasped his teacup handle. "Hurry, son."

Our families knew each other? Did Father know I'd meet Sam in California?

***

Once again, Logan stood at the dining table with his brothers. Their father was passing out books about magic to each of them. "*Freezing Time and What Can Go Wrong?*" Kyle read aloud.

"*Visions of the Future. Dreams of the Past,*" Hayden read. "Really, Dad? You knew about all of us and never told us? Maddi and everyone back in California have been using their powers since they were young. I'm nineteen and I don't even know how to fully use mine."

"As I wanted to tell all of you yesterday…" Their father ran his fingers through his hair, sighing. "Your powers can't be fully activated until I leave. And by leave, I mean leave Earth for good. Your mother and I have struggled with the thought of breaking up the family, especially with the added pressure of you being royal children, but the older you get, the more danger I'm putting everyone in by not letting you have your powers."

"And we can't opt out of having powers?" Liam spoke up. *That's odd. I didn't think Liam would want that. He seemed so excited to practice his powers.* "I don't want to break up the family either." His voice softened.

"Unfortunately, no. Your brother, Logan, needs to step up and learn about his powers. I'm afraid my hesitance to let him may have already cost someone's life."

"What?" Hayden exclaimed.

"Sam. You probably met her. Logan has informed me that nobody is aware of her whereabouts." Their father's eyes became teary.

I didn't think he would know Sam this well. Who was her mother?

"Listen, all of you need to understand how this world works. I won't be here for much longer, and your mother will have to deal with everyone having powers. No matter what, do not stop using them. You lose what you don't use," King Nikolas cautioned.

"Why are you being so cryptic about everything, Dad?" Kyle looked frustrated.

"It's hard to explain. There's a lot you don't know."

"Then tell us! Did Sam know what danger she was in when she went to Athanasía?" Logan insisted.

"Wait, hold on. How is everyone being so casual about the fact that Sam is missing? She was so young," Hayden exclaimed as he looked around at his brothers. Logan could tell that nobody knew what to say. He felt a bit broken inside, thinking about someone his age being gone, yet also unsure how to feel since he had only recently become close to her.

"I don't want to be, but unfortunately her passing means grave danger to the balance of this world, and Logan will have to take on a lot of responsibility in restoring it."

"I can't anymore. What the hell are you saying?" Kyle threw his hands up in the air.

Damn. That was bold.

"Kyle! Be polite. I understand you are frustrated, but this is no way to behave," their mother shouted while walking in. She scolded him in Greek and gestured for him to take a seat. "And, dear, will you tell them already? Even I can't bear to wait any longer."

"Logan will be the other time lord once I leave."

"Other?" Kyle faltered as their mother glared at him.

"The first being Keith, Sam's brother." Their father eyed Logan.

"I don't think I met a Keith." Hayden scrunched his face in confusion. Lines wrinkled his forehead.

"He's much older, and I believe he is estranged from the rest of the family since he chose evil. The point is, however, if Keith killed Sam," their father's voice softened as he cleared his throat, "then he has most likely taken her powers as well, giving him more power than any one person should have, thus tipping the balance towards evil."

"But what can I do? You keep saying I'm the next time lord, but so far, I haven't even demonstrated any of the basic powers that they have." Logan pointed at his brothers who looked back at him.

"Basic?" Kyle asked in amusement.

"Not the point, brother." Logan looked back at his father. "How am I supposed to deal with all of this, especially now that you're leaving?"

"Your brothers. You will have to stick together. For now, I will show you all how to use your powers. The three of you obviously have time-related powers as well."

"I can freeze time," Kyle exclaimed excitedly.

"Okay. Show me what you can do." King Nikolas took a seat, coughing loudly.

"Are you okay, Dad?" Hayden murmured as he rushed to their father's side. He took a hold of his back and helped him sit on a chair.

He's been coughing a lot recently. Should we be worried?

"Never mind me, boy. Let's see what all of you can do. Kyle, make me a sandwich, but I don't want to see you leave."

"Um. Okay. Right now? Or after I show you my powers?" Kyle pointed behind him looking confused.

"No, son." their father sighed. "I have done quite the disservice not discussing your powers sooner. Freeze time and go make the sandwich so that we will not see it."

"Oh. Right. Okay," Kyle said, flustered. Logan and Liam looked at each other with laughter, but Logan couldn't help but see Hayden in the corner of his eye. He stood next to their father's chair with his arms crossed, sulking.

I don't think any of us are processing father's announcement well. Is he really leaving? Logan sank deep into thought.

"Done!" Kyle's voice broke Logan back into reality. He realized his brother had left, his family was frozen, and he had completely failed to notice.

Has it already been a few minutes? Logan looked at Kyle, who was messing around with his frozen siblings, ruffling their hair or moving their arms and legs. "Do you know how to unfreeze them?" Logan inquired.

"Yeah, little bro. I froze everyone back at the mansion when I wanted something for myself. I guess I never really tried to freeze you, though. Damn, if I had, we would have noticed your powers sooner."

That's true. I guess they were right. I hadn't been spending time with them in Malibu much. I was so focused on exploring or running into Sam. Oh. Sam. I really hope Seth is right about you. Father seems convinced you're dead. "Okay let's bring them back, then." Liam unfroze mid-laughter and Hayden's face softened from the distressed look he had.

"Good, thank you!" King Nikolas took the sandwich and opened it up. "Now, which one of you can age things? In other words, manipulate time on objects." Liam stepped towards their father, raising his hand. "I want you to make this sandwich taste fresher."

That seems kind of complex. I wonder if Liam can do it.

"Sounds good." Liam lifted the piece of bread off the top and focused. Logan could see the lettuce unwrinkle and become greener. The room began to smell like fresh turkey as Liam unaged the meat in the sandwich.

Have they already mastered these powers? Why didn't I realize how much they already knew? Logan crinkled his shirt in his sweaty palms. *I really hope that I can get a grasp on my powers this fast. Why would Father want me to be the king and whatever this time lord thing is? I'm not even the oldest.*

"Very good, son. Now, Hayden, we will use your powers to teach you and your brothers about the magical dimensions."

"How will seeing the future or past help with that?" Hayden pouted.

"Have you noticed that touching certain objects triggers your ability to see things?" their father stood. His legs trembled. Hayden nodded as he hovered his hands around the king frantically trying to catch him if he fell. "That's because those things have been gifted with visions. The person who owned them intended to leave a message, and you, son, are one of the few in the world who can access those messages."

"Can I leave a message?" Kyle nearly jumped as he asked.

"Yes, you can. Another day, I will show you the library in detail and you can explore all the different ways people use magic. However, today, we only have an hour before we must all be ready for the gala, so I want to take you somewhere that will give you the most insight into how people use magic."

"In an hour?" Logan asked. *How will an hour be enough time to go to a place, explore it, and come back? Mother will be so mad at me if I am not presentation-ready tonight.*

"Don't worry, son. You will be alright. Mother and I have already agreed that all of us will take this trip. Now, follow me."

Since when did Mother become so on board with magic?

***

The four of them walked through the villa's library. Logan couldn't believe how many magic books were sandwiched between the school novels he had read. He'd never given much thought to them, writing them off as fiction. *Mother did a great job at making us not interested in magic, didn't she?*

"This here is one of those objects that was intended to send a message," their father announced. His hoarse voice and cough echoed through the circular room.

"Father, are you sure your health is alright?" Logan was becoming more concerned. King Nikolas' physical appearance had started visibly deteriorating to the point that the royal make-up couldn't hide it.

"My son, I am fine. I must leave soon. That's all." Logan tried to get in another word, but the king continued with his speech. "Hayden, come. Touch this compass. What is it saying to you?"

"Travel." He closed his eyes and spoke as if instinctively.

"Good. This is the device that allows people to travel between dimensions. We're going to visit one where magic is the central force in everyone's lives."

"Which one?" Logan's eyes grew wide. *Maybe I can use this device to find Sam.*

"As per your mother's instructions, I cannot disclose that information. But look closely at how people live there. Now come and think of your full names as you walk through." A bright light flashed in front of Logan's eyes and warmth surrounded him. *Logan Green.* His father recited an incantation, but Logan was too distracted by the momentary nothingness around him to hear.

The world looked very different. *Is the sky actually purple here? Or am I still stunned from that light?* Logan held his head as he tried to regain his balance.

"Dad, what is this place?" Kyle shouted and looked confused, which made Logan feel better. "Since when is the sky and the ground purple?" He tipped to the side as the ground formed below them and almost fell.

The ground too? Logan looked down and to his amazement, Kyle was right. This world looked so different from Earth. It felt unreal.

"Don't worry. You will get used to it. To the citizens here, Earth looks weird." King Nikolas coughed but quickly recovered to point at a shop. "Go explore this street and the markets. You will notice that magic is everywhere. Meet me back here in thirty minutes. These pagers will tell you when to come back. Have fun."

"We just leave you?" Kyle gushed.

"Go in pairs."

"Kyle!" Logan looked at his brother, and they made eye contact. "Let's go." Liam and Hayden left immediately, and Logan made his way to the closest shop with Kyle.

"I can't believe Dad just let us go by ourselves," Kyle murmured.

"Yeah. He must either trust us a lot or even we can't mess up here."

"Woah. Did you see that?"

"What?"

"That person snapped, and that guy's groceries just appeared." Kyle looked at the cashier in awe. He walked towards her in an almost trance-like state. "Hello. Can I ask you how you did that?"

"Kyle!" Logan blurted out, embarrassed.

"I'm a mind controller. My specialty is in reading peoples' minds and materializing their needs," the tall blonde woman said with a smile. Logan couldn't help but be enamored by her pointy ears and sharp nose.

"What?" Logan forgot about being embarrassed.

"Can you do me?" Kyle walked up to the register. Immediately, a cake appeared in front of them, along with carrots.

"Here. Your desire and what you truly need. Cake and Vitamin A."

"That's amazing." Logan looked up at his older brother.

"How will you be paying? Magic?" Kyle fished out a few dollars he had in his pocket. "Earthlings?" The cashier giggled. The boys nodded. She smiled in understanding and said, "Here, just take it."

"Thank you!" Kyle cheered. The boys ran outside. "That was wild. Dad wasn't kidding about magic being the main mode of operating here." Kyle opened his cake box.

"Yeah. Let's see what else we can find," Logan said, his voice trailing off. He was distracted by a sign in the distance. *Athanasía's Oldest Museum Now Open!* "Let's go that way. I want to see the museum."

"It looks like that sign's been there for ages. Do you think it's still open?" The sign was falling over, and the wood was badly scraped.

"Yeah. Let's go check it out." *I can't believe Father left us alone in Athanasía after knowing Sam was last seen here.* Logan got his new phone out. *I wonder if cell service works across dimensions.* He sent a text to Seth:

~ This is Logan. In Athanasía. Going to look for Sam. Any updates back in California? ~

"Okay. Let's go." Kyle jumped in excitement, dropping some cake frosting on the ground. They made their way up the path beyond the sign.

This purple ground is throwing me off. Does time work the same here? Is it day or night? That's rich, Logan. You're the time lord and you can't even tell time.

"You good, brother?" Kyle paused.

Logan realized he was clenching his fists. He released them to find nail indents on his palms. He turned towards Kyle and shook his head.

"To be honest, I don't really care about the museum. I think Sam is alive, and I want to find out where her brother lives. I'm hoping the museum will have some maps or something."

"Okay, good. I wasn't really into the idea of looking at a museum." He sighed in relief and then put his arm around Logan's shoulder. "An adventure sounds way more fun!"

"That's what you took away from that?" Logan chuckled.

"But Sam, you care a lot about her?"

"I don't have to care a lot to want to help someone."

"Fair enough, brother. Fair enough, but do you?"

"I don't know. I just met her, but she was nice to be around. Really nice."

"Oh. Okay, I see." Kyle smiled and eyed Logan. "Let's go find this museum." He laughed.

"It's not like that, okay. She's the first friend I've had that Mother hasn't picked out for me," Logan snapped.

"I know Mom is tough on you, but she means well."

The two of them walked for a few minutes more and found a tall metal gate. "Is this the museum?" Kyle pulled Logan back by his shoulder.

"I don't kn—" Logan got cut off by his father's buzzer ringing loudly. "Already?" He cursed in Greek.

"We have to go, Logan. Let's just tell Dad that you think she's alive."

"Wait. Look! There's someone there." Logan pointed through the gate's bars. A girl with dark hair was running off in the distance. She jumped off a rock, landing after a mid-air somersault. "Is that her?"

"We have no way of knowing that. It could be anyone. We have to go." Kyle looked at the ringing buzzer. "Come on." Kyle took Logan's arm and began running. Logan ran but kept looking back. The girl glanced over towards them, but was too far for Logan to make out her face.

"What if she's in trouble?" Logan scrambled as he caught up to Kyle.

"Logan, we don't even know if that's Sam. What if we just watched some random girl living in her house?"

"Maybe, but I have a feeling—"

"The feeling has to wait. Dad may have let us roam free, but if we're late going back for the gala, Mom will kill us.

"You're right." Logan sighed, eyeing the buzzer with anger. *I'm coming back without you next time.*

CHAPTER 18

CAN YOU TRUST TIME LORDS?

———

"There. Done." The seamstress stood up after sewing Logan's dress pants. He awkwardly held his hands up for the multiple stylists working on his suit. Logan was tired of looking at the boring yellow walls of his dressing room. His mother had made him leave his brothers to get ready. *They're probably getting to ask Father questions about magic and other realms. I really wish I could focus on learning my powers and helping people with them rather than if my suit is exactly one inch below my ankle.* He groaned. *Wouldn't that make me a better king?*

"Your suit has been tailored to you perfectly, my boy." Queen Iris patted her son's back. "Don't ruin it. No food tonight. Wait 'til after the big announcement." She turned and thanked the tailors in Greek.

"Okay, Mother." Logan sighed. He had lost the little interest he had in the family's royal affairs ever since he had seen that girl running. *She was too far to know for sure, but she looked like Sam. I have to go back.*

"I'm bringing your brothers in for their fittings. Stay here."

"As you wish." Logan took a seat at the make-up counter and immediately a man came in to touch up his appearance. *Father put his compass in his bedroom. I just need to sneak in.*

"Hey, little brother. Looking good." Kyle walked in with Liam and Hayden.

"Ready to be announced as the next king?" Hayden came in behind Logan's chair.

"No." Logan didn't even try to hide his lack of interest. "Bel's more interested in royalty than I'll ever be. I'm just hoping I can help the people here."

"I'm sure you will. You have the biggest heart of all of us." The three brothers took their seats next to Logan.

"Kyle? So, about the girl we saw, I need to go back and confirm it's not Sam," Logan whispered.

"Really? You're still on that?" Kyle waved his hands in disbelief. "I told you. She could've been anyone."

"Would just anyone be running around in a dark old museum behind a tall gate?"

"I mean, the ground was purple, and the cashier gave me carrots by magically assessing my needs. I don't think we can really judge by our standards." Kyle chuckled.

"You're not even slightly concerned?" *How is he okay not knowing for sure? I can't focus on anything else if someone's life is at risk.*

"I am, but how do we go back? And what about this gala?"

"You can freeze time. We saw where Father put the compass. Come on. Let's try," Logan pleaded.

"I don't think we can, Logan. I've frozen a few people for a few minutes. I don't think I can freeze a whole event. And we also saw Dad lock the compass in a drawer."

"I agree with Kyle. It's going to be hard getting the key for that drawer. If you do though, let us know. We wanted to go back too," Liam mocked his brothers' whispering.

"You heard all of that?" Logan trusted Kyle to keep his secrets, but Liam and Hayden were the older brothers. They were always much more strict about his safety.

"Secret's safe with us. Don't worry." Hayden gestured as if he was closing a zipper on his mouth.

"Thank you, brother," he sighed. "Efharistó," Logan said, thanking and dismissing his make-up artist. He got up excitedly. "After they announce us tonight, you can freeze them, Kyle." Logan couldn't help but grin.

He walked out and headed to the ballroom. *I'll be the next king and the next time lord soon. This seems more stressful than not knowing my powers.* He walked past the guards, who bowed to him. After tonight, everyone would be bowing to him. *I wish I didn't have to be treated so formally everywhere, but I guess I'll finally have the power to help people without others ruling my actions.*

The rest of his brothers followed behind him. They stood next to the large, open bronze doors waiting to be announced. Logan's palms were becoming sweatier at the thought of his citizens waiting for him.

"I present to you Logan Green, the next heir to the throne." Queen Iris proudly gestured for Logan to walk out as the party cheered for him. He could see nothing but flashing lights bouncing off of peoples' expensive jewelry. *I can't even tell who's here.* "And the rest of the royal court." His brothers and sister walked out and stood beside him.

"Thank you, everyone, for coming," King Nikolas announced. "I am very proud to present my son as the next King of Aiónios. From a young age, he has taken an interest in the well-being of our citizens. More so than even half of my court at times. He won't sleep with even one person struggling under him." Logan felt weird having his father talk about him to the island's citizens. Sure, he cared about the country and would never let the people suffer, but the truth was that he only agreed to be the next king because the rest of his brothers had said no and Mother wouldn't let them consider Bel.

Maybe the others didn't even say no, though. I have a feeling Mother and Father wanted to force me into this position.

"You're right, brother. We can't stay here knowing Sam's alive and in trouble," Kyle whispered as he turned to Logan.

"Ready to freeze everyone?"

"We'll just have to try and hope it works. Let's go find Sam!"

***

The boys waited to be dismissed from the stage. Logan eyed Kyle, who promptly froze the people around them. "Shouldn't you unfreeze Liam and Hayden too?" Logan asked pointing at his brothers. "They wanted to come."

"No. They leave me out of all of their fun adventures in boarding school. Now it's our turn!" Kyle winked. "Now hurry. I don't know how long this will last."

"Grab the keys from Father's front pocket, Kyle." Their father was frozen still with his microphone. Logan could see his face patted with makeup. *He seems really weak now. Is that what happens when he gives up his powers to us?*

"Got 'em." Kyle leaped past their dad and joined Logan.

"I really hope Seth was right about Sam being alive."

"Wait, you got me here and you aren't even one hundred percent sure she's alive?" Kyle stopped in his tracks.

Damn. I shouldn't have let that slip. She has to be alive, doesn't she? "Seth was so sure. I had to believe in what he said. I need to believe."

"And Seth is who to you?" Kyle waved his hands. "You trust him because of what?"

"He's Sam's friend." Logan faltered realizing the fault in his words. Kyle rolled his eyes.

"Oh, great. So we know nothing about him."

"Okay, sure, we don't, but what's the point in turning back now?" Logan motioned to the room full of frozen people.

"Let's just get that compass and be done with this. Mom will rain hellfire on us if she finds out." They ran to their parents' room and to the ancient-looking dresser. Kyle jiggled the key into the wooden drawer and pulled it open. "Perfect. Dad hasn't moved it." Kyle tossed it to Logan.

Now what was Father's incantation? Oh, it's written on the back! "Prithvi Asana Athanasía." A similar warmth and bright light flashed in front of Logan. For a moment, he felt weightless, and then familiar dark skies appeared. "This place really has no concept of a sun rising or setting, does it?" he mumbled.

"Wait. This isn't where we landed last time. I don't see the shop we got the cake from." Kyle looked at Logan, who cursed in Greek. They seemed to be in a park or a cemetery. "Is this a graveyard?"

"You're from Earth, aren't you?" an old man said as he approached them. Except he wasn't just an old man. He had claw-like nails and a hairy snout protruding above his well-defined jaw.

Why is it so obvious to everyone here?

"How'd you know?" Kyle asked innocently.

"We don't have graveyards here." Logan heard the man's words, but he couldn't focus. He titled his head and stared at the man's strange animal-like features.

Is he a werewolf? First sirens, now werewolves. What other creatures really exist?

"Also, no, I'm not a werewolf." The man snickered as if his words should have been obvious.

"What are you?" Logan asked, realizing too late how rude that sounded. The man laughed, brushing off the comment.

"I'm a shapeshifter. Werewolves are a subspecies of my kind."

"Woah!" Kyle blurted out.

"What brought you here today?"

"Can you help us find a museum?" Logan intercepted. *A local may know where the museum is.*

"Why would you go there? You know it's no longer a museum. Not since the original family moved back in."

"Who's the original family? I'm looking for a friend."

"You're friends with Keith?" A look of fear washed over the man's face.

"No. Sam." Logan looked at the man who had completely changed his body language. He was now looking at Logan like the citizens of Aiónios did when they found out that Logan would be king soon—straightened posture with a demure voice. He didn't like it.

"Sam Bleu! That's amazing. Um. They stay in the castle in the upper half of the city." He pointed behind him and towards a line of people. "They're all waiting for the shuttle that goes north. Catch it and you'll be dropped off right by the marketplace in front of the castle grounds."

"She's alive!" Logan shouted. He looked excitedly at Kyle and then back at the shapeshifter. "Thank you!"

"Be careful. Good luck." The man bowed to Logan, who began running towards the line.

"Wow. A different dimension and people still treat you like royalty." Kyle laughed.

"I wonder what that was all about. Why did he get scared of us after I mentioned Keith and Sam?"

"I mean, Sam's powers seem to be something really important, right?"

"Yeah, that's true. I didn't think her having control of fire would warrant that, though." The boys stepped in line behind a few children who all seemed to be heading home from school.

They held books titled: *Witchcraft Is A Myth, but What Truths Is It Based On?*, *What Mind Control Powers Do We All Have?*, *How To Unlock Your True Power.* The last book caught Logan's attention.

"Hey, can I see that book?" Logan asked the girls without thinking. They all looked back, confused, but as soon as they saw Logan they began smiling and giggling.

"Sure, take mine." The tallest one handed Logan her book, and the two others gave her dirty looks.

"Uh, thank you." Logan smiled back and immediately opened it up.

"You're really torn up about your powers, aren't you?" Kyle put his hand on Logan's shoulder.

"I just don't understand how I can be the time lord and not even know the slightest about my powers. I mean, all three of you can already do cool tricks. I just know other people can't affect me."

"Sometimes the best defense is a good offense." Kyle shrugged.

"Yeah, but I'm hoping this book might have something about that defense, too." *Your powers are you. As counterintuitive as it seems, try to put yourself in danger that is somewhat safe. Your adrenaline might just cause you to trick your body into activating your powers.* Logan closed the book in frustration. *How is that going to help me?*

"Already giving up?" Kyle joked.

"Everyone keeps telling me that in time I'll learn, but what can I do to be actively involved in this learning pro—"

"Um. Can I have my book back? The shuttle is here." The girl interrupted Logan and looked at him, concerned. He still had the book he'd slammed shut between his hands.

"Oh. Yeah, sorry." He gave the book back and turned to Kyle. "Let's just get on this shuttle and get Sam."

"We got this." Kyle patted Logan's back as they entered the shuttle, which was more of a bunch of individual pods. Kyle and Logan had one to themselves, and the inside was extremely posh. White couches and black lighting gave the pods a futuristic look in terms of Earth's standards.

"Woah. Look outside." Logan could see the pods moving in formations across the land, carefully avoiding the infrastructure and other beings. "I couldn't even tell we had started moving."

"Damn. This is impressive. I wonder what kind of powers this takes to control." Kyle joined his brother at the window sides. "Look at this dashboard." Kyle pushed a button that had a symbol of a window on it. Immediately the walls seemed to melt around them.

"Woah. What did you do?" Logan climbed on the couch in fear.

"I don't know. I just pressed the window button." The boys held onto each other but slowly realized that the pods around them looked similar. Logan extended his hand to where the wall used to be.

"Oh. It's still there. It's just invisible."

"This gives indoor-outdoor a whole new meaning." Kyle laughed.

"Wait, look! I think we're here." Logan could see the dome building and the large metal gates that he saw the girl through last time. This time he saw the path from the marketplace to the castle more clearly. The pod passed by the old, broken museum sign and then landed in front of the grocery store where Kyle had gotten cake.

"Okay, so while you go get her, I'm going back to the shop."

"What? You're leaving me? You don't even have any money."

"Don't I, though?" Kyle waved some cards in front of Logan's face. "I found these in the drawer with the compass. One of these has to be the magical payment the cashier was talking about, right?"

"Fine. Whatever. I'll meet you back here. Get ready to run, depending on how this goes." The two of them exited the pod as it came to a halt. Logan quickly began running towards the sign and up the path to the castle. "Ouch!" Logan said, tripping over something protruding from the dirt. *What is this?* He picked up a card-like object. *MagNesium ~ hold for payment.* He read the card and got up, dusting the dirt off of his vest. *That's funny. I guess instead of a platinum card they have magnesium? Is that supposed to be a pun on the word "magic?"* He pocketed the card and kept running.

The gate looked more daunting today. There was something darker about the sky in this part of the city. *How do I find Sam again?* Logan put his foot on a ledge in the gate, seeing if he could sneak in, but quickly decided against it. The top of the gate was covered in tall arrow-like spikes. He wouldn't be able to make it across them. He looked at the edge where the gate met the wall. There was a large rock that Logan could try to throw onto the gate to make noise. *What if Keith hears instead of Sam? I guess it's the only choice I have, though.*

"Sam! Sam!" He threw the rock at the gate, making a thunderous noise as the metal clanged. *This is dumb. What are the chances she will be running near here again?* He slid down to the ground and leaned on the gate, sighing. *There has to be another entrance. Maybe around the corner. This place is huge, I'm sure this wall has other gates.*

Logan stood up, straightening his back. The new idea gave him energy again. He looked to the left and saw how far the wall stretched. Its end was hidden. It seemed to curve in eventually. He took a deep breath and walked towards the edge.

Its gray bricks made the castle look like a prison under the grim sky. For a world run by magic, it sure was dark and depressing. *People on Earth wish for magic all the time, but I would trade not having powers for life on Earth over this any day.*

Logan ran his hands over the wall as he walked. Gray dust covered his fingertips. *Huh. How old is this wall?* He chipped away at one brick and he was able to make a decent dent within its side. *It's weakening with time.*

A pile of dust fell in front of Logan as he jumped back. Where the brick had been was now a window-like opening in the wall. *Did I do that?* He choked on the dust, but his eyes grew wide. Logan's blood rushed through his veins. *Did I actually use my powers?* His heart was racing, and his stomach felt tighter; he felt like he had control.

He looked at the bricks around the one that he had destroyed and focused on the rest, watching them turn to dust one by one. *I didn't think time control could lead to this.* He hopped through the human-sized hole that now existed in the wall and looked around. *I did it! I'm in.*

Logan headed towards the dome-shaped building first. It had caught his eye every time he looked at the castle. The dome was an atypical choice compared to the rest of the buildings. The fact that it was made completely of glass, but he still couldn't see through it, intrigued Logan. He walked to its edge and looked at the world's reflections around him in the glass.

He could see a big, bright sphere in the sky, as well as other buildings, yet not himself. The clouds moved through over the glass surface but no matter how much Logan moved around, he couldn't see his reflection. *That's weird.* Turning around, he realized that the sphere was actually that big and bright. It wasn't distorted in the reflection. *That planet must be really close to this one to look that large, but why is it blue?*

He looked around at the other buildings hoping to find a way in, but they all seemed to lack doors. And when he tried the few that had marked entrances, they were immune to Logan's newfound time acceleration powers. *Great. I finally learn how to use some of my powers in the one place they don't work.*

Logan peered through what seemed like a window on the ground floor of a tower, but before being able to see inside, the glass shattered. He jumped, falling on his back.

"Logan?" A familiar voice yelled. "Is that you? Are you okay?"

"Sam!" He turned around to see her holding a dagger. She had a few more on her belt.

"I didn't mean to throw that there. I was training. Are you hurt?" She lifted him and put her hands on his shoulders, examining him.

"No, you missed me, thankfully." He enveloped her in a hug. Sam's hands awkwardly flailed around him.

"Um, hey. So, uh, what are you doing here?" She stretched her hand behind her head.

"I'm here to take you back."

"I can't do that."

"Yes, you can. You're coming with me. Seth came looking for you and told me everything."

"Everything?" Sam faltered.

"Yes, you came on a mission, and Derek and Sky left with Mia after Keith said you and Ethan died, but Seth didn't believe it. Keith slipped up in front of Seth."

"I can't believe you met Seth." Sam bit her lip, but her face changed to have a frightful expression instead when she heard a bang behind Logan. "Listen. You have to leave. Keith and I are training right now. If he sees you, I don't know what he'll do."

"No. You're coming with me. I'm not leaving you with him any longer."

"You don't get it. He won't let me leave."

"We'll make a run for it."

"Logan, he has a spell on me. Anytime I leave, time flips back thirty seconds to when I was still in the castle. Even if I leave, I'll just be back, and he'll be angrier than he already is."

"Do you trust me?" Logan smiled, knowing he could break the spell. *This is when I need my powers to work. I'm immune to his powers, so this shouldn't be a problem, right?*

"Um…" Sam looked unsure.

"We don't have time for this!" Logan took her hand and pulled her to run with him. They ran past the large gates, towards the shop where Kyle was waiting. Sam turned her head to see the castle getting smaller and smaller.

"How did you…"

"I'm the other time lord," Logan declared.

"What?" Sam exclaimed, stopping in her tracks and making Logan stop, too.

"We don't have time for this."

"You're the other one? The only person who Keith can't control? Is that why—"

"Yes. He couldn't freeze me in California because he can't touch me." Logan felt a wave of power rush over him. He had never realized what being the other time lord had meant until now.

"You know what I would give to be able to say that. I've spent the last entire year trying to become more powerful than him."

"He can't touch you now either, Sam, but we have to go." Logan exclaimed. Sam let go of Logan's hand.

"Okay, let's go." She started sprinting.

PART 7

SAM BLEU

CHAPTER 19

PILLS AND SHARKS CLASS

———

Sam looked back at the castle anxiously as she waited for Logan to open the portal for Earth. *Keith will notice I'm gone soon. I need to be strong enough to fight him if he comes after me.*

"Think of your magic name!" Kyle came running to them. "Hurry, Logan. The chant to go home is on the back of the compass."

"I don't know where this is going to take us back to, but here goes nothing." Logan shrugged.

"What?" Sam and Kyle shouted in unison.

Trust is going a long way here. Logan opened the compass casing and rang the dial back, shouting in some unknown language. *Sameera.*

"Prithvi Asana Terra."

That sounds like what Derek and Sky said bringing me here. Did they send Logan to get me? They knew this whole time that I was okay and left me here? Sam suddenly saw the world around her become bright gold and magenta. Her vision began clearing up and she realized that they had landed at the entrance of a banquet. A flower arch stood above them and waiters were buzzing past, handing out honey cakes. They stood on a hill overlooking the ocean. Logan cursed something in a foreign language to Sam. *Is that Greek? Are we in Greece?*

"We have to leave before they see us," Logan muttered.

"You guys go back there." Kyle pointed towards a hallway that led into the house. "I'll go in and distract them."

Is this his house? They have a backyard big enough to host a banquet outside their house? She marveled over the white stone and glass windows. *What is Logan doing here? This clearly isn't Sweden.*

"Thanks, brother." Logan took Sam's hand, and they started running away from the loud music and people.

I guess his clothes make sense now, at least. Sam finally had a second to process the fact that Logan was in dress pants with a matching shirt and vest. They were covered in dirt and wrinkled from running, but they still looked more appropriate than the tank top, black shorts, and matching knee-high socks and boots Sam was wearing. They stopped abruptly as they saw a room to their right.

"Let's go in here. I promise I'll explain," Logan whispered. As he opened the tall bronze door, a woman appeared in front of them. "Mother!"

"Logan. What have you done to your vest?" She looked at the scuff marks all over his clothing. "And who are you? Didn't you read the invitation? Today's event is formal wear." Sam looked down at her training attire. There were cuts and mud all over her arms and legs since she had been in the middle of a training session.

"Mother. No worries. I am going to take her to change into something more suitable now."

"I wonder how you got an invitation. Never show up in front of me like this. I'm the—"

"We have to go now." Logan pushed Sam to the side and into the room.

The what? Why was his mom so mad at me? "Dude. Who are you, and what is happening?"

"I'm Logan." He laughed, but his eyes looked serious.

"Ha, ha," she said, rolling her eyes. "Okay, but seriously, you live in a hilltop mansion which is clearly not in Sweden, right? And what was your mom saying about showing up in front of her?"

"Don't worry about her. She is just very..." Logan hesitated. "Conscious about how she looks to society."

Conscious or just mean?

"I can't believe you're alive. Seth and I were so worried. Your family was crying back home. None of us thought Keith would let you live."

Trust me, I didn't, either. For some reason, he seems to think Derek and Sky are the bad ones. I don't want to believe any of them are bad. "I'm still confused about that. How'd you even find me after this entire year?"

"What do you mean by year?"

"This whole year that I've been stuck in Athanasía, I trained both with Keith and alone. I didn't know how I was going to leave, but I knew if I ever did, I didn't want to be scared of him coming to get me again."

"You've only been gone for a month." Logan looked at her, concerned.

"What?" *Is he messing with me?*

"It's only starting to be fall here."

"That's because time works differently in Athanasía." a tall man who looked like an older Logan walked in, making Sam and Logan flinch. "Sam Bleu. It's really you! You're alive! I didn't believe it when we saw you at the gala, but it's true." He smiled, looking pleased with himself.

"Hello?" Sam said, confused. *How does he know who I am?*

"This is my father." Logan looked up at the man. "I know you said not to steal your things, Father, but I couldn't leave knowing she may be alive."

"I'm proud of you, son." Mr. Green smiled. Logan looked up, raising his eyebrows.

"You are?"

"Sometimes doing the right thing is dangerous, and sadly, you'll be in danger often." He eyed Sam who sank down, feeling guilty that every time Logan was in danger, it was usually her fault. "I don't want to scare you off from the world of magic. We just have to be realistic."

"Wow. Can you talk to my brothers for me?" Sam mumbled, not realizing how loud she was talking.

"Ah, Derek always looked after you so well."

"Wait. You know Derek?" She stood up straight again and furrowed her brows.

"Yes. Sorry. I must explain. I knew your mother and your father." Mr. Green looked into Sam's eyes.

Does Logan know about my father being the devil?

"Your mom had only told me and Sky's mother about wanting to give her powers to you. She never said why, and I couldn't ask before she left."

Shoot. I don't want Logan to know about me. It's too much. I want to become friends with him before he gets scared off by all of this.

"You knew my mother? Do you know what happened to her?"

"Logan, dear, why don't you head back to the event. I think they're expecting you." Mr. Green gestured to the door and made eye contact with his son.

"Oh, yes. Um, my friend needs me there while he gets presented as the next heir to the throne." Logan shifted nervously as he looked at his father and then Sam.

"Your friend. Um, yes, he was looking for you," Mr. Green stuttered as he said "friend."

Does everyone here just casually know royalty? The room we passed by seemed to be filled with important people. They were all in suits or ball gowns. Looked like a fairytale.

"I will help get Sam settled here. I'm sure she has a lot of questions." Mr. Green guided his son out. Logan nodded and swiftly left them alone.

"So, my mother?" Sam inquired.

"I did know her, and don't worry. Logan knows nothing about your powers or your father. I understand that it is a very heavy secret to give out."

"Thank you."

"Of course, Sameera." Mr. Green's tone shifted to be more serious.

He knows my true name? She looked at him wide-eyed.

"As for your mother, I'm afraid I only know so much. I told her that I would keep an eye out for you if we were ever to meet, and I could not be happier that you got away from Keith." He took a seat on the armchair by a bookcase. "It's such a shame. He used to be such a nice kid."

"We're all confused about that." *Damn. I was hoping he knew something about Keith and why he turned evil.*

"Did he take your pow—"

"No. I don't know why, but no," Sam interrupted. Mr. Green furrowed his brows and squinted his eyes.

"He kept you for a year and didn't take your powers?"

"In fact, he started training me. I would train on my own to try to get stronger than him, but it was almost as if he wanted to help me defeat him."

"This is not good."

"Why?"

"If he didn't take your powers…" Mr. Green coughed into his handkerchief. Sam could see red drops covering the small, otherwise white cloth.

"Are you okay?" She rushed to his side.

"I'm sorry. Sameera. I must leave and take care of some things. Please stay within this house until then. I'm afraid Keith has something more sinister up his sleeve if he felt confident enough to train you in your powers for a year."

He's right. What could his motivation be, though? How would keeping my powers help him? Sam slid down to the ground and sat with her hands on her head. *It won't take long for him to know I'm gone. I hope he won't go back to Malibu and hurt anyone.*

***

"Here's a shirt and some new boxers," Logan said, tossing the clothes at Sam. He had brought her to a guest room that looked more lavish than any of the rooms she'd ever lived in. Even Keith's somber castle paled in comparison to the glamour of this villa.

Boxers? Sam caught the clothes and glanced up at him, confused.

"Sorry, I didn't know what to give you. I don't think Bel's clothes will fit you, but these are new, don't worry."

"Thanks," Sam laughed.

"Father will have some actual clothes for you by morning. He said that you should stay with us for a few days since Keith won't think to come here for you. He already called Sky to convince him to let you stay here and told them to be on the lookout in case Keith shows up."

"Your mom must be happy." Sam rolled her eyes.

"She'll have to come around," Logan said, smirking.

"Tell your parents thanks, though. And thank you for coming back for me. I can't believe you found me there." Sam walked into the bathroom and started changing. It had paper napkins with personalized engravings. *Welcome Guests of the Green Residence!* There were also seashell-shaped soaps laid out on a rose gold tray.

"Seth and I were planning to find you no matter what. He's the one who suspected you were still alive. I just got lucky that Father took me to Athanasía," Logan called out from the room.

"You know, boxers are kind of comfortable." Sam walked out, crinkling her oversized shirt and spinning to show off the style.

"They look good on you," Logan laughed. Sam blushed and turned around. She collected her old clothes and came back out.

"I think I should sleep now. See you tomorrow?"

"Good night." he nodded.

"Good night, Logan." Sam smiled and closed the door as he left. *I never thought that I'd be living with the boy from the window.* Sam heard a knock on the door. "Hello?"

"Sorry, actually, can I ask you a question?" Logan peered into the door.

"Sure."

"The year you spent training, how did you learn so much about your powers? I was in Malibu for the summer and couldn't even figure out what my powers were."

"It's fine. I only found out when I accidentally set a building on fire." Logan's eyes widened in shock. "But for learning? Honestly, it was a lot of reading and just using my powers without holding back." Sam walked back to her bed and tapped on the covers. "In Athanasía, they don't have science. They have magic. Nobody fears their powers. They just use them. When I trained with Sky and Derek, everyone was so concerned with using the safe side of our powers, but one thing I learned was that it wasn't the powers that were evil. It's how we use that power, so I immersed myself in the magic."

"I haven't read a single thing about magic. Mother wouldn't let us talk about it until fairly recently."

"Do you have a library here? I mean, how could you not? This place is huge," Sam gushed. Logan laughed.

"Yeah. We have a really nice one downstairs."

"Okay, you know what? We can sleep tomorrow. Let's go down there. Let's see what you can do, time lord," Sam teased and bowed. "Do you trust me?" She held out her hand, winking.

"No way. I can't." Logan shifted back uncomfortably. "I'm nobody's king or lord," he said flustered, shaking his head.

"Too bad, I trusted you. Now it's your turn." She got up and gestured for him to guide her to the library. "Time to own your powers." Logan reluctantly got up and walked outside.

"Shhh." He tiptoed around past the master bedroom. The oak stairs creaked as they made their way down. "Here. Father used to lock this library when we were younger, but he stopped since we came back from California."

"Perfect. Hurry, close the door," Sam whispered as she roamed inside, looking at the gorgeous paintings on the dome above. Books lined the walls from the floor to the ceiling. *It's double the size of the library back home.* "Looks like a Malibu mansion was a downgrade for you."

"Yeah, I can't say I haven't been privileged growing up here." Logan walked in and started looking through books. Sam perused a section of novels for finding your powers. Instead of the books filling up the walls, her eyes landed on one half-open on a side table in the middle of the room.

"Someone's been reading here lately."

"Wait—is that?" Logan turned to see the book in Sam's hand. "I found that book in Athanasía when I came to get you." He turned the pages finding a specific section. "Your powers are you," he read sarcastically.

"I hate it when people say that. Like yes, they are, but how do I use them?" Sam quipped.

"Exactly." Logan gave Sam a boyish smile. "It gets worse." He continued reading from the book. "As counterintuitive as it seems, try to put yourself in danger that is somewhat safe. Your adrenaline pumping might just cause you to trick your body into activating your powers." The sarcasm in his voice made Sam laugh uncontrollably.

"Okay. Don't hate me. But that advice is actually very true."

"No. They've converted you too," Logan said, disappointed. He gave Sam a fake look of concern. She giggled.

"No. Okay, kind of. But think about it. For you to really break that time rewind spell Keith had on me, all it took was a sense of danger and necessity."

"That's true, but I can't recreate that feeling here."

"Sure we can." Sam had a cheek-to-cheek smile on her face as she created a fireball in her hand. "Try to freeze the flame as I throw it at you."

"No. No way. Sam, we can't."

"Danger, right?" She tossed it at him, but Logan fell to the floor to dodge it instead of freezing it. "Shoot, Logan!" She quickly had the fireball disappear into thin air and rushed to him.

"The goal was for you to try using your powers, not to help me burn down your library." She laughed as she helped him up. "You okay?"

"Yeah. I don't think I'm so good with danger." Logan looked at Sam as she put her hands on both of his shoulders.

"Says the guy who went to another dimension and risked running into the only other time lord to save a girl he met a month ago. Yeah, I don't believe it." Sam dropped her hands and broke eye contact.

"Maybe we read more and then try again," Logan uttered.

"You're avoiding the inevitable, but okay. I'll rein in the flames for now." Sam tossed him another book. "Read up."

***

For the next several days, the two of them made it a habit to sneak into the library at night. They would practice the books' tips in hopes that nobody would find them.

"Okay, let's try this again." Sam pointed at the books on the top shelves. She climbed the library's ladder. "Try freezing these books as they fall." Sam dropped the books one by one.

Logan raised his hands over his face and looked between his fingers. Two of the books froze but the others fell to the ground with a thud. "Oops. I really tried, Sam."

"Okay, you clearly know how to use your powers. You just can't control them;" Sam sighed.

"Let's read another book?" Logan shrugged.

"Wait! Look at this one." Sam crouched down by one of the fallen books. It had opened to reveal journal entries and envelopes.

"This is Father's handwriting." Logan picked up the journal. "And these letters are from an Avni Bleu. Is that your mother?" He handed her the letters.

My mom and his dad wrote each other letters? She opened the top one and read it:

Dear Nikolas,

I'm afraid we must call upon our circle again. It's back, and we have to vanquish it from Earth, no matter the cost. This demon can and will destroy Earth if we don't.

Love,
Avni

"Our parents fought demons together?" Logan peered over her shoulder and gasped. "That explains why Father knew who you were."

"What demon do you think they're referring to? Do you think they defeated it?" Sam's hand shook as she opened the second envelope.

Dear Nikolas,

We did it. I still miss the others, but I hope we can stay. I don't want us to leave our families, and isn't it okay if good stays while evil is gone? Our children might need us if anything like the demon that took our friends comes back. We have to make sure they can fight and vanquish anything else trying to take over Earth. This planet must stay neutral, or the magical realms will be in trouble.

Love,
Avni

"Does this make any sense to you?" Logan asked, running his hands through his hair.

"Keith and I fought a lot of demons in the last year, but none of them were powerful enough to take over Earth. Well—" Sam faltered. Logan looked at her worried. "Keith could be powerful enough. He didn't get my powers, but he has been stealing spells from different magical realms."

"Then we have to be ready for when he comes back for you." Logan put his hand on her shoulder. "Our parents did it back then, and we will do it now," he proclaimed, but then looked down. "Just once I figure out how to use my powers." His face was distraught. Sam felt for him because she remembered the feeling of having so much potential and everyone telling her she wasn't using it all. *I need to help him learn them. It's the least I can do after he brought me into his home.*

"Let's go adventure around the island. We'll find something to help you."

"How about reading more?" He grinned at Sam pleadingly.

"You've been reading all week long. It's time for action, my dude." Logan looked at her doubtfully. "Okay. Worse comes to worst, you'll have just taken a break from reading to show me your hometown. The books aren't going anywhere, and I need to clear my head from these letters."

"Okay, sure. Aiónios beaches are even better than Malibu's."

"So I've been meaning to ask. We're in Greece!" Sam laughed at Logan. "Why did you say you were from Sweden?" Logan stopped in his tracks. He looked at her with a blank face and then finally replied.

"This is just our summer home. We're here because my friend asked us to host his gala," he muttered.

Okay, if this is a summer home, then I really want to know what his actual house looks like.

***

The two of them walked outside through the streets. Sea breeze filled the air. *It's funny how the ocean smells different around the world. It's more natural here.* Sam looked at the cobblestone pavement below them and the beautiful cottage-like homes on the hill. *Looks like the perfect place to settle down.*

"You want to see some ancient Greek ruins?" Logan reached out his hand to Sam as they stood above a wide stairway.

"Of course." She eagerly took his hand, and they rushed down the steps towards an open green space littered with the remains of stone structures. "It's crazy to think that entire civilizations have been reduced to just this. Imagine the knowledge that wasn't passed down."

"The Library of Alexandria burning is the greatest tragedy I can think of."

That's such an intellectual response. Guess he really does like to read, even when it isn't to escape training. Sam smiled and felt butterflies in her stomach. She hadn't met many people who knew about the library. Mia would tell her stories about Alexander and the knowledge lost in the library. Sam never got enough of it. "Do you believe in the myths and stories passed down about these ruins?"

"I'd like to think that every myth in the world has some truth to it. We might all be receiving different ends of the same telephone game," Logan replied.

"Yeah, and fighting over our interpretations even though the initial call was the same." Sam walked through a series of broken pillars.

"Exactly." Logan gave Sam another boyish smile.

Damn. Maybe he should be the next king instead of his friend. I feel like he could actually bring peace to this world.

"Ready for the next part of this adventure?"

"Ah, I like that you're on board now." She smiled profusely. "And yes, let's go."

"So I think this will bring about that danger you want us to seek." Logan laughed as he made eye contact with Sam.

"You make it sound like I'm crazy." She joined in on the laughter.

"I think we're both crazy if we do what I have planned."

"Okay, spill."

"Follow me and you'll soon see." Logan smirked. "But first, I want to show you the island, too." He extended his arm, gesturing for Sam to follow him.

"Fine." Sam rolled her eyes and jogged up to him. They walked past the street shops. Sam took in the new environment. Little mom-and-pop stores were littered around the island. She motioned for Logan to wait as he kept walking. Some people on the street stopped and looked at her in disgust as she had her arm raised and palm open towards him.

"Oh. Um, don't do that here." He laughed and closed her hand into a fist. "That doesn't mean stop here." He muttered some words in Greek to the passersby. They laughed and left.

"Oh, shoot," Sam said, flushed in embarrassment. She felt her head get hotter. "I just wanted to ask if we could see one of these shops."

"There's a bakery around the corner that has my favorite breakfast on the island." Logan smiled. "They should be open now."

The two of them walked to the shop Logan was referring to. He went in and came out with a bag full of pastries. "That smells amazing." Sam eagerly took the bag from him.

"These are called bougatsa. Custard pie, if you will." He beamed. They took a seat in the outdoor courtyard by the shops.

"Greece is gorgeous, Logan," Sam said as she took a bite of their food. "And this is yum." She licked her lips. Logan chuckled and they watched as a street musician played his guitar.

"Let's dance?" Logan took her pastry and set it down. Sam looked up in shock.

"Um, what? Here?"

"It's another type of danger, isn't it?" Logan jogged backwards towards the musician. "Come on, everyone is enjoying the music."

He was right. Some others had started to dance to the music too, clapping in sync with the stringed instruments. I guess. *Why not?* Sam joined him on the stone streets. They danced with several others circling around them. Sam awkwardly tried to follow the steps Logan was making.

"This is called the Zorba," he yelled out to her over the music.

"This is fun, but it doesn't get you off the hook for our magic training." Sam winked at him as she finally got in the hang of the dance. A flower shop caught her eye as she danced. The shop had fake blue roses that reminded Sam of Keith and Ethan. *Shoot, Sam. You're getting too distracted here. Keith's still out there.* She frowned and stumbled next to an elderly man. "Sorry, sir."

"Are you alright?" Logan pulled her aside.

"Yeah, that was really fun, but we should finish your plan before your parents figure out we aren't home."

"You're right." He continued smiling, but Sam could tell he was concerned about her. "Let's go. Don't worry, it shouldn't be too scary. I hope."

No matter which street they turned to, they could see the water. The island felt peaceful, but Sam couldn't get rid of her anxious feeling. *Forget Keith. All I can do is train and prepare for his arrival, which is what we're doing right now.* She nervously tapped the side of her clothes with her fingers as they walked to their next destination.

"Okay, so past this alley, there is a great view of the ocean." Logan gestured for Sam to follow him down a stone path. The alley had a bike rental shop at one end and a bar at the next. "Most people need liquid courage, but since we're trying to find something to fear, I think we can do this without anything."

"What are you referring to?" Sam was getting suspicious.

"We're cliff jumping," he replied nonchalantly.

Sam's eyes widened. *I guess I was basically asking for something like this.* "Is this even safe here?"

"Kind of. But remember you're the one who said danger will help me."

"I can't believe how well you can twist my words around." She laughed and they both walked towards the cliffs reluctantly. "I'll go first."

"I'm good with that." Logan looked at her surprised. "I'd rather not go first."

"Wow, thanks for the concern. This is your plan, you know." Sam walked up to the edge and looked over. *Must be a thirty-five foot drop. Don't fall on one of those ledges, Sam.* Her heart started racing as she thought of all the things that could go wrong. "People do this drunk all the time?" She wiped her sweaty palms on her shorts. *You fight demons. If mortals do this, I can too.*

"Yes, but I don't know if that makes us dumber or smarter." Logan pointed at a few teenagers jumping from a cliff in the distance. Sam walked back, took a deep breath, and ran towards the edge. She made a leap and, for a second, she thought she was clear. The cliff was a few feet behind her as she fell, but as the water came closer, she saw that there was a ledge that reached out and she was headed straight towards it.

Shoot! She made contact with the water, but her leg had scraped the side of the rocky ledge cutting the side of her left thigh. "Ow!"

"Sam? You okay?" Logan called from above.

"Yeah, so danger was correct."

"Hold up. I'm coming in," Logan yelled. Sam watched as Logan moved out of sight getting ready to jump. She tried hard to stay above the surface of the water and braced her leg that was shooting in pain. Sam could see the water around her turning red.

Get on that ledge, Sam. How bad is this cut? She couldn't tell if she was actually losing a lot of blood or the sight of the bloody water was making her dizzy. Sam went underwater for a second to try to get a look at her leg. *Okay. It's not too bad. It's just a cut. You're fine.* She tried to swim out to where the water wasn't completely red yet. As she struggled, she could see a few fish swimming by.

"Sam!" A hand grabbed her shoulder.

"I'm fine, Logan. Don't worry."

"Let's get you out of the water."

"Wait, look at this. We're right next to a school of red fish. They're gorgeous." Sam went underwater, but instead of seeing more fish, her heart dropped. A large gray shark was swimming a few feet away from her. She came crashing out of the water. "Did you see that?"

"Yeah. We need to get out now!"

"Let's go." Sam's heart pounded. The dizziness hadn't subsided, and her vision was starting to blur. *A shark? Sam, you should've never agreed to anything water related. You know that's Mia's zone.*

"Sam, take my hand." Logan turned, seeing her lag behind. He dipped below the water and the next thing Sam knew she was lying down on the rocky ledge.

"What happened?"

"You're right. Danger really does help, just apparently not danger aimed at me."

"What?" Sam felt a bit dazed. *I'm pretty sure I didn't lose consciousness. How'd I end up here? Is my leg worse than I thought?*

"I froze time. I looked underwater, and the shark was headed straight towards us."

"I can't blame it. We were here for its feeding hour." Sam ran her hand through her hair and Logan laughed. "Thank you. And congrats, you did it. I told you it would happen."

"I don't think you can really pull off an 'I told you so' right now." Logan teased, pointing at her leg.

"Shoot. I need to bandage this up." Sam looked down at the shirt she was wearing. *I could easily rip off the bottom and make it a crop top.* "Sorry in advance. I'll promise I'll buy you a new shirt."

"What?" Logan sat confused. His eyes widened as Sam stretched and tore the bottom half of the oversized shirt. She started wrapping it around her leg.

"Where did you learn to take care of yourself so well?" He looked amazed.

"I lived with Keith for a year. If I didn't take care of myself, nobody would. He called it tough love."

"That's more like no love. I'm sorry you went through that." He began helping her tie the cloth.

"Don't worry. It forced me to become who I wanted to be. I finally realized that I couldn't just complain about the rules people and my powers had set for me. I just had to do what I had to do."

"I still need to learn that."

"I think you're learning. As I recall, someone just froze time and saved me, yet again." Logan laughed as they both stood up. "You got to let me save you for a change," Sam joked.

"Let's call us even from the demon encounter in the forest." He laughed.

"Now it makes sense why you just stood there. I thought you were too scared to do anything."

"I wasn't not scared." Logan stammered, pursing his lips. "But I didn't know what to do. And then you threw that knife. I still don't understand."

"Yeah, you're right. We're even now." Sam blushed.

"I think it's time we head back. Are you good to start walking?"

"My leg hurts like hell, but also I want to get as far away from that shark as possible."

Logan let out a silent laugh. "Here. Hold onto my shoulder, and I'll take us the short way back." He took a hold of her waist, and they started hiking up the cliffside to get back.

***

"I can't believe we just did that," Sam laughed as she and Logan made their way into the pool bathroom.

"I told you that Aiónios beaches were more fun than Malibu."

"Yeah, fun when you're not in the water." They started grabbing towels from the cupboards and drying themselves. "I really would have been screwed without you. Thank you."

"You need to stop thanking me. I had fun too, you know." The two of them laughed and shushed each other simultaneously. "I don't want my mother to hear us."

"Yeah, wouldn't want to give her another reason to hate me."

"She doesn't hate you." Logan looked at Sam. "Or at least I hope not." He burst into laughter as Sam stared him down.

"Wow, thanks for that. Makes me feel so much better," she said sarcastically.

"Again with the thanking," Logan teased. Sam rolled her eyes and hit him with her towel. She looked at her leg that was bandaged in her own shirt. "Let's go to the infirmary for that?"

"Yes please. And can I get a new shirt? Your mother will definitely not like me if she sees me in this homemade crop top."

"Sure." He giggled. Sam followed him out the door, which led them to an outdoor passageway and towards the second half of the house. She could see the infinity pool below them on both sides of the railing.

This house is so big. I can't believe they're this rich. I guess Logan did say he was friends with the soon-to-be king, so being wealthy is probably a given. Logan took out his keys for the door at the end of the passageway. "So why was that the first time you went to California and met everyone?"

"As I recall, that was the first time you met your family, too?" He wiggled the key into the door.

"Fair enough." *I guess that's a touchy topic. Oops.*

"But I guess Mother doesn't really like us being involved with magic."

That can't be the only reason. Right? What's he hiding? "Yeah, I got that from the way she greeted me. She really didn't want magic at that event." *Even after getting close to him and meeting his family he seems to have so many secrets.*

"She's really close to my friend, so she gets overly invested in his image and thinks magic only leads to trouble."

"She needs to see the side of you that helps people then."

"What?" Logan turned around tilting his head to the side.

"Sorry, I was looking at the photos of you in the room I was staying in. All of them showed you helping someone. I mean, soup kitchens, reading to the elderly, teaching kids. You're a poster child for the college admissions philanthropy section. Your magic isn't bad. It's going to help you help even more people."

Logan looked down but didn't answer. They walked into the infirmary and he walked towards the blue metal cupboards. "Here are some antiseptic wipes." He handed her the pouch.

"You know you don't have to be scared of your magic? I'm still trying to fully believe it for myself, but it's true," Sam emphasized.

"But how do I know I won't mess up when it matters most?"

"You don't, but even if you do, you keep trying to do good. You can't save everything and everyone," she hesitated as she cleaned her leg up. "But every one life you try to save is better than not trying at all, right?" Sam had to live by this advice. If she didn't, she would never be able to get over Ethan's death.

"Right." Logan moved back, trying get something from the drawer next to him, but he accidentally ran into a plastic drawer set. A few bottles spilled open on the ground along with a prescription description. "What is this?"

Sam got closer to the ground. "Alecensa?" She read out the name on one of the bottles.

"Wait, it says it here. Stage three lung cancer treatment plan." Logan translated the prescription. His eyes read further down the page. "No. No." His mouth dropped open.

"What?" Sam asked, concerned.

"This can't be real." Logan's voice was choking up. "It's for my father. He's leaving because he's dying." Tears came rushing down Logan's face. Sam moved closer towards him and placed a hand on his knee.

"I'm so sorry," she said softly. *This can't be. Surely angels are immune to something like this. Or is this how they all leave, maybe even Mom?* She remembered seeing her mother on the floor again. *Was she sick too?*

"This is why he has been coughing and looking so weak lately. How could I have been so dumb to ignore it all?" Sam gave him a side hug and to her surprise he leaned in, hiding his face in her arm. They sat without uttering another word as she held him and he cried.

CHAPTER 20

THE RING OF LIFE

———

"Think about this. Think about how it's going to affect your siblings." Sam rushed after Logan back through the passageway. Wind came through the pillars, blowing the sky blue curtains around.

"I don't even know that they don't know. If it's anything like before, they probably only hid it from me because I'm one of the youngest."

Boy, I wish you knew how much I can relate to that. Sam finally caught up and took Logan's wrist. "Stop. One second, Logan."

"How could he hide this?" Tears streamed down his face again.

"I don't know. I don't know why they hide things from us, but is this really what will be best for your brothers and sister?"

"Won't it hurt more if they find out after he is dead? I think I have to. I need answers, Sam."

I can't argue with that. "Okay, then let's go. I got your back." Sam let go of his wrist, sliding her hand into his. They walked towards the kitchen where everyone would be for breakfast.

"How could you not tell us, Father?" Logan slammed the door open even surprising Sam. "How could you not tell us you were sick?"

"Sick?" Hayden nearly dropped his plate.

"What?" Liam got up from his seat.

"Logan, not now." Ms. Green gave him a death stare. "Parakaló kathíste káto," she commanded.

"I'm not taking a seat, Mother." Logan snapped.

"Sam, what happened to your leg?" Mr. Green seemingly ignored Logan's accusations. Sam looked at Logan. She didn't know how she fit into this conversation. *I can't tell him the truth, can I? I'm just here to support Logan, keep quiet.*

"Let me guess, this girl got you both in trouble, didn't she? Are you hurt, too?" Ms. Green rushed by Logan's side and started examining him up and down. "If you got him hurt, I swear." She started mumbling more in Greek under her breath. "After I let you stay here." She pointed a finger at Sam's chest.

"Mother! Stop. She got hurt because of me. She did nothing wrong." Logan got in between his mother and Sam.

"I think I should go, Logan. I'll meet you back in the guest room?" Sam fretted. *His mom will never like me. I represent magic to her.*

"No, please stay," Logan said in a soft voice. His eyes were visibly tearing up. Sam stood still and nodded, squeezing his hand as she stood behind him. "Father. Please. Just for once, can you answer my questions clearly?" Logan's voice was calmer than before. He let out a deep breath.

"Yes, I am. I have lung cancer. It's not looking good, but I have time." He sighed and picked at his breakfast.

"That's why you're leaving?" Liam chimed in. "Would you even have had to leave if your health was fine? Was that all a lie too?"

"No, my time on Earth was always meant to be limited. Angels don't stay in mortal realms for long. We come and go as figures of prominence, but we all have to leave in the end," he sighed. "I stayed longer than I should have, which is *why* I'm sick. It's the balance restoring itself." Mr. Green looked longingly at Ms. Green and his children and then looked towards the ground.

"What is this balance you keep talking about?" Logan asked.

"You're one time lord. Keith is another. It's a balance to make sure no one person has too much power." Mr. Green looked at Sam. She was well aware of the need for the universe to have balance. She was also aware that her powers threw off that balance entirely.

"In the same way, all powers have an opposite or an equal power to make sure that no one person in the universe can take control. Angels and demons are part of that balance. Some angels are more powerful, like Sam's mother, and some demons are more powerful. Those are the ones you often hear in stories referred to as the devil." Mr. Green spoke with a stern voice.

Thank you for not revealing any of that to everyone. Sam projected her thoughts into Mr. Green's head. He looked at her and smiled. Logan saw the smile and turned around to look at Sam with a look of confusion.

"That's enough for now, Logan. Your father's health can be discussed later. You need to get ready for—" Ms. Green tried pushing Logan out of the room.

"Yes. I know. I know." He looked down.

How is his mom focusing on anything other than Mr. Green's health right now?

"What about the rest of us?" Hayden stumbled, looking at his parents. Kyle and Liam got up and stood by him. "What about answers for us?"

"Your father will give you answers slowly. He needs extreme rest, and this is too much stress for him right now." Ms. Green walked up to Mr. Green and started checking his forehead.

"I'm fine, dear." He tried to calm her. All the boys reluctantly left the room. Sam followed Logan out, but before she made it out the door, Ms. Green called out to her.

"Sam. You stay. We need to talk to you."

Shoot. She let go of Logan's hand and nodded for him to leave. "Hello," Sam said timidly. *Ms. Green scares me more than Keith sometimes.*

"Sky called this morning. He wants you to come back, fast. We already booked you a flight for tonight." Ms. Green took out a few papers from the kitchen drawers and threw them on the table.

"Dear, I'll take it from here." Mr. Green intercepted the papers and gave his wife a dirty look. "Sky said that Keith had reached out to him and that it's important for you to be with them. If you don't feel safe, you are welcome to stay here as long as you want." Ms. Green's face was growing redder with every word Mr. Green spoke.

I don't think I can stay. "Thank you. Really, but I think I should go back to everyone. They already lost Ethan. We need to be together now and figure out our next steps." Sam tried hard to avoid Ms. Green's glare. Mr. Green's face lit up in a smile.

"You're really strong, you know."

"I wasn't always like this."

"You're still young. You're allowed to make mistakes in your life, Sam. Don't let fear stop you and don't let the past dictate the future."

"Unfortunately, it took me so long to figure out my powers, and Ethan isn't here because of my mistakes. I took away his future." Sam couldn't help her voice cracking as she tried desperately not to break down in front of Logan's dad.

"Death is only a concept on Earth. He may not have a future here, but trust me that he has one."

"Logan's right. Your answers aren't very clear."

"Unfortunately, some things you will have to figure out on your own. We angels come and give knowledge, but it's how mortals on Earth have interpreted the knowledge that has dictated their future." Mr. Green picked up the tickets on the table and gathered them. "Buddha, Christ, Allah, Vishnu, Zeus and others came to Earth and mortals interpreted religion. Earthlings interpreted science from angels like Newton and Einstein and philosophy from Socrates, Locke, Sartre, and Plato."

"They were all angels?"

"Yes, and they still exist, just devoid of a mortal form."

"Are you suggesting that people exist in different realms?" *Is that what the book I found on Athanasía was about?*

"You're a smart girl. I think you'll figure it out." He passed her the tickets. "I'm glad I was able to meet you while I still have my mortal form, and thank you for taking care of Logan. You two will need each other now more than ever."

"You mean to fight demons?" Sam looked up at him. *This is my chance to get answers about those letters.* Ms. Green's eyes looked like they were about to fall out of her eyes as Sam said the word demon.

"Ah, I knew you would find those letters if you kept snooping around the library," Mr. Green chuckled. "You can keep them if you'd like, but yes. We kept Earth safe, which is why we came. Now it is your turn. You and Logan have great power, and it would be best if you stayed together." He looked at Ms. Green wearily. "He will be back in California soon, don't worry."

That's the clearest thing he has said all day, but I agree. If Keith's powers don't work on Logan, then we'll need both of us to defeat him. Mr. Green gave her a hug and then had a maid escort him out of the room. Sam quickly said thanks to Ms. Green and left, not wanting to start any more conversations. *I don't know what I did to her, but she definitely hates me.* Sam headed back to her guest room hoping Logan was still there.

"What are you going to do when you get back?" Logan had a sad look on his face. He was sitting on her bed, sulking.

"How'd you know I was leaving?" Sam was confused as she entered the room.

"Plane tickets usually don't mean people are staying."

Oh, right. She looked at the papers in her hand.

"I kind of expected it when Mother and Father pulled you aside."

"Honestly, I think I'm going to find demons and get rid of them. Living with Keith, I realized that we've all been so worried about us, but humans are being attacked and they don't even have powers. I mean, we live in privileged mansions while people around us are barely making it. Yes, we have horrible struggles, but I don't want to dwell in my problems anymore. I need to fix them and use the privileges I do have to help those who don't even have that." Sam ranted. She saw Logan's sad eyes and toned herself down. "I think if I go after the demons, I'll also be able to get stronger and work my way up to fighting Keith."

"Be safe, Sam. We can't lose you again." Logan looked straight into her eyes. Sam reached forward and hugged him.

"Please tell me you know when you're coming back to California? I need my best friend," she whispered into his ear and held onto him. She didn't want to let go.

"Hopefully soon."

"If you ever need saving, I'll be the first one there." She kissed his cheek, cupping his other in her hand. As Sam pulled away, she felt Logan catch her hand and hold it to his chest. Her breath escaped her.

"You already are," he said with teary eyes. She gave him a sad smile as his words filled her with warmth.

It's always his blue eyes, catching me at my worst.

***

Sam looked up at the mansion in front of her. *It's been a year. A month? Well, both. I didn't think I'd see this place again.* She could see the main doors open and familiar faces emerged. She surged forward and hugged Sky and Mia. She wanted to break down and cry about Ethan with them, but she had to be strong for them.

They all looked like they had broken four times over when she was missing. She also knew that she had to talk to Sky and Derek about her training and how much she'd learned about her powers and herself. One by one, everyone gave her a hug. She hadn't realized how much she missed them all until now. Seeing them, she felt a sense of family. It was a feeling stronger than she'd felt before they left for Athanasia. *Losing someone does really make you want them more.*

She turned to Sky. "Can we talk for a moment?" Her voice changed to become firmer and more assertive. "I need to talk to you and Derek."

"Yeah, about that." Sky cleared his throat and then lost his train of thought as he looked at her. "I can't believe you're home, Sam." He had a warm smile.

"Listen. I know you both were trying to do the best for me, and I appreciate everything you did to help me grow up and train, but things have to change. Derek was right about Keith and his intentions, but he also taught me a lot." Sky looked up surprised to hear her say that. "He didn't train me on his terms. He gave me free access to the books and devices. He locked me up physically, but being there forced me to work on myself, without distractions."

"Are you saying you like what he did?" Sky asked.

"No. He's the reason Ethan's dead, and I can't figure out what his agenda is or why he didn't take my powers this last year." Sam looked down. "But being trapped with him made me realize that the way we were training before was never going to work." She looked up at the mansion and the familiar forestry where she had fought her first demon. "Sky, I need to be able to protect myself. I know you don't want me involved in this dangerous lifestyle, but I don't have a choice. It's the world we live in. And I know Derek-"

"About him—" Sky tried to interject, but Sam wouldn't let him.

"He wanted me to train by only learning particular things, but the truth is, I'm the only one who can understand the gift. I don't mean to hurt you both, but I need to train on my own terms. I can't continue to only use my powers in the way you want me to. Derek always said that they're a part of me not an addition to me. So I need to learn to control every part of them. I can't rely on the safe side of my powers." Sam knew she sounded harsh, but she couldn't go back to being the shy and unconfident person she was before. She would never be the same person, but she wanted this new her to be better.

"Sam—" Sky started saying something, but Sam noticed she couldn't find Derek in the crowd of her family.

"Where is Derek, anyway?" she asked. Everyone fell silent.

"That's what I need to talk to you about. He left. None of us know where he went."

"You didn't go after him?" Sam didn't understand why Derek would leave. She looked at Mia. *There's no way Mia would let him leave. And he just left her, too? With me and Ethan already gone?"*

"He and I got into a fight about what had happened to you and Ethan. It got heated, and he left. After a few days, I was going to go look for him, but we got this." Sky handed her a letter that had a familiar picture on the black envelope.

"This is from Keith?" Sam recognized the castle on the envelope. It was where she had just escaped from.

"Yes. Read it." Sky nodded.

Dear Sky,

I have been reexamining where life has taken us recently. I thought that Sam may have been alive and came back to Athanasía hoping to get her back. When I arrived, I found her gone, but I talked to Keith. We have come to realize that we want the same things. I won't be returning. Keith and I see eye-to-eye more so than you and I do, Sky. We want the best for Sam and her powers.

> We understand that we cannot control her, but we know she will return on her own.
>
> Love,
> Derek Bleu
>
> P.S. This is Keith. I won't be coming for Sam anymore, but I know she agrees that nobody helped her like I did. Tell her to think about that. She is always welcome to come back and see her brothers.

"This doesn't make any sense." Sam shook her head. *Derek was just as horrified when we found Keith's stolen spells. This can't be true.* "I don't think this is him writing." Sam handed the letter back to Sky.

"I want to think that, but it all adds up. He rushed us to go to Athanasía."

"Sky. You know we needed to go."

"Maybe with a better plan, we could have had you both coming back to us."

"Stop, Sky. I can't do this right now. I can't think about Ethan in what-ifs."

"You know it's true," Sky pressed.

"Is this what you did with Derek too? Drove him away with your accusations." Sam waved her hands in the air.

"That's not fair. You weren't here, Sam."

"Thank the angels I wasn't." Sam ran away towards the woods between the mansions. *Back for five minutes and already running away. Sam, that's got to be a new record.*

"Wait up, sis." Mia ran and caught up to Sam.

"Why did Derek really leave?" Sam looked at her, clenching her fists.

"I thought he was going to go get you, but he also was mad at Sky. They kept fighting about who was going to get your powers."

"Get my powers?"

"They knew that they couldn't let Keith have them."

"Ethan and I were gone, and they were worried about the powers. I don't think it's the powers we have to be afraid of. It's all the people after them instead."

"I know. I can't tell when Sky and Derek are looking out for you or for themselves anymore. I don't want to believe that Derek is working with Keith," Mia said, flustered.

"That wouldn't make sense, would it? He's the one who turned us against him."

"Yeah, but he also had so many secret meetings. How do we know he wasn't always working with Keith?" Mia looked at Sam.

"Something's telling me there is more to the story. There has to be." Sam walked towards the cabin in front of the Greens' mansion. She knocked on the door and waited.

"What are you doing?"

"Logan told me Seth is staying here."

"Your merman friend?"

"Why isn't he opening the door?" She opened the lock on the door with her mind and walked in. "Yes."

"Woah. How did you do that?"

"Keith wasn't lying about one thing in his letter, and it's that he really did teach me how to use my powers." Sam looked around the dusty cabin. "Damn. He isn't here." She turned to the bed and found a cellphone. She picked it up and flipped it open, finding nothing and slammed it shut. Sam sighed.

"He taught you how to use the powers he wanted to steal?"

"You know, at the end of the day, all of our brothers left us. I don't know who to trust, but I'm tired of trying to figure it out. Mia, we're the only ones we can trust." Sam opened the bedside drawers in hopes for finding something from Seth. The top one had nothing, and she slammed it shut in frustration, falling on the bed.

"Wait, look!" Mia pointed at the coffee table in the center of the apartment. There was a note sticking out of a book. Sam rushed over and read it:

Dear Sam,

Keith sent me a letter after I met Logan. He said that, as a trade for helping me get legs, he has taken over my planet. I know I didn't grow up there, but I couldn't let the people fall under his control, so I begged Derek to take me. He was already on his way to save you.

I don't know why he and Sky were fighting, but Derek felt really bad and was dead set on making sure you would be safe. If you ever get back with him and find this note, I wanted to tell you that I'll be back as soon as I help my people.

Until then, I hope you and Logan figure out your powers. We're going to need them to beat Keith. I think he'll be coming after Earth once he gets all the magical realms under his control.

Love,
Seth

Shoot, did I help Keith get control of Seth's home planet when we found the coral? Is that what the piece of wood he took was for? Sam's heart raced. She hoped she hadn't accidentally done Keith a favor.

"So what do we do from here?" Mia looked concerned. "Is Keith really powerful enough to take over Earth? And did Derek really change his mind or is he trapped there?" She rambled.

"I think we figure out how to get Derek back and ask him." Sam walked to the door and kept rereading Seth's words. "You want answers, right?"

"Yes."

Sam looked at Mia with cold eyes. She shuffled her hands through her pockets, feeling a few broken pieces of a metal ring. "Then we're going to have to find them for ourselves."

THE END

ACKNOWLEDGEMENTS

Writing a book truly takes a village. I could not be more grateful for everyone who has ever believed in me or helped me on this journey. This book would not exist without sixteen years' worth of interaction with amazing family, friends, even strangers, or without all the amazing literature that already exists and has fueled a creative passion within me.

I'd like acknowledge those who have given this book, and the stories within it, legs strong enough to move forward. It's been a sixteen-year process, and it wouldn't have been possible without:

My mother, Seema, who read the earliest drafts and has stayed up countless nights, helping me make all my dreams come true—thank you for always having my back.

My father, Sanjiv, whose life advice I will never forget and has helped me find success.

My sister, Swati, who played Mario to entertain me while giving me life lectures that allowed me to be who I am today—and for giving me a Greek mythology book when I was six years old to spark my obsession.

My brother-in-law, Alex, for always trolling us and keeping me entertained.

My Nani, for being the first one to see the creativity in me and never letting me compromise it for anything else, and my Nana, for reading me all those stories at bedtime. Ram Ram.

My aunt, Alka Maasi, for being the first one to read the final book and give me feedback in the late hours of the night.

My aunt, Neeta Mami, for listening to me tell her stories as I grew up and always believing in the storyteller within me.

Sarita Nani, Anuj Mama, Sumesh Chacha, and Alka Maasi, for spreading the word about this book—without whom I wouldn't have been able to get published.

My roommate, Cassidy, who sat through me ranting about my book that wasn't even written at the time and has been such an amazing, and very much needed, source of support throughout the process.

My friend Lindsay, who would write with me at 3 a.m. with chicken nuggets and grounded me as a writer while pursuing data science in school.

My friend Aanya, for being the best little and taking care of me when I drowned in college work and writing.

My friend Alexandra, who spent hours acting out characters and putting up with my Greek mythology obsession—and for letting me borrow her character names, thank you.

My friend Ananya, who never failed to bring life to scenes and act out storylines with me. Chipmunks have nothing on us now.

My friend Jasmine, who biked around the neighborhood having book club with me; I don't even know what the neighbors think of us at this point.

My friend Emily, who may be the only person who will do ab workouts on a hammock with me and then five minutes later discuss why we are getting errors in our code. Thanks for adventuring around with me.

My friend Halie, for roasting my book so I could improve it and drawing/writing with me.

My cousins, Isha and Ria, for acting out scenes from Winx Club and creating a desire in me to write stories about magic.

My fellow authors, Nivita Chaliki and Nina Raman, who struggled with college and book deadlines with me. Looking forward to our writer's retreat.

My editors, Alexander Pyles, Venus Bradley, Jessica Drake-Thomas, and Michelle Felich, who have helped me become a better writer and guided me through my book journey.

My cover artists/designers, Gjorgji Pejkovski, Milan Krstevski, and Noemi Bažon who crafted the gorgeous cover art and layout.

An amazing author and life strategy coach, Joyce Teo, who beautifully captured what I had hoped for readers to see in this novel.

My aunt, Geeta Sehgal, who, as a best-selling author, guided me in the book process.

The program director, Eric Koester, without whom this book could not have come to fruition.

Special thanks to all my beta readers:

Seema Sehgal, Alka Goutam, Swati Sehgal, Anuj Rajput, Sanjiv Sehgal, Lindsay Klenk, Halie Nam, Cassidy Samovar, Annika Johnson, Veronica G. Thousand, Shagun Taneja, Isha Rajput, Ria Rajput, Ria Sehgal, Geeta Sehgal, Nivita Chaliki, and Aanya Jhaveri

I'd also like to acknowledge everyone that supported this book:

Seema Sehgal, Sanjiv Sehgal, Swati Sehgal, Alex Riabov, Apollo, Sage, Alka Goutam, Shafali Goutam, Yugesh Goutam, Sumesh Sehgal, Ritu Sehgal, Abhishek Sehgal, Ria Sehgal, Anuj Rajput, Isha Rajput, Ria Rajput, Ajay Rajput, Anu

Rajput, Neeta Rajput, Sanjay Rajput, Aman Rajput, Renu
Malik, Neelam Sikka, Suresh Sikka, Dipali Kapoor, Samar
Sikka, Subhash Sikka, Kamal Chugh, Abhinav Handa, Sarita
Handa, Geeta Sehgal, Shelly Thakur, Nina Raman, Cassidy
Samovar, Avinav Budhraja, Jasmine Jambusaria, Mira Jam-
busaria, Subrat Mishra, Rita Chickabasaviah, Jason Keltgen,
Sarika Katyal, Muralidhar Pochiraju, Amy Doan, Heather
Spaun, Ruby Tazim, Augusto Gonzalez, Shubhechha Dhar,
Sarah Hoffman, Mayura Jain, Ashley Cavuto, Ananya Pochi-
raju, Zev Burton, Giuliana Carrozza, Torrance Teng, Cannis
Meng, Eric Koester, Aanya Jhaveri, Will Fritz, Allen Stub-
blefield, Thanh-Thao (Sue) Do, Neelu Bajaj, Sunil Dhodhi,
Monica Dhodhi, Amit Talwar, Nivita Chaliki, Annika John-
son, Sohini Shah, Sanjiv Puri, Lindsay Klenk, Riddhi Jain,
Keri Vornadore, Meghan Stern, Veronica G. Thousand, Erik
Mitchell, Catherine Bryson, Sanjana Sharma, Ria Paliwal,
Katie Casey-Anderson, Patricia Fleetwood, Namrata Deva,
Arthur Miranda-huicochea, Megha Chouthai, Khandker
Hasan, Alisa Fang, Shravan Suresh, Lydia Chan, Emily
Ferguson, Lara Obedin, Andy Xie, Almi Berhane, Santoshi
Nadimpalli, Maya Hankin, Gamble Yeung, Jennifer Heuer-
man, Andrea Harvey, Justin Nguyen, Hayley Amo, Lauryn
Edwards, Anthony Perez Vargas, Amy Conway-Hatcher,
Blake Burum, Sebastian Guevara, Darsh Thakker, Riley
Reeder, Kaylee Luc, Zane Catlin, Prabha Jhamb, Josselinne
Lima, Rhiannon Lang, Santino Espiritu, Francesca Goble,
Samantha Smith, Anna Grace Krebs, Dazie Miller, Jenni-
fer Bono, Hanna Katsiapis, Sally Rong, Alexandra Weiss,
Shruti Vakharia, Titan Ngo, Samantha Marcus, Rajesh Nay-
yar, Amit Sinha, Matthew Mercurio, Misha Hoang, Claire
Hyon, Anant Gandhi, Ritika Bajaj, Nicholas D'Souza, Eliana
Schulner, Grant Webster, Elizabeth Chang, Olivia Koutsky,

Gitanjali Kamra, Gaurav Gombar, Tejvir Singh, Kaleigh Garraffa, Eli Mendoza, Adina Keeling, Anjani Sinha, Manjit Kahlon, Andrew Benser, Achal Malik, Gowri Malik, Vanessa J Mechem, Lyle Lalunio, Jarred Allen, Jinha Kim, Vivian Than, Wesley Zhen, Hailey Suh, Stephanie Gomez, Sapna Srivastava, Sam Magpantay, Arya Nair, Janae Escarez, Kanas Huynh, Christian Roberts, Carmina Gomez, Fariha Faeezah, Jasmine Mounphoxay, Srinivasan Rangarajan, Neil Prajapati, Alice Lu, Sarah Adams, Naomi Magpantay, Andrew Nguyen, Jitendra Verma, Smita Pawar, Gillian McMahon, Katelyn Cleveland, Mark Hunter, Shagun Taneja

Lastly, I'd like to acknowledge a few sources of inspiration:

Rick Riordan, Mary Pope Osborne, Amanda Lovelace, Suzanne Collins, Lilly Singh, Iginio Straffi, Bradley Bredeweg, Joanna Johnson, Peter Paige, Jennie Snyder Urman, Aldous Huxley, Laura Esquivel, and Lois Lowry

Made in the USA
Middletown, DE
13 May 2021

39677266R00157